MEMORY ADDICT

Tracy Nadeau

ISBN: 0692850058
ISBN 13: 9780692850053
Library of Congress Control Number: 2017902747
Bet on Yourself, Clinton Township, MI

CHAPTER ONE

When you have what I have, you learn to hide it early on. Of course, it takes a while to know that there is anything different about you; you just assume that everyone's mind works the same way. All the things people say to you and all the shows on TV that march by hour after hour and all the things in your house and your backyard and down the block. It's a relatively tiny world, after all, even though you don't comprehend that when you're a child.

Even when I was little, I realized that I could remember things better than the people around me. I could never understand why my mom couldn't remember the street directions that my dad gave her, and I couldn't understand why we were always lost. I would be strapped into the back seat with my fuzzy white stuffed cat clutched in my hands, calling out directions with my little voice while my mom largely ignored me. "No, right on Beacon and *left* on Sunnyside Street. Daddy said to go past the bakery. You didn't go past the bakery, Mom."

I knew where Aunt Suzie lived because we had been there before, and I remembered the bakery and the big willow tree on the corner and the black driveway and the gray roof and white aluminum siding. If I remembered it, then everyone remembered it, so why was there so much confusion?

Once we found the house and sat down for lunch, my mom would always laugh about how I knew the directions all along, and wasn't it funny how I could remember it? And she's so *young*! My mom thought it was a cute parlor trick of sorts that she could show off before moving on to more interesting topics of conversation.

So began a brief honeymoon period when I was young enough to still be cute and my ability to notice and remember everything was novel. I became the oracle of the house because I always knew exactly where everything was: keys, Scotch tape, pens, that black button that fell off my winter coat. I remembered which coupons my mom had in her coupon keeper and what the expiration dates were. I also knew where the *TV Guide* was, but once the crossword puzzle was done, you really didn't need a *TV Guide* with me around because I knew exactly what time and what channel every show was on.

Grocery shopping with my mom and grandma was a breeze because I remembered where almost everything in the store was located. My mom would make a list before we went, and I remember being confused that she had to keep checking it. What was she looking for? Green beans and laundry detergent were the next items. If she got in line and forgot the instant mashed potatoes? No problem: I knew exactly which aisle and which shelf to grab them from.

I had bags of plastic animals and knew exactly what was in each bag. Four cows: two daddies, one mommy, and one calf. Three lions: one lion, one lioness, and one cub. And so it went. *Phil Donahue* was on in the mornings, and the ice-cream truck came by at around eleven on Tuesday mornings, and I could remember the name of every bird that landed in our yard. But that was how everyone was, right?

As it turns out—no.

The first hint I had that there could be anything wrong with me were the dirty looks, hand squeezes, and occasional swats I would earn for correcting people. Adults, to be specific. I would be listening to my mom or dad recount a story and couldn't help but interject with a few corrections because they never seemed to get the facts right. The car was gray, not white. It happened on Wednesday afternoon, not Friday. Aunt Suzie's dog is a teacup poodle, not a miniature poodle. And so on. This was helpful information I was supplying after all, so shouldn't people be appreciative?

As it turns out—no.

And correcting other adults was a whole other ball of wax. Telling Mrs. Kaplin the correct store hours for the Winn-Dixie or correcting Mr. Haney that male baby horses were foals and females were fillies, for instance. Correcting the checkout woman at the supermarket when she said we had to buy two boxes of Hostess Ding Dongs to use the coupon when I knew the fine print said "each box." Without realizing it, I had absorbed a ridiculous amount of information about everything around me. Everything I saw, read, felt, or did lodged itself inside my brain. I was the very definition of a sponge, and I had no way of knowing that I was unique in any way. It was always confusing to me that the adults around me didn't already know all of this stuff. Wasn't that what being an adult was all about? Knowing everything?

As it turns out—no.

As I got older and less cute, I began to catch that look in their eyes and shift in their body language that told me I had crossed a line and my useful information was not needed or appreciated. My parents cautioned me over and over to be quiet and not correct anyone unless I was asked. So I sat quietly and listened to people using the wrong facts and struggling to remember the name of a street or a car or a person.

My mom was terrible with names. We would have lunch with someone on Tuesday, and then I would have to sit quietly and listen to my mom struggle to remember her name on Saturday night. *How could you forget someone's name?* I wondered with astonishment. Her name was Elizabeth Barton, and she had red hair and wore a green-and-black jacket with gold buttons. Had a little gold pinkie ring with an emerald in it and a gold charm bracelet with cat charms. One charm had red eyes, and she told me that she bought it because it reminded her of her cat Rusty, who died a few years back. She ordered chicken croquette and iced tea for lunch. The waiter's name was Bill, and he was in for the summer from North Carolina, and he had a large Band-Aid on his left hand (although we never found out for what).

I was still young and didn't realize how different I was from other kids—or even other adults—but for the first time, I started to sense that what I had wasn't a good thing. Once I started school, I learned that lesson the hard way.

CHAPTER TWO

B efore you start school, you spend all your time trying to win the attention and approval of the adults in your life. My brothers were quite a bit older than I was, so they and their friends were practically nonexistent to me. OK, I was nonexistent to them. Other than the almost constant teasing I endured, my brothers were just these kids who seemed to come and go as they pleased and could reach stuff on tall shelves.

There was also a slow parade of cousins that appeared on holidays and some kids down the street that I occasionally played with while our mothers sat on the porch drinking coffee and talking. I was always fascinated by their rooms and toys and books and how they organized, or rather *didn't* organize, their stuff. I loved walking through their houses and looking at the furniture and knick-knacks, and of course, after one lap through their houses, it was all committed to memory.

Kindergarten was my first introduction to a new group called my *peers*. My excitement at meeting other kids like me was soon dashed as I met the twenty or so paste eaters in my class. They ran and played like feral dogs. They rolled on the ground and got muddy during recess. They were loud and picked their noses and ate baloney at lunch. None of them were familiar with Phil Donahue.

My ability to notice and remember everything was on overdrive. I noticed what everyone wore, what was in their desks, how they smelled, what they ate, when they were sick, which cars they got into at the end of the day, and every other ridiculous detail. Their conversations swirled around me in a constant stream of words dancing in front of my eyes.

They seemed to have trouble understanding the lessons that were being taught—the same lessons that I absorbed and regurgitated without effort. My ability to learn things quickly soon caught the attention of my teachers, and I became teacher's pet. At first, this seemed like a great honor. I got to do all sorts of chores like leading the Pledge of Allegiance, collecting homework from everyone, writing examples on the board, going to the office to deliver important communications, and getting equipment from the A/V room.

In later grades, the teachers moved my desk up next to their desks, and I corrected everyone's papers and tutored students who were struggling. It was thought they might learn better from one of their peers, so a paper sign with the words *Teacher's Assistant* was adorned with flower stickers and taped to the front of my desk.

In turn, I was privy to all kinds of adult conversation between the teachers and administrators, and I could walk the halls anytime I wanted without being stopped and forced to produce a hall pass. I got extra candy from the teacher's secret drawer and an extra hot dog on hot-dog day, and I was allowed to leave early on Fridays and skip quizzes because I already knew the material. I was also allowed to skip gym class whenever I wanted and didn't have to go outside for recess when it was really cold or wet.

I knew whose parents were getting a divorce, which kids were being abused, whose father was an alcoholic, and whose mother the administrators thought was a "bitch." I knew which teachers were "going to get canned" or had gotten drunk at the Christmas party. I overheard every conversation in the office and between the teachers as they passed one another in the hallways and caught every eye roll and knowing look they exchanged. Sounds like I had the world by the butt in elementary school, right?

As it turns out—no.

My peers hated me. I was the one who made them look bad at every turn. I was the one who wrecked the curve for everyone by scoring 100 percent every time. I was the one who remembered to bring her boots when it rained and her permission slips on time. I returned all my books to the library, and I brought enough gum for everyone. I was the one who remembered to do the extra credit and to ask the teacher for the homework assignment she'd promised us for the long weekend.

In short, I was an alien to them. Oh, I tried to assimilate as best I could by talking about the things they talked about and playing the same games and occasionally getting dirty at recess and "forgetting" my gym shoes at home so I could be punished just like everyone else, but there was no getting around the fact that I was different.

Because I absorbed every conversation around me, I also heard about every playdate and birthday party and pool party that I wasn't invited to and heard every whisper of gossip that was aimed at me. While my peers paired off after school to play or study, I walked home alone and spent my afternoons reading books or watching TV.

When kids did walk home with me, it was usually to yell insults or toss crab apples at me. Then there was the time that some of the boys tore off my mittens, jacket, and hat and shoved snow down my pants and up my shirt and left me half-buried in a snowbank.

They tore up my books and homework and ruined my macaroni diorama, too.

None of this was lost on my teachers or my parents, and sometime during fourth grade, they staged an intervention with some of the other parents, asking them to involve me in their children's activities. I was just "mature" for my age, it was explained to them. Couldn't they make an effort to build a bridge? My parents reminded me that no one likes a know-it-all and asked me to act more my age and try to do the things the other girls were doing. And so I made my way to a couple of birthday parties, softball games, and study sessions.

It was at the study sessions that I first learned how to harness my true power: I had access to the answers to every test. It occurred to me that trying to actually teach them the information paled in comparison to just giving them the answer key and teaching them to memorize the answers. Boom—instant friendship!

Suddenly, they wanted to be around me, wanted me to come over and hang out. It was a win-win because their grades improved, and I looked like a successful tutor because my "students" were improving so rapidly.

I also learned not to talk about everything I noticed and not to recount everything that ever happened to me in such vivid detail. I learned how to fake saying "I'm not sure" and "I don't remember," which were all lies, of course. I stopped thinking that knowing things was an asset.

When my friend's mother "lost" her baby, I didn't explain what a miscarriage was, even though I knew exactly what it meant. I didn't argue with my friends when they recounted a story incorrectly or said that I had worn my red jeans to the roller arena last Saturday or that *Happy Days* was on TV on Monday nights.

Kids kissed my ass and bribed me with Twinkies and lip gloss and *TigerBeat* magazines in order to get test answers or have me change the incorrect answers on their tests when I was correcting them or let them know when the next pop quiz would be held. Don't get me wrong—I didn't exactly feel good about this arrangement—but for the first time, I felt like I belonged to a group of people. And that felt good—even if it was all fake.

Of course, it all came crashing down when my sixth-grade teacher figured it all out and I was exposed. For the first time, the adults in my life were disappointed in me. Parents, teachers, and administrators sat across the table from me, shaking their heads in disgust. I was devastated and elated all at once. Devastated for being so careless with the trust that had been placed in me. For trading in my integrity for a couple of friends who I really didn't even like that much. But elated that I was such a bad girl. I was someone who had done something wrong and gotten into trouble, just like everyone else. I was normal! I couldn't wait to find out what my punishment would be, and I couldn't wait for my friends to see me being punished so they would know that I was just like them.

I couldn't answer the adults when they wanted to know why I did what I did. I just sat with tears in my eyes and shook my head, and as I sat and let their disapproval wash over me, something bizarre happened: they started to make excuses for me. They knew I was different, even if they didn't understand exactly how differently my mind worked. They knew I had done it to win approval from my peers. They understood my motivation and blamed themselves for not helping me to fit in better. They blamed themselves for elevating me to a position over my peers.

They apologized to me and set up appointments with the school social worker. They assured me things would get better in middle school because there would be other kids to whom I could relate. There was no punishment. I sat and stared at them in utter disbelief. Didn't they understand that I needed to be taught a lesson? Didn't they know that letting me get away with my indiscretions was the worst thing they could do to me?

They took the *Teacher's Assistant* sign off my desk and pushed it from the front of the room to the end of the first row, taking care to explain to me that it was all for the best and would help me assimilate with my peers. I walked behind them with a look of resignation on my face, but I was secretly happy because now I could hide in the back of the room and pass notes back and forth like I had seen everyone else do.

My "teacher's pet" status stripped, I tried to pass through the rest of sixth grade like everyone else but found that now that I didn't have the answers, I also didn't have many friends to pass notes with, so I sat at the back of the room and listened to everyone's conversations and watched them pass notes and draw hearts on one another's books and counted down the days until the end of the school year. Middle school would be different, I thought. It had to be better than this.

CHAPTER THREE

I magine your brain is a radio receiver, able to switch from channel to channel and receive information from each source separately. When you are talking to someone or watching a TV show or reading a book, everything else fades into the background of white noise and escapes your notice. Now imagine that you are like me and you can't simply choose one channel at a time; they all come spilling into your receiver at once. Being in crowded places is like being assaulted with noise, color, sounds, and smells until you think you will explode. When you are talking with one person, you are still aware of the people and conversations going on around you and can follow them with startling accuracy. You hear the dog barking and the car drive by and the music being played and notice that the girl who just walked by has a limp and wears a pink bracelet, even though she is no one to you and you will never see her again.

Now imagine that you are locked in a building called "school" with a thousand other people each day and you notice and absorb everything. Every conversation you walk by in the hallway jams itself into your head in vignettes of teenage angst. Every blouse and skirt and T-shirt and the sound of shoes on the tile floor is committed to memory. Lockers slamming, basketballs bouncing, chalk on chalkboards, and bells signaling the beginning and end of each class are a constant. The smell of lunch cooking each day, gym clothes left in lockers too long, and kids who eat a lot of garlic and onions at home mingle with a million scents of perfume and deodorant and hair spray and AXE, all leaving an imprint on you.

I had already caught on that no one else seemed to have what I had, and I stopped trying to explain it to other kids or teachers. There was always that certain point in the conversation when they would get that creeped-out look in their eyes, and I knew I was alone in my affliction. Other kids just thought I was weird and dismissed me. Adults were very predictable, one after another telling me to learn to focus and suggesting some type of medication to help me block out the world around me.

Instead, I learned to keep my head down and walk through the hallways as quickly as possible to get into the relative quiet of the classroom. I always sat in the first row because that kept me from being able to see most everyone else. I also tried my best to keep my back to the windows so the birds, squirrels, trees, and clouds were out of sight. That meant I only had to deal with the teacher and the front of the room, along with whatever was going on in the hallway during class.

Although I was friendly with everybody, I wasn't very good at making friends. Most of my classmates had best friends with whom they shared secrets and lockers, hung out after school, and styled each other's hair and traded clothes. To be honest, I really didn't relate to the kids around me. To me, they seemed immature and superficial. They formed cliques and said mean things about one another. They were forever hurting one another with word or action or deed, and then they would start hanging out again, as if none of it had ever happened. I could never understand how they could do that, because I remembered every nasty thing that was said, along with the look in their eyes, what they wearing, and who was audience to it.

I overheard countless arguments and declarations of innocence, and I could have put an end to every one of them by just walking up and unleashing my memory. But I knew that no one would appreciate my input, so I just kept it all to myself.

I continued to score As on everything I touched and successfully destroyed the curve in class after class. I was soon lumped into the "accelerated program" and pushed into honors classes with the smart kids.

I was initially very happy about this because the honors wing was separate from the rest of the school, down a quiet little hallway off the music annex, and it meant that I might actually discover more people like me. I designed a little experiment to see if I could find another freak like me. I wore a different color bangle bracelet to classes each day and waited until I had an interaction with someone. The next day I would ask that person if they remembered the color of the bracelet I had worn the day before. Of course, no one remembered it, and everyone thought I was weird for asking. I was going in the wrong direction.

I had almost given up hope until the day Ann Wong lost her gold earrings. It was fourth period in honors English when she let out a scream and said that she forgot to put her earrings back on after gym class and that they had fallen out of her purse and were now missing. I had honors economics with Ann first period, and she didn't have the earrings on that day. I remembered that very clearly, but there was no sense in bringing this fact up because I knew no one would believe me. Ann went into a frenzy, and Ms. Thomas sent her with two other students back to the gym to retrace her steps and find the earrings. She also directed all of us to check the classroom floor and hallway outside. We all dutifully complied, and another girl named Chelsea and I combed the corridor.

"I wondered what happened to them," I said, attempting to make normal-people conversation.

"Nothing. She didn't wear them today," Chelsea said flatly.

My breath caught in my throat. "How do you know that?"

"I saw her this morning, and she didn't have them on. Her locker is right next to mine," she said confidently.

My heart raced just a bit faster. "Well, you can't be sure. How could you remember that?"

"I remember everything. I have a photographic memory. Once I see something, I can practically draw you a picture of it, and she didn't have any earrings on this morning."

My mind reeled, and I regarded her carefully. "Really? OK, then what color bracelet did I have on yesterday?"

"Blue," she said, without hesitation. "You change colors every day, but you almost always wear the blue one on Mondays."

Wow was all I could say back. She was the real deal.

"Don't get freaked out on me. My mom says I'm not supposed to tell people because it freaks them out, but I don't care who knows."

"What else do you remember?" I asked.

"Just about everything I see and a lot of what I hear. That's how I get such good grades; once I see something, I can recall it perfectly. The answer, where it was on the page, what the cover of the book looks like, where I was when I read it, and lots of other stuff. I can't help it; it just happens that way."

"I've got the same thing," I admitted.

Chelsea stopped scanning the floor and looked me up and down. "I doubt it. It is very rare, you know."

"I know. I've never met anyone else with it before. I've always had it."

"You don't have to say that. I'll still be your friend if you want," Chelsea offered.

I began to feel angry. I had just told someone my biggest secret, and she didn't believe me. I walked up and faced Chelsea squarely. "OK, ask me anything you want, and I'll tell you to prove it."

She smiled with surprise and thought for a moment. "What are the books on Ms. Howard's desk? In order."

This was going to be easy. "From top to bottom or bottom to top?"

I could see the surprise in her eyes. "Bottom to top."

"*Hamlet, The House of Mirth, The Raven, Elements of Style, The Little Brown Handbook,* and *Clan of the Cave Bear,*" I shot back, as fast as I could.

"That's pretty good, but you sit right up front." She thought for a moment and then asked, "What are the years of the basketball championship flags that hang in the gym?"

"1968, 1970, 1971, 1972, 1973, and 1978."

She smiled and nodded approvingly. "Mr. Barrett's wife died last month. What was her name?"

"Jean Anne."

"Who was the thirty-second president of the United States?"

"Franklin Roosevelt."

"Who were the member nations of NATO during World War II?"

"It's a trick question; NATO wasn't formed until 1949." My body tingled with excitement as I rattled off the founding member nations. "Founding nations were Belgium, Canada, Denmark, France, Iceland, Italy, Luxembourg, the Netherlands, Norway, Portugal, the United Kingdom, and the United States."

We stood toe to toe in the hallway, firing questions at each other. "What did I wear last Friday?" I asked.

"White shirt, untucked, and blue jeans. You had a hummingbird pin on your collar. What did I wear last Friday?"

"Yellow cardigan with a white shirt underneath, yellow pants, and brown clogs. You had a yellow-and-white scrunchie in your hair."

"What did I wear the Monday before that?" she challenged.

"I don't know; you weren't here on that Monday," I shot back. "Your mom had to take your grandma to the doctor's in Toledo, and your dad was in Tacoma on business, so you went with them. It's your dad's mom, not your mom's mom, and her name is Grandma Page. Your mom's name is Mary, and your dad's name is Russell."

Chelsea took a step back. "OK, how did you know that stuff about my grandma? Did you see it in the office or something?"

"No, I heard you telling Rebecca Miller during lunch on the Friday before. I remember most of what I hear, unless I force myself not to remember it, but I can usually remember everything if I think about it for a minute. Can you do that, too?"

Ms. Howard peeked her head around the corner and called us back to class.

"Sometimes. I'm better with things I see," she admitted.

We stood there and smiled at each other, both exhilarated at the discovery of another one of our own species. We exchanged phone numbers after class and talked on the phone for three hours that night. My mom was so happy I had a friend that she didn't even yell at me to get off the phone like she usually did to my brothers.

The next day, Ann Wong apologized to the class for getting everyone upset and admitted that she had forgotten to wear her earrings that day and that they had been sitting on her dresser, safe and sound.

CHAPTER FOUR

C helsea and I became best friends in no time. We were both voracious readers and tore through books in one sitting. We both loved movies and hanging out at the mall and spent the next few years almost inseparable. We formed a tight clique of two and spoke in a shorthand code that consisted mostly of quoting lines from books and movies. None of our peers could follow our conversations, and few cared to try.

We sailed along in the accelerated-program bubble as if the rest of the school didn't exist, until that fateful day when James entered the picture. James was a jock, and in a time when the name that was embroidered on your jeans was the most important statement you could make, he wore ripped Levi's, T-shirts, and the same tennis shoes every day.

Our honors calculus teacher had volunteered several students to tutor kids from the regular classes that were struggling, and James was struggling. From 2:00 p.m. to 2:45 p.m. each day, we met in one of the study rooms off the library. I was immediately disgusted by him and immediately drawn to him.

First off, he was very cute. He had thick arms and shoulders; even his forearms and hands were muscular. He had light-brown hair that was never combed or styled but still looked good. He had these beautiful blue eyes and a very direct way of looking at me that invariably made me turn away in embarrassment.

Besides his undeniable good looks, he was not like anyone I had ever met before. He didn't care about school or grades or rules or what adults had to say about anything. He thought I was ridiculous for trying so hard and told me so every chance he got.

"None of this means anything," he would say dismissively.

"How are you going to get into a good college?" I would challenge.

"I ain't going to college. None of my brothers went to college, and they are doing just fine."

The logic was hard to argue with until I found out one brother was in jail, one cleaned a chain of porn shops, and one was a mechanic.

So instead of learning simple algebraic formulas and how to apply them, he spent the forty-five minutes telling me I had nice boobs, rubbing my leg, and offering to show me his penis. I was smitten. I couldn't wait for two o'clock to come each day, and on days when he skipped school or forgot to meet me, I would mope around for the rest of the afternoon.

One week, he skipped out on me two days in a row, and I was devastated. I had seen him in the hallway both days, so I knew he was there somewhere. Instead of assuming it was the math he was avoiding, I took it personally. On the third day, I walked around with my stomach in knots, holding back tears until 2:00 p.m. I sat nervously in the meeting room waiting for him to arrive. When he didn't, I became furious. I knew he hung out in the parking lot behind the auditorium with the rest of the burnouts when he skipped so I marched out there.

I had never left school without permission before, but I was on a mission. I walked past the hall monitors without pausing and exited through one of the side doors. I could see several students leaning against the wall smoking. I recognized them but didn't know any of them. I don't know what I thought they would do to me for intruding on their space, but I was scared. Still, I walked up and forced myself to talk.

"Hey, what's up?"

They looked at me with curiosity, and one or two nodded in my direction.

"James around?"

One of the girls, Rhonda, I think, jerked her thumb behind her. "See the blue car?"

"Yep. Thanks."

The parking lot was mostly filled with old beaters that were the only cars most kids could afford, and the blue car was no exception. It was an old Lincoln that was as big as a boat and full of rust. I couldn't see anyone inside until I got up close, but I could hear Led Zeppelin playing through the open windows. John had the driver's seat fully reclined and was smoking a cigarette.

"This is what you do when you skip out on me?"

He sat up, slightly startled. "Hey, hey, what's up?"

"Nothing's up, just haven't seen you in like three days."

"And you missed me?" He smiled and blew a buff of smoke out at me. "Get in."

I was unsure of what to say because I did miss him, but I didn't want him to know that I missed him. "I can't get in. I'm not even supposed to be out here. No one is supposed to be out here right now."

He laughed at me. "What, do you think you're gonna get in trouble or something? Silly, get in." He reached over and unlocked the passenger-side door.

I walked around to the passenger side and leaned in the window. "Come on, you're gonna make me smell like smoke. Let's go back to the study room."

He flicked the cigarette out onto the concrete. "Get your butt in here."

The old, cracked leather groaned as I sat next to him and closed the door. "Happy?"

"Getting there." He slid over the bench seat so he was right next to me and put his arm around my shoulders. "How's this?"

I could barely talk. My heart was racing. I had imagined this moment so many times over the past few weeks.

"I won't do it if you don't want me to," he said and started to blow in my ear.

I let out a loud giggle. "Stop that! On my god, that tickles!"

"Yeah? What about this?" He leaned over and began kissing my lips softly.

I kissed him back, my lips meeting his more and more urgently. His mouth tasted like cigarettes, but it was warm and wet, and it felt so good. I could feel him working his hand up my thigh as we kissed and pushed it away as soon as he got too far up.

By the time we stopped kissing, I didn't know if ten minutes or ten hours had gone by.

"I like how you kiss," he said, simply.

"Me too. I mean, *you*. I like how *you* kiss," I stammered and pushed my hair back in place.

"See, isn't this more fun than math?" He dug a ChapStick out of his pocket and put some on before offering it to me.

"So that's why your lips are so soft." My whole perspective had changed: he wasn't the kid who couldn't do math anymore; he was the man with the soft lips.

"I aim to please. I'm not the first guy you ever kissed before, right?"

I didn't know what to say so I just stared at him for a few moments and finally said, "Kinda."

"Kinda? *Kinda* means *yes*. You never kissed anyone before?" He gave a high whistle. "Not even your girlfriends?"

"Stop! I have never kissed a girl! Why would you say that?" I punched him in the arm.

"Oh, shut up; I know you girls do all that kind of stuff at camp." He laughed.

"Not this girl! God, I can't believe you even said that. Don't ruin it." I was having a hard time telling if he was joking or not.

"OK, OK, I should have known. Maybe we should stop talking and kiss some more."

I noticed the time on his dashboard. "Is that the right time?"

"Don't get all freaked out, Ms. Smarty Pants; the school won't burn to the ground if you're not inside."

"I have to go back right now. I can't miss English," I said, the panic rising in me. I had missed school only twice in the last three years.

He slid back over to his side and took the keys out of the ignition. "OK, let's go. I'll show you which door opens so you don't have to walk all the way back around the school."

"What? You mean the doors don't open?"

"Not from the outside. Don't worry; I'll show you the way, but then you'll owe me another kiss."

He carried my book bag as we walked back past the same group I had seen on the way out. I wondered if I looked different to them; could tell that I had been kissed? I was with James now, so I met their eyes with more confidence.

James took me to a door at the far end that someone had propped open with a small rock. "As promised," he said and leaned down to kiss me again. I grabbed him around the waist and pushed my body up against his. I was afraid the spell would be broken if we went back into the school, and he wouldn't want to kiss me again.

When we finally parted, he said, "Yum, I definitely want some more of that."

My heart soared. "That can be arranged."

And just like that, I was in my first boyfriend/girlfriend relationship. He convinced me to meet him at his house after school, where he got me to smoke cigarettes and look at his brother's porn magazines and tried to get me to ride his motorcycle. Hormones had taken over my sixteen-year-old brain, and it was all very exciting to me. My senses, perpetually tuned to a heightened state, were now in overdrive, and I felt like my entire being was vibrating. Every kiss and touch was like being shocked with electricity. My fingers memorized the soft hair on the back of his neck, the smooth skin on his lower back, the rough stubble on his face, the hard muscles of his thighs, and the feeling of his hard penis straining against his Levi's.

Both his parents worked, so each day we would lie on the couch and make out until half past five, when we heard them drive up. I knew about sex and orgasms from the hundreds of books that I had read, but I considered my virginity a prized possession that I needed to keep, so I explained to James that he had to settle for mutual masturbation for now.

I would run home each day and immediately call Chelsea to tell her everything that had happened. At first, she was excited for me and listened with great interest. But she soon got jealous of all the time I was spending with James, and she got irritated with the whole thing. I pushed James to set her up with his friends, and he did, but James's friends were a little rough around the edges, and Chelsea wasn't into the whole "bad-boy" thing.

So the three of us ended up being the Three Musketeers. Chelsea and I included James in our trips to the mall, movies, and pool, and James included us in a world we knew existed but had never ventured into before: parties.

Most of these parties consisted of a bunch of people smoking pot and drinking beer in a backyard or basement of whoever's parents were gone for the weekend. It was quite a bit different from the parties thrown by those in the accelerated group, which consisted of playing Dungeons & Dragons or watching *Monty Python* movies in the company of adults who were more than happy to supply soda and pizza and drive us home afterward.

At the first party James took us to, I noticed a lot of kids who I had seen before in class or in the hallway at school or in yearbook pictures, and thanks to my flawless memory, I knew who they all were, but I was still nervous about entering their territory. I noticed the double takes as I said hello to them by name because most of them clearly had no idea who I was, so I switched off that part of my brain and simply waved as we made our way through the basement and over to the keg in the corner.

The basement was loud and smelled like beer, smoke, sweat, and mildew. Chelsea and I sat on an old couch that was too soft, and we sunk down immediately. James pumped beer after beer into Solo cups until we each had one. The first sip was warm and bitter and nasty. It tasted exactly like the basement smelled, and I gagged a bit. James laughed at me and downed his beer in one gulp before returning to the keg to get another. Chelsea and I smiled at each other and forced ourselves to drink.

The first thing I noticed was that my knees felt warm, and muscles that I didn't even know I had begun to relax. I was smiling and wasn't sure why. All the people and noises around me seemed to fall into order. Instead of a jumble of movement and noise and color coming at me, the people fell into separate groups who were talking and laughing, and their conversations bounced by me. It was like looking at people through a shield: I could see them and hear them, but their auras didn't touch me. My mind had stopped trying to figure them out and file them away for future reference. My eyes skipped over the room again and again without absorbing anything.

For the first time, I didn't feel the need to tell anybody anything. I didn't need to explain or defend my actions or thoughts. I didn't feel the need to understand and categorize the things around me. I laughed and giggled without really knowing why. My head buzzed with a lightness that I had never felt before.

I hugged Chelsea and James and giggled and said, "I love this! Isn't it great? I love this!" over and over again.

Without knowing it, I had just discovered the magic elixir that would set my busy mind free.

CHAPTER FIVE

James was a bad influence—there was no arguing that point—but kissing him on the couch was the greatest feeling I'd ever had in my life, and I had no intention of stopping. Ever. In just a few short weeks, he had turned me from a genius into an idiot who was extremely open to suggestion. I soon discovered that there were many magic elixirs: vodka, whiskey, rum, pot, hash, mushrooms, and various pills that had no names but all made my busy mind relax.

The first time I arrived at school without my homework, I felt like a true gangster. The first time I skipped class, I thought helicopters would descend on my house, and police would kick the door in to find me. But nothing happened. The teachers would just give me a knowing nod, and my parents were never notified. My chemistry teacher, Mr. Hamilton, kept me after class one day and gave me a short lecture on keeping my values and watching the company that I keep, but they all knew they were no match for the hormones of a sixteen-year-old.

James taught me how to shoplift and roll joints and hot-wire cars. It never really occurred to me that we were actually stealing a car—we were just borrowing it for a while, right? Chelsea was an unwilling participant in most of our hijinks. She was the moral compass that sipped one beer all night, refused to take drugs of any kind, and made sure I made it home before midnight.

When I drank too much, she took me to her house and hid me in her basement, where I puked in a garbage bag all night. When I blew off my homework too many times, she made copies of hers and turned it in with my name on the top. When I skipped school, she typed my name on the excused attendance list. When I contemplated giving up my virginity to James, she talked me out of it.

She was my best friend in every sense of the word. So when I noticed a few looks pass between her and James, I dismissed them. When James's and Chelsea's phone lines were busy at the same time, I ignored it. When I overheard a few whispers between them, I convinced myself that the pot must be making me paranoid.

But by the time I took a ten-day trip to Hilton Head with my parents that spring, a feeling of dread had settled into my system. My innate ability to perceive everything around me, although dulled by alcohol and drugs over the past few months, had kicked in, and I knew the truth.

I sat in the back seat of my dad's car on the way home from North Carolina, feeling like my life was over. I jumped on my bike as soon as the trunk of the car was unpacked and rode over to Chelsea's house. I could see James's car as soon as I turned onto her street. I jumped off my bike at the neighbor's house and laid it in the bushes and tiptoed into the garage and up to the back door. I carefully opened the screen door and stood on the landing. Two steps up to the kitchen, fifteen steps down into the basement. I listened until I heard breathing coming from the basement. I knew the basement steps creaked badly and I would lose the element of

Memory Addict

surprise as soon as I stepped down, so I slowly sat on the top step and bent over to get a view of the couch.

It took a few minutes for my eyes to adjust and for my mind to accept that they were completely naked and having sex. All while she was convincing me not to give up my virginity, Chelsea had apparently decided to give hers to James. I wanted to throw up. I wanted to run downstairs and confront them. I wanted to sneak back out and pedal as fast as I could home.

Wow was what I finally said out loud.

James didn't hear me, but Chelsea's head swung around, and she saw me. Her eyes opened wide, and she tried to push James off of her. He protested in surprise before he saw me, too, and understood. He jumped up, his still-hard penis bouncing in front of him.

I jumped up, ran out of the house, retrieved my bike from the bushes, and rode home like the devil himself was chasing me.

I spent the rest of the summer avoiding Chelsea and James. I hung up on them when they called. I refused to open the door when they came over. I threw away the letters and notes that came through the mail. I refused to talk about them when they sent third-string friends over to talk to me on their behalf. I hung out with a few people from the accelerated program and played D&D on Fridays and smoked weed and drank beer with some of the kids from James's crowd on Saturdays. James had gotten into a fight with his friend Kirk early in the summer, so his house was safe harbor for me. Kirk wasn't a jock. He was a burnout, and he was skinny and didn't kiss as well as James. But I drank his warm beer, smoked his weed, laughed at his jokes, and took my pants off for him. I remember everything about my first time: the way the vinyl in the back seat felt on my naked skin, the way the condom smelled, the way he held his hands under my head to form a pillow, how his penis felt sliding in and out, how my orgasm exploded inside me, and how I wanted more when it was done.

When it was time to select classes for my senior year, I shocked everyone by choosing a variety of art and shop classes and nothing from the accelerated program. My parents protested. The teachers and counselors called me into the school, and I sat on the other side of a long table while they tried to convince me to change my mind. My future hung in the balance, they said, with very serious looks on their faces, and this was no time to be irresponsible.

They knew that Chelsea and James were together now and talked to me in soft tones about how I must feel and how my feelings would pass in time. I nodded and ultimately relented. I added a few honors courses to my curriculum to give them what they wanted and get out from behind the long table and back out into the warm sunshine of that August day.

So I went through that fall split pretty evenly between the honors hallway and the corridor behind the gym where the burnouts hung out. I learned that if you smoked and drank and swore, you blended in with the rest of the student body, and people stopped being intimidated by your presence. I skipped class and smoked weed in the parking lot. I wore blue jeans, flannel shirts, and tennis shoes every day. I stopped writing for the school paper or participating in any after-school activities. I said shitty things about my teachers and taped *Kick Me* signs on fellow classmates.

The first time I heard some of the underclassmen refer to me as a loser, I almost danced home. When the Collins family stopped using me to babysit their three kids without any explanation, I was overjoyed. The first time I noticed an older woman at the store clutching her purse tightly when I walked by, I smiled in self-satisfaction. Mission accomplished. I was now a part of the "unwashed masses," and I realized that life was much easier when I no longer had to live up to everyone else's high expectations.

Dating was rough for me. As it turns out, guys frequently lie and bend the truth to suit their needs and try to manipulate and convince you of things, and when you have the ability to memorize every word, action, and promise that someone ever makes, that can be rough. I found that the only way to get through all the bullshit was by disconnecting my feelings to avoid the almost constant disappointment. After Kirk, I slept with Robert, and after Robert, I slept with Joe, and after Joe, I slept with Jimmy, but I never made the mistake of ever believing what any of them said to me.

I walked past Chelsea and James holding hands in the hallway without reacting for months. I heard all the rumors about their relationship, and I knew when they broke up. Of course, he cheated on her with a new girl who had transferred over for senior year. She smoked and wore leather jackets and drove an old Corvette, so Chelsea was no match.

After they broke up, Chelsea would appear at my locker at regular intervals crying and asking for my forgiveness, and I would tell her to fuck off and slam the door and sulk away to my watercolor class while she returned, dejected, to the honors hallway. I suppose I should have taken mercy on her. Despite smoking weed before class every day, my brain could still grasp the big picture, and I knew that it was all a moment in time that would pass and that the right thing to do would be to forgive her. Then we would go to U of M together and share an apartment like we had planned before things got so complicated. Guys were crap anyway, I reasoned, and it was ridiculous to let one come between true friends, but I just couldn't bring myself to reach out to her.

When her mother called mine to try to arrange a reunion on her birthday in January, I flatly refused to go, even after my mom bought and wrapped a blouse for her. She lectured me on forgiveness and kindness and reminded me that Chelsea's mind was like mine, and her feelings were amplified a thousand times, so she didn't just feel bad but felt bad times a thousand. I walked past the pink-and-white-wrapped box on the counter for a week without relenting. The box made me feel angry; I was the one who was the victim, and yet all the pressure was on me to make things right between us, and that just didn't make sense to me.

"Take the high road," my mom would say. "Be the better person, and you'll never regret your decision." And when her words of wisdom still didn't change my mind, she just called me a stubborn ass and said that I would be sorry someday when I did something wrong and needed to be forgiven myself. *Impossible*, I thought. I would never do anything to hurt another person. Well, not on purpose.

She killed herself just after her seventeenth birthday. I knew it was something serious when they pulled me out of shop class and instructed me to bring my books and jacket to the office, where my mom was waiting for me. She told me in the car, and I remember that it was very cold, and there were little ice crystals on the windows because my mom hadn't waited for the car to warm up before she drove over to the school. The pink-and-white-wrapped box wasn't on the counter when we got home.

CHAPTER SIX

I remember the funeral and the smell of the flowers and the mass of students filing past the casket. The girls in their black dresses and the boys in their suits that didn't quite fit. Her family sitting quietly on the green-and-gold couch in the front row, wiping away tears. James didn't come to the funeral, and I never saw him again; he wasn't eligible to graduate anyway, so he drifted into night school with the youth offenders and the pregnant girls and was gone.

I had no reason to talk to him again, but I did wonder if he felt guilty at all. My own emotions swung between guilt and anger. I admonished myself for not forgiving her and wondered if it would have made a difference. But at the same time, it was all her fault. She was the one who had lied and made the situation happen in the first place and then couldn't handle it. She was the coward who checked out early instead of facing her feelings.

My busy mind ran through a thousand scenarios of how things could have worked out differently, if only. If only I had done this or if only she had said that or if only it hadn't been her birthday or if only James had taken her back. It was a never-ending, constant playlist that occupied my waking hours and kept me up most of the night.

The adults in my life spent months wondering why Chelsea killed herself. I knew why, but it was difficult to explain to people whose minds didn't work like Chelsea's and mine. She killed herself because she couldn't shut her mind down. She couldn't stop remembering everything that went right and everything that went wrong. When she did sleep, her mind ran through scenarios nonstop and she woke up exhausted.

She never learned to turn her brain off or to use weed or alcohol to dull the constant chatter, and so she did the only thing she thought would work.

After the funeral, everyone began to talk to me in soft tones. It was suggested that I see the school counselor each day and that I attend college nearby so I could "keep a solid home base" under me. Tests revealed that I didn't exactly have a photographic memory or an eidetic memory, but I was somewhere on the exceptional memory spectrum, and combined with a hypervigilance disorder, it explained why I absorbed all outside stimuli.

With my GPA and natural abilities, the adults in my life pushed me toward a future in medicine or law, but I was becoming more and more fascinated by how people's minds worked. Why did some people sense everything while others seemed to float through life untouched? Was it possible to train yourself not to feel? Not to notice? Not to breathe? To me, it really did seem like ignorance was bliss. Or if not blissful, at least it seemed peaceful.

I imagined that my mind looked like a huge room filled with file cabinets of information, all cataloged and arranged and waiting to be recalled at any moment, while I imagined everyone else's mind to be a single-file box with a set of manila folders that can never expand. Each new folder takes the place of an old folder, and the box fits neatly on an otherwise empty shelf.

I know that this sounds overly simplistic and maybe a bit condescending, but it is the best analogy I can come up with, and besides, I was beginning to truly envy those with that single-file box.

In college, I met a number of people who were very happy to be smarter than everyone else. They took pride in being overachievers and joined all the clubs and organized meetings and protests. They wore sweatpants to class and knew all the professors by first name. The girls didn't shave their legs or their armpits and wore sandals everywhere but still always seemed to have boyfriends. The guys wore the same jeans and T-shirts to class every day and never shaved the scruff that masqueraded as beards on their faces. They were overly serious, talked about politics in the Ukraine with incredible confidence, and thought they knew more about sex than they actually did.

In this environment, I was not special, and I did not stand out. I enjoyed how easy it was to disappear in the mass of students that came and went every day. I interned for a psychology professor and mostly kept to myself. I discovered that most of the professors did not care whether you came to class, and I made it my habit to show up only to take tests and turn in papers.

I managed to get a job bartending at a topless bar a couple of nights a week, and that was where I truly found my element. I was fascinated by the steady stream of dancers, waitresses, bartenders, DJs, and kitchen staff that made up the microcosm of the topless bar. It was a banquet of lost, disenfranchised, abused, and addicted souls that had all floated together for a moment in time to form a makeshift family.

An incredibly transient bunch, there were forty to fifty dancers at the club that seemed to come and go as they pleased, working for ten days straight and then disappearing for a month and showing up again driving a Mercedes and talking about a role in a TV show they would be starting in the fall. They made hundreds of dollars a night and spent it all on cocaine while they allowed their phones to be disconnected for nonpayment. They met a guy on Friday, moved in with him on Tuesday, and couldn't understand when they broke up a week later and had to move back out.

They made up the rules of their lives as they went along, usually with less-than-successful results yet were imbued with almost limitless confidence. They slept with the customers, other employees, and one another with stunning frequency, and it never occurred to them to hide it or be ashamed of it.

I was appalled by them and envious of them at the same time. They were the very definition of ignorance being bliss. They were fascinated with my vocabulary and all the miscellaneous facts I knew and used me to settle just about every argument they ever got into that could be solved by knowing the name of the actor who played Barney Miller or the capital of California or where Indonesia is on the map. They called me Bookworm and shared their cocaine with me and tried to get me to sleep with them.

Back at school the next day, I would watch the girls in their Birkenstocks and the guys with their sketchy beards make cardboard signs with thick markers on the floor of the student center with such an incredible sense of importance. How could all these people with all these different realities exist just miles apart?

I straddled the line with gusto. I wore combat boots and old blue jeans and oversize flannel shirts to school and attended support rallies for the Chinese students at Tiananmen Square and cheered when the Berlin Wall came down as if my own mother were going to pop through the hole. I quoted Shakespeare and John Cheever and interned at a children's magazine and tried my best to forget about Chelsea and James and all the rest of my past. I never talked about it and tried to keep myself from thinking about it and let it all pass slowly into the rearview mirror.

At night, I wore black thigh-high boots and stockings and bustiers and thick eyeliner and red lipstick and crawled across the top of the bar on my hands and knees while a dancer named Dominix pretended to whip me with a cat-o'-nine-tails. I enjoyed the big reaction we always got from our dog-and-pony show just as much as I enjoyed all of the money stuffed in my clothes. I drank and smoked weed and did coke with an ever-changing collection of coworkers who accepted me as I was, didn't care where I had been or where I was going, and never challenged me.

When I finally got my degree, I didn't bother to attend the actual graduation ceremony; I just had them send my diploma in the mail, and I tossed it in a drawer at my mom's house.

CHAPTER SEVEN

I met guys here and there and dated a little but never made it past the three-month mark with most of them. I wasn't attracted to the super-ambitious guys at all. The wannabe doctors and lawyers and financiers that sat around the student center using big words and acting self-important were boring to talk with and clumsy in bed. The socially conscious guys with their need to educate everyone on how the world needed saving just annoyed me, and they spent more time talking than kissing.

The bouncers at the bar were much more attractive and better in bed, but they had a habit of sleeping with every girl in the bar, so they didn't make for very good boyfriend material, although they made for some interesting hookups and friends with benefits.

I met Craig at my friend Nancy's wedding shower. I was a bridesmaid, and at first I was annoyed when she announced that they would be having a couple's shower. I couldn't understand why you would want the guys there to watch you open wooden spoons and bedsheets. But when the guys showed up with a bottle of Jack

Daniel's and started forcing everyone to do shots before the shower even started, I began to change my mind.

Craig was in the wedding party, although I wasn't standing up with him. My guy was one of Nancy's brothers, who was already married. Once I met Craig, I quickly and quietly began to campaign for a change in partners. He had beautiful green eyes and a head of thick light-brown hair and an athletic body with muscular forearms and strong hands. At first I thought he probably worked in construction or was a gym instructor of some kind, so I was surprised to find out he was an IT guy. A hot IT guy was a rare thing, plus he had a mischievous sparkle in his eyes and a wicked sense of humor that got my attention.

After the presents were all opened and the bows were all fed through a paper plate and what was left of the sheet cake sat on a back table going stale, Craig and I sat facing each other with our knees touching, telling stories and sipping wine. It was one of those weird days of day drinking when it was only five o'clock at night but felt like midnight. The guests were gone, and the rest of the wedding party was next door at the bar.

I wanted to sleep with him that day but kept thinking that I would have to face him several more times over the course of the next month for wedding functions, so I held myself back, although his forearms were driving me crazy. I thought about him a lot in the days following the shower and told myself that he was drunk and probably didn't even remember me, but one day Nancy called me and told me that she was rearranging the wedding party so I could stand up with Craig because Craig kept asking her fiancé, Jeff, to make the change so he could spend some more time with me. I was elated and, for the first time in a long time, allowed myself to feel excited about a guy.

We slept together after the rehearsal dinner and then again the morning of the wedding and then again after the reception. We became a couple without ever really talking about it. I went from not knowing him at all to spending every free moment with him. The lack of drama and uncertainty in our relationship threw me a bit off-balance. I wasn't used to everything being so easy and feeling so comfortable. I was used to guys who lied and disappeared unexpectedly. I was used to finding guys I was dating sitting at restaurants with other girls. I was used to not knowing if the guy I was dating really liked me or not. I was used to being stuck in the friend zone.

Although he never admitted it, I knew he hated that I worked at the strip bar, so I quit after I graduated that fall. The magazine I interned for had started paying me for articles, and the parent company connected me with several other publications in their family, plus I started doing some freelance writing for a local PR firm, so I was actually living life as a professional writer, although a poor one.

We got engaged about a year after Nancy's wedding, right around the time she became pregnant with her first daughter. The bubblegum pink dresses I picked for my bridesmaids hid her baby bump, but she was still self-conscious standing next to the rail-thin stripper friends who also stood up for me.

After our honeymoon in Hawaii, we moved into a two-bedroom apartment while we saved money for a house. We got a cat and went to our friends' houses for barbecues on the weekends.

I loved Craig and enjoyed being with him, and the sex was great, but the way everything came together like one domino hitting the next and the next and so on without a hitch just seemed too good to be true. After a few years, we bought a house with a postage-stamp front lawn, and I planted impatiens and geraniums in the front and tomato plants and basil out back, and I sat on my deck drinking wine each night, waiting for the other shoe to drop.

I was very excited to be accepted as a contributor at a local travel magazine, and one of my first assignments was to write three installments on winter vacation getaways in a column called "Snowbird Confidential." I soon found myself drinking rum punch in Islamorada and searching for the most economical salad bar in town. It was my first trip away from Craig since we had gotten married, and I felt a sense of freedom that I hadn't realized I had been missing.

On the second day, I took a fishing charter and drank beer with four older men from Boston and watched fishermen gut fish on the docks. On the third day, I spent hours wandering through the souvenir shops looking at cheesy T-shirts, shells, and colorful towels and ate lobster pizza for lunch and fell asleep in a hammock at the resort.

I woke up just in time to shower and walk down the side of the road to the last restaurant on my list that I had to visit. A favorite of locals and tourists for over thirty years, Sea Glass was a large wooden tiki-style building on stilts. Cars and RVs were parked in no particular pattern in the sand around the building as if they had been abandoned in a hurry. I shook the sand out of my flip-flops and walked up the ramp and into the bar. All the barstools were filled with vacationers in shorts and tank tops, talking and laughing together as if they were all part of the same family, although I knew they weren't.

The bartender looked over the crowd at me and pointed to an empty stool at the other end. I shook my head and said, "I'm looking for Ted. The owner, Ted."

He nodded and came around the bar. "Are you the food critic?"

I laughed. "Not really a food critic. I'm a travel writer. I'm supposed to eat here tonight."

"Yeah, yeah, yeah. I got you. Come on." He walked me past the bar, into the main dining room, and over to a table on the porch that overlooked the ocean. He plucked a *reserved* sign off the middle of the table and smiled broadly. "It doesn't get much better than this!"

Like most bartenders, he was cute. Brown, curly hair tipped blond from the sun, broad shoulders, well-defined arms, brown legs, and muscular calves. I wiped the sweat off of my face, hoping he didn't notice, and sat down.

"Can I get you a cocktail or glass of wine?" he asked.

"Oh, I'll wait for Ted in case he wants to recommend any pairings. Water is good right now," I said.

"OK, I'll get him for you." I noticed that he had a nice ass as he walked away, and I realized that I'd forgotten to ask his name.

The main dining room was mostly full—more tourists in beach clothes with floppy hats and sunburns. A heavy gray-haired man carrying two large glasses of white wine worked his way around the tables and chairs and over to me.

"Hello and welcome! Hello and welcome!" he called as he put the glasses down on the table and worked his bulk into the chair across from me. He wore a loud red, black, and white Hawaiian shirt and khaki shorts, and he had sweated through all of it. I noticed that he had slim white scars from knee-replacement surgery on both knees and wore green Crocs. Something about him told me that he hadn't worn hard-soled shoes in many years.

"You've got to be Ted," I said.

"Yes, of course, of course I am Ted. Who else would I be?" He laughed heartily and reached over the wine to shake my hand. His hand was very warm and moist. "This is a lovely crisp sauvignon blanc with notes of pear and a clean finish," he said, picking up his glass and waiting for me to join him.

I took a sip, and it was delicious. "Wonderful," I admitted.

"Yes, this is one of my favorites. Don't get me wrong; I'm not some kind of wine fag. I like my Coors Light and Crown Royal, but I can appreciate a nice glass, too." He took a large drink from his glass. His ruddy complexion and cauliflower nose told me his story, and I suspected that this was not his first drink of the day.

The bartender returned with two glasses of water. "Well, do you know what you are going to start with?" he asked.

I took the menu out of the holder on the table and started to open it when Ted grabbed it out of my hands and tossed it over the railing and into the sand below. "Fuck that menu," he said, with a laugh. The bartender looked uncomfortable but not surprised.

"I'm gonna tell you what to eat, and he'll bring it, and you'll love it, and then you can write about it. OK?" I could hear what was left of an East Coast accent in his speech, probably New Jersey or New York, I guessed.

I wasn't sure that this was as objective as it was supposed to be but didn't feel like I could argue. "Sure, sounds great."

"You are goddamn right it sounds great!" he shouted and then turned back to the bartender. "Lobster pizza and calamari to start, the sea bass with the mango sauce, of course, and then key lime pie, of course." The bartender nodded and smiled at me with a look that almost said he felt sorry for me and disappeared.

It was a great place, lively and breezy with Jimmy Buffett music playing in the background and a constant stream of people coming and going. Occasionally the people at the bar linked arms and began singing to the music or raised shot glasses and toasted to something and then banged their glasses loudly on the bar. The sun twinkled off the ocean, and the breeze kicked sand into the air, and although Ted never stopped talking, I was thoroughly enjoying myself.

He told stories about living in New Jersey and building the bar and rebuilding it after a hurricane and rebuilding it again after a disgruntled employee had set it on fire. The food came, and the wine never stopped coming, and I ate and took sloppy notes that would be impossible to decipher the next day and decided that it was the best meal I had ever eaten.

Ted switched to Crown Royal on the rocks at some point, and his New Jersey accent got thicker while his speech grew harder and

harder to understand. Around eleven at night, one of the waitresses, who I later found out was Ted's daughter, coaxed him from the
table and led him away. I knew it was a scene that probably played
itself out each night.

I wasn't sure exactly how much wine I'd had to drink during
dinner, but my legs felt pretty wobbly as I made my way over to the
bar and arranged myself on a barstool. Most everyone was gone
by now except an older couple who were making out and a small
group of bikers drinking Budweiser.

The bartender smiled as I approached. "You survived," he said.

"The food or Ted?" I joked.

"Ted, of course. He's a good guy, but he can be a little…" He
struggled to find the right word.

"Ted," I offered.

"Yeah, that's it. Another glass of wine?"

"Oh God, no, I am wined out for tonight. Something simple
like a vodka cranberry or a Crown and ginger."

"Wow, that's my girl. Going to the hard stuff." He laughed and
made two Crown and gingers; he gave me one and started drinking the other himself.

"Hey, what's your name?" I asked.

"Nick. You're Megan, right?"

"Well, I am what is left of Megan," I joked, and he laughed. I
liked his laugh. I was very attracted to him. I hadn't flirted with
anyone for years, and I felt a little clumsy and out of my element.
"How did you get stuck waiting on us?"

"I always get stuck with Ted and his exploits. I'm the manager,
so it comes with the territory." He leaned across the bar on his
elbows while he talked to me. I could see his shoulder and back
muscles through his T-shirt. He was slightly sweaty, but in a good
way, and I wanted to reach out and touch him.

"Hey, honey, wanna join us?" one of the bikers yelled from the
other side of the bar. "We're fun, I swear!"

"I bet you are; I just bet you are. Thanks, anyway." I waved back.

"Oh, come on. Have a drink," he said.

I held mine up. "Thanks, I just got one. Besides, I'm going home with this bartender tonight." Nick smiled and clinked his glass off mine and took a big drink.

"Ah shit, I can do better than that skinny guy! My dick is bigger than his arm!" Everyone who was left at the bar laughed, including Nick.

I was excited and filled with nervousness at the same time. I had opened a door, but could I walk through it? I thought about my options and knew I could easily leave without going any further. I could make an excuse or just say I was kidding or blame the alcohol or pretend to be sick, but I didn't do any of those things. I sat at the bar until the couple drifted away and the bikers left, and I chatted with Nick while he restocked the beer coolers and wiped down the bottles and pulled the shutters down.

When he was done, he came around the bar and stood in front of me and smiled. "So, are you really going home with the bartender?"

"I'm seriously thinking about it." I reached out and put my finger in the belt loop of his shorts. I noticed him looking at my wedding ring. "Yes, I guess I am kind of married. Does that bother you?"

"If it doesn't bother you, why should it bother me?" he said simply. He reached out and took a few strands of my hair in his fingers and twirled it around. "You have great hair."

I pulled him between my legs and wrapped my arms around him, and he bent down and started kissing me. Everything about him was different from Craig—the way he felt and moved and tasted—and I did not want to stop. We started fucking right there on the barstool, and then he carried me over and put me on top of one of the tables and kept going while he stood in front of me. His hands gripped my hips tightly and then moved up to my breasts and then up to my throat as my orgasm ripped through me. It was hard and fast and slightly out of control and fantastic.

"Well, that was unexpected," he breathed when we were done.

"Yeah, not exactly what I had planned when I came here tonight. You must really want a good review." I punched him lightly in the arm.

"You're funny!" he said and pulled on his pants while I tried to find my underwear on the floor. "I'm gonna grab a beer; want one?"

"Sure, why stop now?" I struggled to pull my wadded clothes back on over my sweaty skin.

"Come on; I'll take you back to your hotel." He locked up and walked me back down the ramp I had walked up a lifetime ago.

We got into his beat-up Toyota, and he drove the short distance to my hotel. I felt great and was still buzzed but struggled to keep the conversation going. He got out and walked me to the door of my bungalow.

"So when do you leave?" he asked, wrapping his arms around me.

"I'm gone tomorrow. You'll never see me again. See, I'm the perfect date."

"Well, if you are ever down here again, I would love to see you." He gave me a big hug.

"You'll be my first stop." I hugged him back and kissed him and opened the door to my room and went inside.

I woke up the next morning and lay in bed and stared at the white ceiling fan trying to get my arms around what I had done. I waited to be overcome with guilt and wracked with tears, but instead I replayed the images of the night before over and over in my head until I was so excited I had to slip my hand between my legs and make myself come.

I showered and checked out and started the drive up to Miami to catch my flight home, stopping along the way to buy aspirin for my wine headache and a tube of Vagisil to use when I got home, just in case. I kicked myself for not even suggesting that Nick use a condom and called my gynecologist and made an appointment for the next week.

It was a slipup, I reasoned, and would never happen again. Nothing would be gained by telling Craig, so I would keep it to myself. I had to acknowledge that sleeping with Nick was an attempt at self-sabotage of my picture-perfect life. I drank too much, I took things for granted, and I allowed myself to drift along in the undercurrent without ever really pushing myself to break through the surface and achieve success.

As the palm trees and crystal-blue waters whizzed past me on the highway, I made a declaration to myself that I was going make positive changes in my life, cut back on the drinking, and never cheat on my husband again.

CHAPTER EIGHT

I was lying in bed listening to the sounds of Craig cooking breakfast and thinking about how to organize my day. It smelled and
sounded like he was making frittata. I wasn't in the mood to talk,
so I allowed myself to drift in and out of sleep while I waited for
him to finish and leave for the day. I heard him walk into the bedroom to see if I was awake twice before he left, but I kept my eyes
shut both times.

Once I had the house to myself, I got up and went into the
kitchen. A Post-it note on the refrigerator told me that the rest
of the frittata was in the oven waiting for me, and I smiled and
felt a little guilty. What kind of wife ignores her husband while
he is in the kitchen making her breakfast? Oh well, I had done
worse things than that and managed not to feel guilty, so I
gave myself a pass and took it out of the oven. It was like something out of a cooking magazine: mushrooms, onions, and red
peppers layered perfectly on top of the potatoes, with slightly
browned feta cheese on top. I ate it right out of the pan, and it
was delicious.

I reviewed my e-mails and rewrote a few paragraphs of my last article based on notes from the editor. I checked the appointments that I had set up for this week in order to start my next piece on people caring for family members with Alzheimer's at home. Four out of the ten referrals given to me by my contact at the Alzheimer's Association had agreed to be a part of the article, so I arranged to go and visit them for several days spread out over the next four weeks.

As difficult as it could be to see people coping with illnesses at the end stages of life, I was actually looking forward to digging into this topic. Me, who couldn't stop myself from remembering almost every detail in life, writing about people who were almost completely unable to make memories. I had distant relatives who had suffered from Alzheimer's and often thought about how ironic it would be if I ended up developing the disease.

My first subject was a seventy-eight-year-old man named Larry Strumble who was diagnosed four years ago. His seventy-two-year-old wife, Carol, was his main caregiver, and they lived in Plymouth. I reviewed the notes from my initial conversation with Carol and called her to confirm my 11:00 a.m. visit today. I pulled my hair back into a high ponytail and threw on my jeans, a simple white button-down shirt that I left untucked and hiking boots. I made sure I had my computer, voice recorder, and notebook in my bag and headed out.

On the drive over, I thought about some of the research that I had already done on dealing with people who were suffering from Alzheimer's and reminded myself to be patient, speak in quiet tones, and not move quickly or try to rush through the interview. I was nervous—I always was before starting a new project—but it was a good kind of nervous that was mostly made up of the anticipation of the unknown.

The Strumbles lived in one of the historic neighborhoods in Plymouth, and their house was a two-story Craftsman with red aluminum siding and white trim around all the windows. The front porch was surrounded with a white handrailing that extended down the small staircase. The front door had a half-moon window above it with a wreath announcing the coming of spring hanging on it.

A lady, who I could only assume was Carol, opened the door before I had a chance to knock and welcomed me inside. It had the smell of an old house. Not offensive, just slightly damp and dusty, mixed with the lemony smell of furniture polish.

Carol was a small woman and very short. I estimated that she was no more than five feet tall. She wore navy-colored knit pants and a white-and-navy knit shirt and white Keds that looked to be brand-new. Her hair was curly and cut short and obviously dyed brown. I shook her hand and followed her into the living room, where she gestured for me to sit on a couch that faced a redbrick fireplace. I could hear a TV running in another room down the hallway.

She sat on a chair next to the couch. "So, I just wanted to find out how this works before we involve Larry," she began.

"Yes, of course. My assignment is for *Michigan Aging* magazine—have you ever read it?"

"No." She shook her head.

"It's a quarterly and has a hard copy as well as an online version," I explained.

"Oh, I don't do anything with the computer really," she said, apologetically.

"No worries, there will be a hard-copy version as well. My assignment is to profile several families who are caring for relatives with Alzheimer's and write about how they are coping, what works, what doesn't work. The general toll the disease takes on the family unit and things of that nature."

"I see. Well, it does take a toll; that's for sure." She smiled sadly. Her fingernails were painted pale pink, and her wedding ring set was silver and sat sideways on her finger as if it were too big for her tiny hand.

"So, I would like to interview you and just observe you interacting with your husband to get a general feel of what a normal day is like for you. Does that sound OK?"

"Sure, I guess. There isn't too much special that goes on here, so I'm not sure we're interesting enough for an actual magazine article. Larry is pretty withdrawn now. He mostly watches movies or works puzzles. He used to be a builder. You know the Greenview Valley condos on Telegraph? His company built those, along with some on the east side, River Crest or River Bluff or something like that. Anyway, that was a while ago."

I took out my notebook and recorder. "Is it OK if I record you talking? It's OK if you don't want me to. I can just take notes if you prefer."

She stared at the recorder on the table for a moment and smiled. "I used to be a secretary for a man—it was a long time ago—and he used a Dictaphone machine. You're young. You probably don't even know what that is, do you?"

"I do." I smiled back and relaxed slightly because I knew that the interview had begun.

"He would sit in his office all day dictating into it, and then I had to transcribe it all for him. I learned to hate the sound of his voice. Do you find yourself hating the sounds of people's voices when you listen back to them?"

"No, but I move from assignment to assignment pretty quickly, so I don't have to listen to any one person talk for too long."

"That makes sense." She nodded. "You can use the recorder. I don't mind."

"OK, great." I clicked it on. "You said that you've been your husband's main caregiver for the four years since his diagnosis?"

"Yes. He didn't need much help at first. He would just forget where he put things or appointments or people's names. He has slowly gotten worse, especially over the last year, I would say, but he can still do most things himself."

"What's the biggest change you notice in him?"

"Oh, his personality. Larry used to be very gregarious. Always telling stories and jokes and talking to people no matter where we went. Have you ever heard the saying 'He never met a stranger'?"

"Yes, I know what you mean."

"Well, that was Larry. Now he is very quiet. I know he can't keep track of what's going on, so he just smiles and nods a lot."

"Is he alone right now?"

"Yes, I put a movie on for him. He has a couple of old movies that seem to make him happy, and he'll sit quietly and watch them over and over again."

"I bet you're pretty tired of those movies by now?"

"To tell you the truth, I don't even hear them anymore. And sometimes, I'll be sitting there and the movie is on, and I'll look up and see a scene that I swear I never saw before, and I think, oh my God, don't tell me I'm getting Alzheimer's, too? How can I see a movie hundreds of times and still find something new in it?"

"It's become white noise for you at this point," I offered.

"I guess. I've tried new movies, but he can't follow the story unless it is something he saw years ago."

"Is now a good time for me to meet him?"

"Sure. It's almost time for his sandwich, so why don't you meet him now? He will probably think that you're our daughter, Beverly. You look like you're around her age, and he does that a lot. I'm just going to say that you are from Dr. Burton's office. That is his favorite doctor."

"No problem. I'll follow your lead."

We got up, and I followed her down a short hallway and into a back bedroom that had been made into a TV room. Two recliners sat side by side facing an entertainment center that held a TV, various knickknacks, and some books. There was also a love seat with a footstool against a wall and an American flag hanging from a flagpole in the corner, along with a stack of tray tables. The movie on the TV looked like it was about World War II.

Larry pushed himself up out of his recliner with some difficulty when I walked in. He was thin and taller than I expected, given Carol's tiny frame. He had a smile on his face, but his eyes darted from her to me with apprehension.

"Larry, this is Megan," she said softly. "She is from Dr. Burton's office, and she is going to visit us a couple of times over the next few weeks to see how good you are doing."

"Hello, Mr. Strumble, I'm Megan. It is nice to meet you." I took his hand and shook it with a big smile.

"Oh yes, Dr. Burton. He is a very good doctor."

"Yes, he is. Thanks for having me over today. Please have a seat," I suggested, and I sat on the love seat and placed the recorder on the armrest.

Larry eased himself back down onto the recliner. "Dr. Burton graduated from U of M, you know. He is a very good doctor." Like his wife, Larry's appearance was neat and clean. He wore tan-color tennis shoes with Velcro closures, khaki pants, and a tucked-in red-checked shirt. He had a thin layer of gray hair that was combed back and held in place with some type of hair gel. He wore a watch and a wedding ring. If you passed him in a restaurant or sitting on a bench, you would never know there was anything wrong with him.

Carol hovered for a minute and then perched herself at the edge of the recliner next to Larry. She placed her hand palm-up on the arm of Larry's recliner, and he reached out and took it immediately. It struck me as a largely unconscious gesture on both of their parts.

"Yes, he is. And how are you doing today?" I asked.

"Oh, wonderful, wonderful," he said, his eyes darting to Carol's.

"Great. Well, I'm visiting several people who have Alzheimer's to see how they're doing," I explained as simply as possible.

"Oh yes, yes." He nodded. "Very important."

The noise of an air battle was coming from the TV, and Larry's eyes drifted over to it.

I looked, too, and I recognized the movie. "Oh, *Midway*. This is a good movie," I said.

"Wonderful movie. About the battle for Midway Island in the Pacific."

"Yes, I do remember it now."

"We lost three hundred and seven men taking that island, but the Japs lost over three thousand defending it." Larry stared at the screen for a few moments before looking back at me. "I was just a boy, of course, but I grew up during the war, so I heard all about it. You're far too young to know much about it."

"Yes, only what I've read in books," I replied.

"Is Ken with you?" he asked suddenly.

"No, that's not Beverly; that's Megan from Dr. Burton's office," Carol said gently.

"Dr. Burton is a wonderful doctor. Wonderful." He smiled at Carol and then at me.

"Ken is our daughter Beverly's husband. They live in California," she explained to me, before turning back to Larry. "Remember that Beverly and Ken are in California. They were here at Christmas, and we went to see the *Christmas Story* play. They are coming back in the summer for a visit."

Larry nodded vacantly and turned his attention back to the TV screen. I quickly Googled the Battle of Midway on my iPhone and found that the casualty numbers that Larry quoted were spot-on. I decided to test him a bit more.

"Mr. Strumble, what date was this battle fought?"

"Well, it was really a series of battles fought between June third and June seventh in the year 1942. Everyone thinks that there is just one big battle, but there is always more to it than that, you know? See him?" he said, gesturing to the TV. "That's Isoroku Yamamoto, the Japanese admiral. He was a tough son of a bitch if there ever was one, but he was no match for Admiral Nimitz."

"I guess not. Interesting."

"Ken likes this movie. You should tell him to come in and watch it, too. The big battle is about to start."

"I think it is time for your sandwich," Carol interjected. "Are you hungry?"

"I don't want the fish today, just the chicken. I don't like the fish."

"OK. You watch the movie, and we'll be back in a few minutes."

"You'll be back before the big battle scene?" he asked, with concern.

"Yes, we'll be back in a few minutes." Carol tapped the face of the watch on his wrist and used her finger to point. "Before this hand gets past here, we'll be back."

Larry studied the watch carefully, and Carol repeated the gesture twice more before he finally nodded and mumbled OK. I got up when she did and followed her into the kitchen just across the hallway.

She took three plates from the cupboard and Tupperware full of what looked to be tuna fish out of the refrigerator.

"Is today a pretty typical day?" I asked.

"Yes. It is Groundhog Day around here. A lot of the same over and over again. It's like his mind is stuck in a groove on a record, and it just plays over and over again. He likes everything the same, and if anything is different, he gets upset."

"Is that tuna fish?" I asked as she spread it on the bread.

"Yes, it's his favorite, but he thinks he doesn't like fish, so I tell him it's chicken, and he eats it. I find I do a lot of lying these days." She smiled at me. "But I think I'll be forgiven by the man upstairs for these little white lies."

"Yes, I agree. Oh, you don't have to make me a sandwich," I told her as I noticed her laying out more bread.

"It's easier if you eat in front of Larry. He won't eat unless everyone is eating. He'll keep getting stuck if you don't have food in front of you, and he'll keep insisting that you eat, so just eat or pretend to eat. It's tuna with regular mayo and a little mustard. No onions or relish."

"Gotcha." I noted how she anticipated and adapted to each situation without missing a beat. It was as if it had always been this way, and I wished that I could have seen them ten years ago, when things were normal, to see what a day in their life was like.

"You have a son, too, right?"

"Yes, Michael. He lives in Ecorse with his wife and my two grandkids. He comes by every Tuesday in the evening and sits with his dad, and I go out with my sister, Pearl. We don't do much, just go to dinner or to a movie, but it gives me one night out. Mostly we go to the Panera Bread by her house. Sometimes we go somewhere to have some wine." She laughed. "He comes over on Saturdays, too, and helps with yard work and things around the house that need to be fixed and stuff like that."

"Did you and Larry used to go out at night before he got sick?"

"Not much, but we would go to dinner once a week or so with our friends. He played euchre, too, and I had a standing bridge game on the same night. Once he retired, we used to go to the park and walk around the track in the mornings. He's a little unsteady on his feet now. We do walk around the block once in a while, but being outside seems to confuse him these days. For some reason, no matter what the temperature is outside, he seems to think it's cold, so he won't go out unless he has his winter coat and hat on."

"Really? That's interesting. Is that common?" I asked.

"I don't know about common, but it's not rare either. The doctor gave me some literature, and I've read a few books, so I know what to expect, but everybody is different. Everybody's brain is affected in a slightly different way, so the literature is really just a guideline." Carol added a handful of pretzels to each plate and poured three short glasses of milk.

We returned to the TV room to set up the tray tables. Larry looked at me with curiosity when I walked back in, but Carol anticipated his reaction and immediately reintroduced me. "OK, Megan and I are back with lunch."

Larry made a move to get up, and I moved forward to extend my hand. "No need to get up, Mr. Strumble; we met earlier today." I shook his hand again, and he settled back.

"OK, sorry. I forget things sometimes now and then. You're from Dr. Burton's office? You're a nurse?" he asked.

"No, I'm just here to observe how you are doing," I explained.

"Oh, wonderful. Carol takes very good care of me, and Ken and Beverly come over all the time." He looked at his wife for reassurance.

"And Mike—your son, Mike—comes over to visit on Tuesdays and Saturdays. Isn't that nice?" she prompted.

"Yes, Mike is a good boy. He rides his bike up and down the street for hours at a time." The look in his eyes clouded over as his brain struggled to make sense of the information it contained. I could tell he knew that what he had just said was incorrect, but he couldn't figure out why. He looked at Carol again, pleading for the right answer with his eyes.

Carol patted his arm. "You're right. Mike loved that bike of his, but that was a long time ago. Back when we lived in Livonia in the white house with the blue shutters. Do you remember that house?"

"Oh yes, that was a nice house with a big yard, where we had the oak trees." He smiled and looked at me. "Nice trees but so messy! I swear I spent every weekend cleaning up after those trees so they wouldn't kill the grass. Messy things!"

"I bet that was a lot of work," I responded. I pointed at the TV. "Did we miss the big battle scene?"

Larry looked up at me with surprise. "Do you like this movie? It's a good one. About the Battle of Midway, you know?"

"Yes. The big battle scene was just about to begin before we went in to make the sandwiches."

"Oh, OK." He looked at Carol and held up his sandwich. "Chicken?"

"Yes, chicken with pretzels, just like you like." She smiled.

Larry went back to watching the movie while he ate his sandwich. I noticed that Carol ate her food with one hand and kept the other on the armrest so that Larry could grab it whenever he wanted.

The sandwich of tuna fish on white bread reminded me of something that my mom made when I was a child. It was plain and simple and traditional with no lettuce or bean sprouts or whole-wheat bread with flaxseeds that you see in tuna sandwiches now.

I studied the various family photos on the walls and entertainment center. The Larry in those photos was tanner and beefier, and there was a spark in his eyes that was now absent. The Larry in the photos had a presence, a bit of mischief that was clearly discernible even when standing in his tux at his daughter's wedding or surrounded by his family at a picnic. His eyes now were still blue but flat.

"Mr. Strumble, your wife tells me that you worked as a builder?" I asked.

"Yes, with Hamilton Builders. It's a big outfit. Do you know them?"

"No, I don't."

"Craig Hamilton founded the company. Of course, he died from cancer a long time ago." Larry looked at his wife. "Craig's gone, right?" She nodded back. "Started with single-family homes, but now they build condo communities. Nice but not enough elbow room for me." Larry stuck his elbows out to underscore his point.

"I agree. I like my space," I said.

"Those places are mostly for old people anyway, and we're not old, are we?" He kidded his wife.

"No, we most certainly are not." She smiled and patted him on the shoulder.

"I might not be able to remember a damn thing sometimes, but I'm not old!" He laughed.

"Good for you!" I said.

The big battle scene started, and we all focused our attention on it until it was over, and then I helped Carol clean the plates and put away the tray tables.

"Are you gonna take your nap now?" she asked her husband.

"No, it's time for the other movie now," he answered.

"But then you are going to fall asleep in the chair during the movie and be all stiff when you wake up. Why don't you lie down for a little while now and then watch the movie?" She put her hands out to help him up.

"I'll sleep after lunch," he protested.

"You just had lunch. It's afternoon now. Come on, let me help you up, and you can walk Megan to the door with me."

I could see the confusion in his eyes as he tried to make sense of everything. His wife waited patiently for a few minutes until he worked out the details in his mind and began to get up. Despite her tiny size, she managed to add just enough leverage for him to rise without much difficulty.

I gathered my stuff and shook Larry's hand again. "It was nice meeting you."

He smiled and nodded and took my hand in both of his. "Oh yes, so nice to see you. Thank you. Thank you."

"I'll come back next week and see you again, if that's OK?" I asked.

He smiled and looked at Carol, and she nodded, and he looked back at me. "Oh yes, yes, come back and meet the kids. Beverly and

Ken will be here, and you can talk to them. He has a real good job with the government. He can tell you about it."

"OK, great. Thank you so much." I walked in front of them to the front room.

"So, is that it?" she asked me as I opened the door.

"Pretty much," I answered. "Thanks for your time. I'll call you Friday to confirm for next week, OK?" I pushed the screen door open and went back out into the chilly spring air.

"Yes, OK. Thank you for coming." She shut the door behind me.

On the drive home, I imagined Carol sitting there next to him in that room with the movie playing and his hand on her hand. It was sweet and sad at the same time. She could almost never leave his presence, yet he wasn't really present at all.

CHAPTER NINE

I met Mr. and Mrs. Phillips at the condo they had recently moved into in Clinton Township. Taking care of a house and his wife had proven too much for Mr. Phillips, and he reluctantly sold the home in Franklin Hills that they had lived in since building it some forty-two years prior.

He was an average-size man, standing about five-nine or so, with a thick head of gray hair that grew down his neck. He wore dark slippers, blue jeans, and a light-blue button-down shirt with a light-blue sweater over it. He looked like a high-school science teacher that you could find in Anytown, USA. He seemed anxious as he welcomed me through the front door to a small landing and the living room. The condo was sparsely decorated, and the walls were still a plain white to go with the beige condo carpeting that ran throughout.

Unopened moving boxes neatly lined the walls on both sides of the room, with names of rooms neatly written on the side of each in thick black marker: *Kitchen. Den. Bedroom.* A stack of either paintings or pictures were wrapped in brown moving paper and piled against one another in the corner of the room, waiting to be unwrapped and hung in their new home.

Mrs. Phillips sat in a wheelchair that had been placed next to the couch. She wore a light-green nightgown and was wrapped in a green-and-white robe. Clean white socks covered her feet. The thin hair that was left on her head was long and silver white and pulled back into a low ponytail. She was slumped slightly over to the right, staring vacantly forward. Her hands were curled into fists on her lap.

Through an archway at the back of the room was a hospital bed in what was supposed to be the dining room. Bolts still protruded from the ceiling where the chandelier had been hanging before it was removed. There was a recliner next to the bed with a pillow and blanket folded neatly on the seat, and I assumed that was where Mr. Phillips slept.

The house was very quiet, uncomfortably so for my taste, and when I spoke, I felt I had to whisper. "Thank you again for your time and your willingness to be involved in the article."

"Of course, of course," he answered quickly. "I am happy to help, but my wife doesn't say much or do much anymore, so I'm not sure how helpful we can be."

"It will be fine. It's important that I get to meet people at all different stages of the illness. The piece is really about how families cope, so your input is truly invaluable."

"OK. Of course." He gestured for me to sit in a light-blue chair across from him, and he sat on the couch next to his wife.

"May I record our conversation for accuracy? It's OK if you don't want me to."

"Of course, of course, it's fine. Whatever you need to do."

I noticed Mrs. Phillips's head shift slightly, and her eyes seemed to focus on me for a moment before turning vacant again. "Hello, Mrs. Phillips, thank you for having me in your home," I offered, but she did not respond. "How aware is she of the people around her?"

"Who can say?" Mr. Phillips bent down to intercept his wife's gaze. "Melly? Can you hear me, Mel?" he asked her softly. Her right hand twitched slightly, and her head moved toward him. She took a deep breath but then went still again.

"Yes, it seems like she knows you."

Mr. Phillips shrugged.

"How long has it been like this?"

"Just the last few months. It's a terribly slow process, and if you are here every day, you don't really notice. She was eating soup and crackers by herself at Christmastime. She put up a terrible fuss when we moved here. The change was hard on her, but I had to do it; the house was just too much to keep up. She just likes to sit in the quiet now."

"Noise bothers her? TV? Music?" I asked.

Mr. Phillips thought for a moment before answering. "It's like her brain doesn't know how to process it, doesn't know how to interpret the sounds. When the TV is on, I don't think she realizes the sound and the picture are coming from the same place. She gets real agitated and looks around like the sounds are coming from all around her. To me, she looks like she is struggling when there is too much noise or commotion going on, so I like to keep it quiet."

"I understand. Do you have anyone who comes in to help you?"

"I have a woman named Claudia who comes by on Mondays, so I can do the grocery shopping and go to the bank and run errands and the like. When we were at home—a while ago, when things were different—I had an aid who would stop by every day to help me. Melanie used to wander a lot and didn't sleep much at night. It was a bear to keep track of her at times, but she doesn't move so much now." He reached over and stroked her arm and shoulder. "She doesn't eat much now either. They talked to me about putting a feeding tube in, but I don't see the point."

"I'm sorry if I asked you before, but do you have any children?"

"We had a son named Kyle. He died in the service."

"I'm so sorry," I said quickly, feeling like this family had drawn the short straw in life.

"He died during a training exercise in San Diego. Helicopter crash. All that was on the helicopter died," he said simply.

"Oh, that's terrible. I'm sorry."

"At least he was at home instead of over in some godforsaken country halfway around the world. He was a good kid. He would have been a real help to me and his mom; it's just how he was. It's why he decided to serve his country."

I looked around the room but did not see any family photos. "Do you have any photos of him that I could see?"

"Photos? Most of 'em are still packed away. I don't think I can get to them too easy right now." He looked like he was about to get up.

"Oh, please don't bother. I just thought I would ask. I'll be coming back a couple more times over the next few weeks, so if you come across one, let me know."

"Of course, of course. I'm sure I can get my hands on one."

"That would be nice, but don't worry if you can't. We would like to feature a photo of each person before the illness and one now, if possible."

"So, do you always write about the Alzheimer's?" he asked.

"No, I have written about it before, but I write all kinds of stuff. I write for a travel magazine and a Michigan-based food and leisure magazine. I've also written for women's magazines. Anything and everything from one time or another."

"Does anyone in your family have it?"

"Yes, my aunt had it, but she lived pretty far away, so I wasn't around her once she went into the nursing home."

"That's good. You get to remember her the way she was instead of the way she ended up." I could detect a bit of anger in his voice.

"I guess that's true. I never thought about it that way before," I admitted.

"It's a hell of a thing. How many other people are you visiting for this article?"

"Four families. All from Michigan. All are doing home care at this point."

"Yeah, the doctors keep telling me to move her to a nursing home, but she would hate that. I don't see the point, either; I'd just be sitting in a nursing home all day. At least this way I can be home while I keep her company." He looked around with a look of exasperation. "Well, my home now, I guess."

While he spoke, I searched the room, trying to figure out how he occupied himself during the day. There were folded pieces of newspaper on most of the tables and a Mike Hammer mystery book on the end of the couch. Unpacking didn't seem to be a priority, but he seemed like the kind of old-fashioned man who would have relied on his wife to put the house together.

"What's the most difficult part of the day?" I asked.

"Oh, I suppose moving her in and out of the bed. There's not much to her anymore. I doubt she weighs more than a hundred pounds these days. She has a hard time moving now, even if I get her started, so I have to lift her and support her. Of course, changing her is also getting more difficult. Claudia bathes her on Mondays. That woman is strong; I'll tell you that."

Mrs. Phillips looked at me again, and her mouth moved as she tried to speak. At first, nothing came out, but then she found her voice, and a series of random noises that weren't quite words came out. It was clear from the rhythm of her voice that she was speaking in sentences, albeit sentences only she could understand.

Her husband watched her and nodded as she spoke, waiting patiently for her to stop before saying, "That's right, Melly. That's just what I was thinking, too."

I didn't quite know how to react to her, so I said, "Well, that is something, isn't it?"

She nodded at me and at her husband, and her eyes went neutral again.

"Do you have any other help? Friends or family that come over?" I asked.

"Not much anymore. I hate to say it, but we've outlived a lot of our friends." He laughed. "Who would have thought that we would be the last ones left? Course, maybe that's the curse. Maybe we'd have been better off if we'd gone early and didn't have this to deal with." He looked down and shook his head. "I'm not sure it's a fair trade, you know?"

"Yes, I understand completely."

"I haven't met very many of the neighbors yet. They seem nice enough, but I can't bother with making friends right now."

"I grew up just a few miles away. It's a nice neighborhood," I offered. I stood up and walked through the makeshift bedroom to look out the sliding doors and into the backyard. There was a small wooden deck. A stack of chairs sat in one corner, covered in dust and leaves. Maple trees lined a wooden fence that bordered the complex, and there was a blue birdbath on the right-hand side. "Cute yard. It's looks very peaceful."

He grunted. "It's nice but not much compared with what we had in Franklin Hills. We had a big piece of property with trees and shrubs and flowers and a winding path and a gazebo. My wife worked and worked on that yard. And bird feeders—you've never seen so many bird feeders. She knew what to put in them to attract certain birds, you know?"

"That sounds beautiful," I said, returning to the couch.

"We sold to a nice couple with teenagers, and the wife said she loved to garden. Of course, we had let it go over the last couple of years because I could never keep up with the weeds and pruning and such, but hopefully she will make it nice again." He chuckled.

"A while back, when Melly started to get really sick, she would go out in the garden with her gloves and her garden clogs and her floppy hat and her little tools and would putter around, but then she wouldn't know how to get back to the house." He patted her hand. "Can you imagine that? She would stand out there as if she had been transported to the middle of the Sahara, and she was standing not more than seventy feet from the house!"

I nodded sympathetically.

"Sometimes, she would think the neighbor's house was ours, and she would just be standing along the fence staring at it. She couldn't figure out how to get around the fence or work the gate. Sometimes she would get upset because she knew that she didn't know and couldn't do anything about it."

I imagined Mrs. Phillips dressed in her gardening outfit. "What did you do when you found her like that?"

"Oh, I would just talk to her until I convinced her to come back to the house. She would resist me sometimes. How do you convince someone that her house is her house if she doesn't really believe that it is?" He shook his head. "It's a damn funny thing, this disease. It doesn't make any sense, so how do you make sense of it?"

"Yes, it is difficult, and it affects everyone differently, so there really isn't any one set of rules to follow," I offered.

"She used to smile sometimes and laugh. I could still feel like she was with me, but now I think she is finally almost gone. It took a long time, but the last bits of her have flaked away, and this is what is left."

I couldn't help but notice how sad he looked, and I wanted to leave. "That is very sad," I said, holding back tears. "What are the next steps?"

"You're asking me?" He snorted. "I haven't had a bit of say in any of this since the beginning; I'm just trying to keep up." He took a deep breath and thought for a moment. "I suppose I'll sit here with her until the end and then do whatever I have to do after that."

I picked up my recorder and clicked it off. "Well, I really appreciate your time today, Mr. Phillips," I said, extending my hand.

He stood up and shook it.

"Goodbye, Mrs. Phillips, it was nice meeting you today," I said to her and paused to see if there was a response. She shifted slightly, and her eyes seemed to be following her husband as he moved to open the door for me.

After I said goodbye, I was filled with the overwhelming desire to have a drink in a place with music and TVs hanging off every wall. It was 3:32 p.m., and I briefly wrestled with the fact that it was too early to start drinking, but I drove to Little Steve's Bar and Grille anyway. The lunch crowd was already gone, and the happy-hour crowd hadn't arrived yet, so I sat alone at the bar and ordered a glass of chardonnay and munched on bar pretzels while I stared at the TVs and listened to top-forty music. A men's tennis match, CNN, a soccer game, *Dr. Phil*, a dog-agility competition, and the movie *Gremlins* filled the screens behind the bar. I wasn't really interested in any of it, but I welcomed the influx of information into my senses.

I thought about Mr. Phillips sitting alone in the silence of that condo with what was left of his wife sitting next to him. She was clearly at the end stages of the disease, and she should've been in a nursing home. I wondered why he sold his house and if he was out of money. She would be gone soon, and he would be left in the white condo with the beige carpeting alone to live out the rest of his days. Would he join the bridge club at the condo community and hook up with a widow down the street? Would he sit on that deck and watch the birds in the birdbath?

I thought about what he said about it being a curse to live longer. I would not want to live like Mrs. Phillips was living, but that was easy to say when you were forty years away from the decision.

I tried to imagine what it would be like to have all your memories wiped away. I tried to imagine what Mrs. Phillips thought about while she was sitting there and what she was trying to tell us when she spoke. I wondered if she had any coherent thoughts or if it was like her mind was chasing dandelion spores across the lawn, and they were always just out of reach.

On one of the screens, a yellow lab ran through an obstacle course. He was bursting with enthusiasm, and when he finished, he jumped on his trainer with unbridled joy. He was a dog, without spoken or written language, but his emotions were unmistakable. The woman I had just left seemed devoid of emotion. Or was she just devoid of the ability to show emotion?

I thought about how awful and ironic it would be if she still felt all her emotions but couldn't express them in any way. I shivered and ordered another glass of wine.

CHAPTER TEN

I woke up the next morning filled with dread. I had to go and meet with another family today, and after my experience with the Phillipses, I wasn't looking forward to it. My husband was already gone for the day, so I got up and went downstairs and sat on the floor in the sunshine that was streaming through the sliding-glass door and practiced breathing deeply for several minutes. I reminded myself that I was an impartial visitor who was there just to absorb the situation and that it would be over in a few weeks.

But I knew that although I wouldn't have to see it, those people would all still be in those houses living that reality day after day. I pushed those thoughts out of my brain again and concentrated on the trees outside my door, the flowers that were just opening on my rhododendrons, and my breathing. It was all part of the circle of life and had to be accepted, I reasoned. It was my job to inform people so that others could learn. I needed to do my job well, and I would be happy. Breathe in, pause, breathe out. Breathe in, pause, breathe out.

I parked on the street in front of the Normans' redbrick house in Saint Clair Shores. The house was on a corner, and it was hard for me to tell whether I should go in the front door or the side door, since both were exposed to the street. I sat drinking my coffee and procrastinating before I got mad at myself for putting off the inevitable and jumped out of the car.

Before I even knocked on the side door, I could hear the yelling. A man's voice, a deep baritone, followed by a woman's voice. I took a deep breath and knocked. No one responded. I knocked again, and I could hear the woman telling the man to shut up. He paused briefly, and I quickly knocked again. I could hear footsteps on a wooden floor and the creaking of boards as someone approached, and then the door jerked open.

The force sucked the metal screen door back, and it made a loud popping noise. I jumped involuntarily and then waved hello. The woman who opened the door was large enough to fill the doorway. She wasn't just heavy; she was tall and broad and big, with brown-and-gray hair tied back.

"You the writer girl?" she asked loudly through the glass.

I nodded. "Yes, I am. Megan."

She motioned for me to come in, and I opened the screen door and walked onto the small landing that led directly downstairs on one side and up into the kitchen on the other side. The woman backed into the kitchen, and I followed her.

"I'm Linda. We talked on the phone." She extended her large hand, and I couldn't help but notice the size of her forearm.

"Yes, great to meet you." I could hear the man yelling from the other room and another woman's voice and what sounded like a TV as well.

In sharp contrast to the Phillipses' house, this house was noisy and active. Something heavy fell, and Linda rolled her eyes and without turning away from me yelled, "Jesus Christ, Dad! Is that the footstool again? Leave the goddamn thing alone!" She shook her head from side to side. "He's got something against the foot-stool. Who knows what? He hates it? He doesn't understand it? He thinks it's going eat him? Who knows? Welcome to the asylum." She threw her hands up in the air.

"Is this a good time? If he is agitated now, maybe I should come back later?" I suggested, my feet firmly planted on the peach-colored linoleum.

"No, no, no, no." She reached out and took me by the shoulder. "Your being here will calm him down. He only acts like this in front of us. If a stranger is here, he remembers his social skills, and he acts like a perfect gentleman."

"Interesting."

"Yes, it's a real hoot. You'll see." She walked me through the kitchen and doorway into the TV room. "Dad, look who is here to see you."

The room was large but did nothing to diminish the size of the man who was pacing between the couch and the bookcase. He wore khaki pants and a blue sweater and black tennis shoes, and he was stooped over as if he were afraid his head would hit the ceiling. He was still yelling, "Shovel the cement! We can't be late, and the cement isn't shoveled yet! Where is the boy to shovel it? We can't be late!"

I noticed a brown footstool lying on its side on the carpet in front of the couch. I also noticed that the carpet he was pacing on was well-worn.

An older woman, his wife, I assumed, sat on a recliner across from the couch. She was a medium-size woman with a full head of white-gray hair, and she wore a white blouse, blue skirt, and panty hose. She had a newspaper folded to the crossword puzzle on her lap and a pencil in her fingers. A game show I didn't recognize was blaring on the TV.

I nodded to his wife and stepped forward to say hello to Mr. Norman. "Hello, Mr. Norman." I offered him my hand.

He stopped pacing and yelling and seem to notice me for the first time. He stood up a little straighter and pulled his sweater down and smoothed the front of his pants. He walked over to me in two long strides and shook my hand very gently. "Hello, I am Charles Norman," he said clearly.

"Hello, I am Megan. Thank you for having me at your house, Mr. Norman."

"Charles. Please, Charles." He smiled warmly. "Won't you sit down?"

I moved to sit and stopped to shake the older woman's hand. "Hello."

"Sophia. Nice to meet you." She shook my hand without getting up. "Now that you're here, we can finally get this puzzle done before we go."

I didn't know exactly what that meant but nodded anyway and took a seat on the couch. Charles sat next to me, his long legs extending far out from the couch. I could see his bony knees pushing against the fabric of his pants. He folded his hands in his lap.

Linda stood near the doorway, leaning against one of the chairs from the dining-room table.

"I usually use a recorder; is that OK?" I asked, looking from one person to the other.

"It's fine," Linda called over.

"Would it be possible to turn the TV down a bit?" I asked, feeling like I was intruding.

"Sure, now that the yelling part of the day is over, right, Dad?" she said and came over and used the remote to turn the sound down. She placed the footstool in its proper position, giving her father a look before returning to stand next to the dining-room chair.

"Chuck. What's another name for a ship? Begins with an *s*. Has eight letters," his wife asked.

Charles thought for a minute and then looked at her and said, "Say it again."

"Another name for a ship? Begins with an *s*. Has eight letters."

"*Schooner* is a ship."

"Oh, I think that's it." She filled the letters in and saw that it fit. "Yes, that's it!" She looked at me. "You can answer these, too, you know. Doesn't matter who gets 'em."

"OK." I had a feeling that the crossword puzzle was serious business in this house.

"Charles. Twenty-third president of the United States?" she asked.

"He knows all the presidents up until Clinton," Linda said to me.

"His name wasn't Clinton," Charles said sharply.

Linda looked at me and rolled her eyes and shook her head.

"Twenty-third," his wife repeated.

"Benjamin Harrison," he responded.

"Yes, Harrison fits," his wife said, with no particular excitement.

"Do you do the crossword puzzle every day?" I asked, looking from husband to wife. Charles looked at me, and his mouth opened as if he were going to answer, but then he deferred to his wife.

"We try to do it every day, but sometimes he gets all riled up about something and won't concentrate, so it takes all day to do it. I like to have it done before he goes to his club in the afternoons."

It was really a day care program at the Oaks Memory Care Center, and I smiled that they called it a "club" for him.

"That boy hasn't shoveled yet, and he needs to do that or we won't be able to go, and we need to go soon," he said in an agitated voice to his wife.

"It is done, Dad!" Linda yelled from across the room. "He did it already. We are leaving very soon." She turned her attention to me. "He has a girlfriend at the club, and he doesn't like to miss her."

"Well, she is waiting for me!" he yelled back, and then, as if remembering that I was present, he smiled and lowered his tone.

"She is a very nice person. Her name is Rosalind, and she grew up in the same neighborhood as me, but she is six years younger so I didn't know her back then."

I had read about relationships forming between patients with dementia. I wanted to know how his wife felt and made a note to revisit the topic.

"I see," I said. "Do you have other friends at the club?"

"There are a lot of people over there. Most of 'em are nice. Some of them are sick and can't eat by themselves. A couple don't have any idea where they are; they just sit and stare, even when the music is playing after lunch."

"Oh, they play music?" I asked, with enthusiasm.

"Yes, and Rosalind likes to dance, so I dance. I could do without it, but she likes to dance." When he spoke, the words came out of his mouth in a quick, staccato rhythm, and I wondered if he always spoke that way or if that was a part of his illness.

"Yes, you are a dancing fool," his wife said to him and then looked at me. "We used to dance when we were first dating. He's a good dancer, but once you have kids and life moves on, you stop having time to dance and forget all about it. I don't think we've danced since Linda's wedding."

"Linda had a fine wedding." He perked up and looked across the room at Linda. "Are we going soon?"

"Yes, Dad, it was a good wedding," Linda said and sat down heavily at the dining-room table. "Bad husband but a good wedding. We'll leave in a few minutes."

"He was a bum, that's all." He tapped me on the arm and whispered, "Owned a tool-and-die shop, but he was still a bum."

I nodded and winked at him.

"Chuck, what's another name for a trout basket? Five letters. Ends with an *l*," his wife called out to him.

"A what?"

"Trout basket. Trout. Fish. Like fishing."

"Trout? Trout. Trout. Trout." He said the word like it had never been in his mouth before, turning it over on his tongue and letting it drift out slowly.

"If you went fishing and you had a little basket that you put the fish in after you caught them, so you could take them home and eat them," she explained, the impatience in her voice growing along with the pitch.

"Maybe you have to come back to that one," Linda suggested. "It's almost time to go anyway. Dad? Use the bathroom now."

"Are we leaving? Is the cement clear enough?" he asked.

"Yes, it's done, it's done, it's done. I told you already. Go to the bathroom," she directed, getting up and pushing the chair into the dining-room table.

Sophia made no move to get up and continued to work on her puzzle.

Charles got up and began to pace behind the couch several times before looking outside. "It looks clear. Is there more weather coming in today? I don't want to slip," he said.

"Go to the bathroom, Chuck," Sophia said without looking up.

He stood for a minute and looked like he wanted to say something more and then disappeared down the hallway.

"So that's my dad," Linda said.

"He is very nice," I replied.

"You said you wanted to go to the day care program, right?"

"Yes, I do, but I think I'll do that next week, if that's OK with you?" She nodded that it was. "I'll come by about the same time and follow you over so I can get a look at the facility and a sense of how the program works."

"It's fine by me, and I'll run it by the nurses in charge today to make sure it's OK," Linda said.

"Thanks for your time, Mrs. Norman," I said to her as I passed. She glanced up and waved me off and muttered something I didn't understand.

"By the way, the answer is *creel*," I said. "Trout basket is *creel*."

She looked up at me with newfound admiration. "Well, thank you. How'd you know that? That was a tough one."

"I know all kinds of goofy stuff. See you next week."

CHAPTER ELEVEN

The Dittmer house was in the old-money part of Grosse Pointe Shores, where the best houses had only two numbers in the address. The trees that had been planted on each side of the street had long since formed a tunnel over the road that extended the length of the street. The metal gates at the bottom of the driveway stood open, and I drove up the winding blacktop driveway and parked in the circular drive that led to the front door. I noticed a few other cars parked along a brick-paved approach in front of the garage. Although it was still early in spring, the landscaping was neat and green, and I could tell that the lawn had recently been aerated.

It was a large stone Tudor-style house that reminded me of something you would see in England or Ireland. Each window on the second floor sat under a peak that pushed up into the steep gray/green roof. The front door sat under another peak that dominated the front of the house and was bordered by thick green shrubs on each side.

I couldn't wait to see the inside of the house, and I kicked myself for never writing about architecture. As I knocked on the massive wooden door, I imagined a tuxedoed butler opening the door and offering me a glass of brandy in the receiving room while I waited. Instead, when the door opened, I was greeted by Justin.

It is hard to say what makes one person interesting to another. Looks are certainly part of it, but there is something else... an energy or a vibe that jumps from one person to another like a virus. The second I looked at Justin, I was infected. He had a cute face with piercing light-blue eyes and a brown beard that looked like it was due for a trim. He wore a Detroit Tigers baseball hat, a red hoodie with a cartoon bear face on it, jeans, and toe shoes. I laughed as soon as I saw the shoes.

"What? The shoes?" His smile was the final nail in my coffin. "You don't like them? Nobody likes them," he said, shifting his feet so I could get a better look.

"No, no, I...well...OK, I hate those kinds of shoes." I giggled like a twelve-year-old girl.

"You hate my shoes? You haven't even said hello yet, and you've told me that you hate my shoes? This is going well!" He laughed and backed up to allow me to enter the house.

"Oh God, I'm sorry. Rude. I'm Megan Connor. I'm here to interview you and your grandmother, Mrs. Dittmer." I could feel the nervous energy running through my body as I extended my hand to shake his.

"It's OK. Truth. I like it. I like truth." He grabbed my hand and shook it, and I could see his eyes looking at my face and hair. He made a little exhale and smiled broadly at me. "Welcome. You look different than I thought you would after talking to you."

"I do?"

"Yeah, you know how you get a mental picture of someone when you talk to them?" he asked.

"I do. So, what did you think I looked like?" I was aware that I was flirting but couldn't stop myself.

"Oh man, I don't know. Different. Not as…" He held his hands up and gestured to indicate my height and weight before shrugging. "I don't know. Just different."

"OK, I'll take it. Thank you, I guess," I said, trying to wipe the grin off of my face and get serious. The foyer was immense and extended all the way up to the roof. There was a large staircase that led up to a landing on the second floor. Family pictures hung on the wall all the way up. A small sitting area was situated under the staircase and looked as if it had never been used. To the left, there was an archway to a room that looked like a library or an office. To the right, a set of closed double doors with glass panels that were covered in white sheer curtains.

I swung around and looked at Justin again, and the words stuck in my mouth. I cleared my throat. "This is a big house."

"Yep, it sure is. Been in the family since it was built in the 1920s or so, I'm told," Justin said. "I can give you a little tour. Gram-Gram stays on the first floor now." He gestured to the double doors. "We have all the rooms on this side of the house situated for her and the caregivers. I stay upstairs. Where do you want to start?"

"Is this a good time to meet Mrs. Dittmer?" I asked, thinking that I needed to get down to business and break whatever spell Justin had cast over me.

"Let's find out," he said and opened the double doors. I followed him and immediately caught the now-familiar scent of antiseptic and laundry soap and urine.

What had once been a living room had now been transformed into a hospital room with an adjustable bed, potty chair, walker, and various kinds of medical equipment. A wooden bookshelf along the wall now held towels, washcloths, and bedding. The walls of the room were still covered with large oil paintings and family photos, and a green-and-white marble fireplace dominated the front wall. Brass candlesticks and figurines adorned the mantel, and a very large green-and-white wreath that was no doubt custom-made for this home hung above it.

"Hello." A middle-aged Filipino man appeared from around the corner and waved. "We're in here. Just finishing up breakfast," he called.

"That's Sanjaya—Sam for short," Justin explained, and we walked through the living room into an adjoining room where Mrs. Dittmer sat in a wheelchair at a dining-room table that looked like it had been lowered to accommodate her. Her gray hair was very thin but had been combed neatly around her face. She was ninety-two, and her face was heavily lined with the wrinkles to prove it. Her blue eyes—the same blue as Justin's—had a dullness to them that I was getting used to seeing now.

Sanjaya—Sam—sat in a chair next to her and held a plastic bag of milky liquid up in the air. It was attached to a tube that fed under Mrs. Dittmer's top, and he squeezed it intermittently.

"This is Megan, the one doing the article that I told you about," Justin said, moving aside.

"It's nice to meet you, Sam. Hello, Mrs. Dittmer." I bent down to meet Mrs. Dittmer's eyes. She blinked, but her eyes remained unresponsive.

"Yes, you too," Sam said back, and I detected the slightest accent. "She probably won't respond to you, but I think she knows you are here." He said it to make me feel better, and I smiled, thinking how good caregivers are at taking care of people.

"Sam is with us from six in the morning to three. His sister Divina comes at one and stays until ten, and his other sister Amparo has the overnight shift from ten to six," Justin said.

"They are all related?" I said with surprise and looked at Sam. "The whole family does this?"

"Yes, we are all nurses. Even my mother, but she's back in the Philippines now with my father. My aunts, too, and I have one more sister who is still in school. She lives with my wife and me."

"Isn't that crazy?" Justin said to me.

"Yes, that's crazy. How did you find them?" I asked.

"Her doctor told us. At first it was just Sam, but Gram-Gram kept needing more help, so then Amparo came to stay the night, and then Dee came so Sam could see his wife and kids once in a while, and here we are now." Justin sat in one of the dining-room chairs and folded his hands in his lap.

"Yes, here we are now," Sam repeated.

"Wow!" I said and sat in one of the other available chairs. "That's just amazing."

"I guess." Sam shrugged. "Yes, it is."

"How long have you worked with Mrs. Dittmer?" I asked Sam.

"Over a year now, I think." He looked at Justin for confirmation. "Maybe eighteen months?"

"You started last year before Thanksgiving. Remember, you were here for Thanksgiving with us," Justin said to him and then looked at me. "It was just us for a while, but then she started having trouble with the stairs, so I moved her stuff into the back bedroom so she didn't have to go upstairs to bed, but then she fell a couple of times, and then she almost burned the whole house down trying to make toast, and she couldn't find the bathroom sometimes, and, you know, so I needed help."

"Understandable," I said.

"She would hate this," Justin said, with a knowing smile. "She always did everything herself. She kept up this whole house herself— never had maids. After Grampa died, she used to get on that riding mower and mow all of this property herself and trim all the hedges. Believe me, people in this neighborhood don't do their own yard work. I took over some of that when I moved in, but she was the one in charge, no doubt about it. Right, Gram-Gram?" he said to her in a soft voice.

"OK, we are done here. Time to move back into the bedroom. Are you doing music today?" Sam asked Justin.

"Of course. Every day is music day." Justin jumped up from his chair. "I hope you enjoy mediocre piano playing," he said to me with a smile.

"Oh boy, sounds great!" I said, not knowing exactly what was in store.

Sam moved Mrs. Dittmer into the bedroom area and placed her wheelchair across from the piano. He arranged her clothing and the blanket and carefully placed her hands on her lap. He then busied himself tidying up the dining room.

I took a seat on an oversize chair next to the fireplace and put my recorder on the arm of the chair. Justin sat behind the piano and began to play a few notes. He started a few songs and stopped. "Don't judge," he said to me, with a wink. "I'm just warming up."

There was something very playful about him that was engaging. He said everything with a smile, like it was all part of a very funny story that he was thinking about but wouldn't tell. I couldn't help but smile back at him, even though I kept reminding myself that this was a very serious subject matter.

"OK, here we go." He launched into an old song that I recognized but didn't know the name of. As he played, I watched as Mrs. Dittmer's posture changed; she sat up a bit straighter and lifted her head to look toward the piano. Her hands and fingers began to move along with the music.

"This is 'Moonlight Becomes You,' one of her favorites," Justin explained to me as he played.

I wasn't sure whether it was the acoustics of the room, his playing, or the piano, but the music sounded wonderful. The song ended, and I clapped. "That was very nice."

"Why, thank you. It is so nice to have such a lovely audience today," he joked and bowed to us and the rest of the invisible audience around the room. "Next up is 'Wrap Your Troubles in Dreams,'" he announced, in a fake radio-announcer voice and began to play again.

I watched as Mrs. Dittmer became more animated as he played each song. The way she moved her hands led me to believe that she used to play the piano herself. I could see her legs and feet moving to the music ever so slightly. Her eyes lit up, and a slight smile crossed her lips. It was as if there was a person trapped inside her almost useless body that was struggling to get out. Something about the music tapped into the little that was actually left of the person named Mrs. Dittmer who sat before me in her beautiful house on her beautiful tree-lined street.

Sam coasted in and out of the room doing chores as Justin played. He stopped and leaned over to me at one point. "Isn't it incredible how she comes alive with the music?"

"Yes, it is. It's lovely," I answered.

"Watch when he stops playing. Watch her eyes, and you'll see tears." He used his finger to draw imaginary tears down his cheeks to underscore his point.

"Really?"

"Yes, we don't know whether she's happy or sad, but we prefer to think that she's happy, of course," he said and drifted away.

Justin began playing a new song, and I couldn't help but shout, "I know the name of this one—'It Had to Be You.' Finally, one I recognize!"

He laughed. "I'll be sure to get you a song list before my next performance."

When he finished playing, he stood up, came up to his grandmother, bent down, took both her hands in his, said, "Thank you for listening today, Gram-Gram," and kissed her cheek.

I had tears in my eyes as I watched the tears form in her eyes. She still looked happy, but a few tears rolled over the wrinkles and down her cheeks and disappeared onto her shirt.

"She always does that," Justin said. "We think they are happy tears, right, Gram-Gram?"

Sam came back into the room and wiped her face with a tissue before moving her chair over to the side of the bed and preparing to move her up into the bed.

"It's nap time now," Justin explained. "Wanna go into the other room?"

"Sure." I said, and I took my recorder and stuff and followed him out through the double doors.

"We can sit up here," he said and started up the staircase. I followed him up and across the landing to a large media room that was dominated by a flat-screen TV that hung on one wall. A large black leather coach, reclining chairs, speakers, audio equipment, and a wet bar made this an official man cave, and I imagined it was where Justin spent the majority of his time.

"Nice man cave." I nodded in approval.

"Thanks. It's comfortable. Do you want anything?" he asked, walking toward the wet bar and opening a counter-size refrigerator.

I couldn't help but smile and felt myself flush as I flirted. "What are you offering?"

He smiled and flirted back. "You're a bad influence, I can tell. I have water and pop and beer and wine and Jack Daniel's and tequila. White tequila—it's very nice and smooth."

"Wow, my kind of guy." I tossed my stuff on the couch and forced myself to not ask for the beer that I wanted. "Water is fine. I am at work, after all. See, maybe I'm not such a bad influence."

He grabbed the water for me and a Bud Light for him, and I regretted not asking for the beer. "Maybe not. I guess we'll have to see, eh?"

We both sat on the couch, and I was again aware that I felt a bit nervous sitting next to him. It had been a while since I'd had that feeling, and I struggled to play it cool. "Did your grandmother used to play the piano, too?"

"Yes, she played her whole life. Made my mom take lessons, and she hated it, but she made us take lessons, too. You know how that goes."

"And where are they? The rest of your family?"

"San Diego. In California."

"Oh, is that where they put San Diego? I had no idea," I joked.

"Yeah, I guess that was kind of obvious." He smiled and took a long drink from his beer.

"OK, and you're here, and they are there, so give me the low-down on that story."

"My dad got a job with a defense contractor out there when I was little, and we all moved. Gram and Grampa stayed here. I got an aunt over in Novi, too, but I don't see her too much. She's kind of a bitch. Anyway, I came back to go to college and moved in with them. Then my grampa died, so I stayed to help out, and then Gram-Gram started getting Alzheimer's, and then this writer chick came to interview us, and here we are."

"Great story," I said, with a laugh.

"And every bit of it is true. Can I ask you something?"

"Of course." I couldn't imagine what he was going to ask me.

"You really wanted a beer, didn't you?" It was more a statement than a question.

I laughed. "Yes, you got me on that one." I liked this guy.

He jumped up and grabbed me a beer out of the refrigerator and plopped back down on the couch. He opened the can and handed it to me. "Thank God. The Filipinos don't drink, so I've got no one to hang with here."

I took a long drink of the cold beer. "Where do you work?"

"Ah, adult questions. No fun. I thought you were going to be fun."

He was definitely flirting with me, and I liked it. "Oh, I can be fun, but I have to TCB, too, you know." I noticed that he had sat down on the couch a little closer to me than he had before.

"OK. I work out of the home." He said it in such a way that I knew something was up. "It's what you would call a home-based business."

I looked at him again—his baseball hat, slightly overgrown beard, and toe shoes—and understood. "You sell pot," I said simply.

He broke into a deep laugh. "You're good! You are good! How did you guess that, girl?"

"Two words: toe shoes," I joked.

"Dead giveaway, eh! Do you smoke?" he asked.

"I'm already drinking a beer in the middle of the afternoon; I'm not smoking with you, too," I protested.

"Calm down, little lady. Calm down. I've not offered just yet—just wanted to know where you stand on that particular subject matter."

"I'm pro that particular subject matter," I admitted, although it had been a while since I had smoked weed.

"Excellent." He nodded his approval. "You know that it helps prevent and slow down Alzheimer's, right?"

"No, I did not know that. Are you kidding?" I asked, truly surprised.

"Of course I'm not kidding. Marijuana has so many health benefits that it is just unbelievable. Why do you think the government is starting to legalize it?"

I could tell that Justin was very serious about the subject matter and that this wasn't just a hobby for him.

"They had to figure out a way to control it and get their paws on all that money, which is total bullshit. They want to regulate everything and control everything and dictate everything, but that's not what weed is all about, and it will never be what it's all about."

"Well, you're obviously passionate about the subject matter," I said, draining the rest of my beer. "Did you ever smoke with your Gram-Gram?"

He finished his beer as well and, without asking me, took my empty can and got up to get us two more.

"Let's not be ridiculous. It's not like I could pass a bong over to her during *Wheel of Fortune* or anything. She never would have gone for that, but I used to give her edibles when we first figured out what was wrong with her." He handed me a beer and sat sideways, facing me on the couch.

"The thing is, I wonder what would have happened if she had been taking it before she got sick. Like, what if she had been a recreational smoker during her lifetime or just took small doses of THC as soon as they suspected that she was losing it? I always wonder if that would have stopped it or at least slowed it down, ya know?"

"Do you think it helped her at all when you gave it to her?"

"It's hard to tell. You have really nice hands."

His compliment caught me off guard. I looked at my own hand holding the beer. "Well, thank you."

"Yeah, all except for the finger with the wedding ring on it." He winked.

"Ah yes, I do have one of those." I held it up and wiggled my fingers, wishing that I didn't have it on. I wondered if he had a girlfriend, but it seemed inappropriate to ask. I struggled to get the conversation back on track. "So how did you know she was getting sick?"

Justin looked at his own hands for a moment, stopping to examine his nails. "I need a manicure," he said.

"Oh really? You don't strike me as the kind of guy who would get a manicure."

"I'm just full of surprises. You wait and see." His eyes twinkled with mischief. I was very attracted to him, and he knew it. I cursed myself for my inability to hide my feelings.

"Now what? What was the question?" he asked.

"When did you notice that there was something—"

"Oh yeah, oh yeah. It's hard to tell at first, ya know? She was like any other old person; she forgot names and stuff sometimes, lost her keys and purse in the house, forgot to get stuff at the grocery store, missed a lunch date or two, couldn't remember what day it was, and stuff like that, but mostly she was OK. I mean, she is rich as fuck and hasn't worked since she was a teenager, so who cares what day it is?"

"I get you," I said.

"So, like two years ago, it got weird, and sometimes at night I could hear her up and moving around her room. See, the next door is my bedroom," he said, pointing down the hallway. "And the one after that is hers. There's a sitting room and an archway, and then the bedroom and bathroom are in the back corner of the house. It's big as fuck; she has windows on three sides of the house, so the light is amazing."

"Don't tell me you use it as a grow room now?" I joked.

"Smart-ass. I wouldn't grow in her room." He slapped me lightly on the arm.

"Of course not. The basement then?"

"Oh my, you are smart! I love it!" He slapped me lightly again, this time on the thigh.

"Sorry, don't let my smartness get in the way. Go ahead with the story," I prompted.

"Yeah, OK, anyway, so I hear her moving around at like two or three in the morning, and I figured she was just getting up to go to the bathroom, but it kept happening night after night. Her light was on, and I started to get worried and wonder what was up, so I got up one night and went to the door and knocked, and she answered right away and told me to come in." He paused to take a long drink from his beer, and I did the same. "She answered like right away, like she was just waiting for me to come in, and I open the door, and she is sitting on one of the chairs by the door all dressed up."

Justin sat up straight on the end of the couch, mimicking the formal way his grandmother was sitting. "She was fully dressed and had a coat, hat, and leather gloves on and her purse in her lap. It was fucking spooky. It was the middle of the night! So I ask her what she's doing, and she says that her mother is coming to get her to go shopping at Hudson's. So I'm thinking that she is sleepwalking, right? I mean, her mother has been dead for a bazillion years. And she says that she has to be ready or her mother will get mad because they can't miss the bus, and I tell her that she is sleepwalking and that her mother is dead, and she gets upset and tells me I'm wrong and stuff." Justin pushed himself back on the couch and turned to face me again. "Spooky, right?"

"Yes, that would freak me out," I admitted.

"So anyway, stuff like that kept happening. She got lost driving. She kept running out of gas because she would forget to put any in the car. She forgot that Grandpa was dead and kept trying to call his old number at work and couldn't understand why it was disconnected. I finally convinced her to ask her doctor, and he diagnosed her, and things just went from there."

"Wow. When you found her up at night, how did you get her to go back to bed?" I asked.

"I didn't. I ended up just leaving her like that, and eventually she would fall asleep in the chair or put her nightgown back on and go to bed. It just made her upset when I tried to tell her the truth, so I let it go. I'd just see her downstairs the next day like nothing happened."

"That gives me the chills," I said.

"I know, right? Anyway, I wasn't kidding about the weed. Look it up. There is research out there to prove THC lowers the markers for Alzheimer's in the brain and increases the mitochondria. This is no shit."

"I will look it up. I think it's very interesting," I admitted.

"It is beyond interesting. Do you want to smoke?" he offered, jumping up from the couch.

"Oh no, I don't think that's such a good idea right now, but maybe next time." I could feel a slight buzz from the two beers, and I wanted to stay and wanted to smoke with him but felt like I needed to leave. I stood up and finished the last of my second beer and handed him the empty can. "I should get going now."

"Do you have another person to interview?" he asked.

I looked at the clock on my phone and saw it was just past two o'clock and struggled to think of an excuse. "No, I don't, but I have to work on writing my notes from this visit."

"Oh, OK." He looked disappointed. "Do you like live music?" he asked, brightening up.

"Yes, I really enjoyed your playing," I said.

"No, not me screwing around on the piano—live music, like bands?"

"Yes, yes, of course I do." I wasn't sure where he was going with this question.

"My buddies have a band called Atomic Depot, and they are playing in Rochester this weekend. You should come and see them. I'll be up there on Saturday just hanging."

My mind raced as I tried to figure out why he was asking me to meet him on Saturday. Was he just being nice, or was he interested in me for some reason? I hadn't even left yet, but I knew I wanted to see him again. "Sounds tempting," I replied. "Not sure what's up for this weekend."

"You can bring the guy who gave you the ring, if you want, but it would probably be more fun if you didn't." He smiled and waited while I gathered my stuff and started for the staircase.

"Well, it has been enjoyable meeting you, Justin. And I did like your piano playing. I look forward to hearing it again next week," I said as I worked my way to the foyer, with him following closely behind me.

"Yeah, thanks for hanging with me and putting up with my toe shoes," he joked.

I laughed and wished that I had asked for another beer. We stood awkwardly in front of the door for several seconds, and finally he reached out and opened it, and I walked out into the sunshine and fresh air.

"Hey," he called from the door, "don't forget Saturday. They're at Pub M. They start at nine."

I nodded and waved back at him, and then I got into my car and made my way back down the long driveway.

I opened another beer when I got home and sat at my desk and looked through my notes. The beginning of a project was sometimes overwhelming until I found the voice of the story, and then things usually fell into place. I typed some of the notes into my computer and wrote down some questions to ask during my next set of visits so I wouldn't forget them, but my mind kept drifting back to Justin.

I dug the recorder out of my purse and listened to him play the piano. I couldn't help but smile at every comment he made. There was something very likable about him. I didn't realize that I was still capable of developing a crush on anyone, but I was definitely crushing on Justin.

I replayed the tape again while I breaded some chicken and put together a salad for dinner. I contemplated meeting Justin on Saturday night. It was a ridiculous thing to even consider, but my mind was already busy thinking up possible alibis. I tried to step back and look at the situation philosophically. Why would I bother lying to my husband to go off to see someone that I had known for about two hours? Was there something about Justin that made him worth the risk, or was I just back in self-destruct mode and looking for a temptation?

I was intoxicated by his blue eyes and his wonderful smile and the way he flirted with me. My body hummed with a low level of excitement that I hadn't felt in years, and I wanted to have sex. I texted Craig to see when he would be home. Sex with my husband,

I reasoned, should put an end to my devious thoughts about sleeping with a stranger.

Craig didn't answer but pulled in about ten minutes later. "Hey," he said, as he walked in and began sorting the mail on the counter.

"Hey back at you. Did you get my text?" I worked my way around the counter and stood close to him.

"What? What text? When?" He sounded tired and hadn't looked directly at me yet.

"Just a bit ago. I was eager for you to come home." I wanted him to ask me why, but he was staring at a letter, oblivious to me. I put my hand out and covered the letter until he looked up at me.

"Eh? What? What are you doing?" he said, slightly annoyed.

"Stop looking at that, and pay attention to me." I wedged myself between him and the counter and put my hands around his waist.

"Oh boy, what are you up to?" he said and pushed himself away from me.

"Don't push away. I promise you'll like what I'm up to," I said, grabbing his waist again.

"Are you pregnant?" he asked, half smiling.

"Well, that's a mood killer. No, I'm not pregnant, but I am in the mood to practice trying." I was slightly annoyed that he had brought it up, but nothing was going to stop me at this point.

"Oh, come on, not now," he said and tried to back away again.

"Come on, we've got about a half hour before the chicken is done, so let's get going."

"I just got home. Let me relax. Maybe after dinner." He started walking away.

I grabbed his belt buckle and held him back. "Maybe nothing." I grabbed one of the chairs from the dining-room table and swung it around and pushed Craig down onto it. "Just have a seat, and I'll do all the work."

"Wow, you are in a mood tonight, aren't you?" he said and pushed his shoes off while I unbuckled his belt and unzipped his pants.

I pulled my jeans and underwear off and straddled him. I slowly moved my hips back and forth until he got hard, and then I put his penis inside me with my hand and began to ride him harder and harder.

"Fuck, you are crazy hot tonight," he breathed as he pushed himself up to meet my thrusts. He pulled my shirt over my head and grabbed my breasts and squeezed my nipples just hard enough to make me cry out.

"Yes, yes, yes!" I screamed.

"Oh yeah, that feels so good." Craig said, kissing my breasts and biting on my nipples.

"See, aren't you glad you came home?" I joked.

"Oh yeah," he groaned.

I got up and turned around so my back was facing him and used my hand to reinsert his penis.

"Oh yeah!" he yelled and grabbed my hips and pulled me down on him while he thrusted up into me.

I was incredibly turned on, and I could feel my orgasm building. Craig's rhythm quickened, and his groaning got deeper, and I knew he was almost ready to come. I jumped off him again and turned back around to straddle him face-to-face. "Grab my tits!" I yelled as I pushed myself into him over and over again. We both came hard and sat entangled on the chair, trying to catch our breath for several minutes after we were done.

"Yeah, that was good. Very good," I said, kissing his neck.

"I'll say. Thank God for kitchen chairs," he said.

"Yeah, it's been a while since we did that," I said and climbed off him and gathered my clothes off the floor.

"Chicken? Did you say we were having chicken?" he asked.

I laughed and kissed him. "Yes, chicken."

CHAPTER TWELVE

Rumors of a supervirus that was going to cripple networks across the globe kept Craig and his team working late every night to develop and implement an antivirus for their clients, which meant that I was left sitting at home alone, working on my article and daydreaming about Justin. I could not stop thinking about him. I wanted to know what it was like to touch him and kiss him and be touched by him.

I tried calling and texting Craig several times to remind myself that I was married and that I loved my husband, but he was very busy and short with me. Besides a couple of instances of harmless flirting at hotel bars and one particularly heavy session of mutual masturbation with a paddleboard instructor in Annapolis, I had kept my vow and hadn't cheated in the four years since the bartender in Islamorada.

By Saturday, I had almost convinced myself that it was all in my head. I blamed the beers and told myself that Justin was one of those guys who flirted with every girl on the planet and couldn't be taken seriously. I told myself that there was no harm in flirting with him and using that excitement for my romp on the kitchen chair.

Then he texted me. *Hey girl—how are you?*

I stared at the text for a few moments, knowing the correct thing to do was to ignore it, but my heart was racing, and I couldn't help but feel happy. *Hey right back. I'm good. U?*

I got even more excited as I saw the text bubble appear almost immediately: *Living the dream. U going up to the bar later?*

I paused for a moment because I hadn't bothered to figure out an alibi yet but then responded, *Not sure but think so.*

K. Just wanted to make sure you weren't blowing me off.

I smiled and read his response over. I felt like a schoolgirl all over again. *Wouldn't do that to you. I'm not that kind of girl.*

Can't wait to find out what kind of girl you are...

U R a bad influence, I typed.

C U later, he typed back.

I reread the texts and then deleted them all off my phone and went into the back bedroom, where Craig was working. He had a computer and three laptops spread across the top of the desk, and his body language told me that he was engrossed in what he was working on.

"Hey," I said quietly.

"Yeah. Busy," he said, without looking up.

"I know. I'm gonna get out of your hair and head out for a drink or two, maybe see a band."

"Yeah. Use Uber, OK? I can't come pick you up tonight," he said curtly.

"OK." I couldn't believe it was that easy. I drifted away from the door and into my bedroom closet to try to find something to wear. I kept reminding myself that this wasn't a date, so there was no reason for me to dress up or wear something sexy. In fact, I tried to make myself wear something shapeless and boring on purpose. After trying on about ten tops, I compromised and chose a purple top that made my breasts look big but fit loosely at the waist. I threw on my most comfortable jeans and sandals and put on minimal makeup and drank a beer while I waited for the Uber driver to arrive.

Justin was standing at the bar with a beer and shot of Jack when I first saw him. He wore faded blue jeans, a Captain America T-shirt with a black hoodie, and a different pair of toe shoes that he was quick to point out to me when I approached. He ordered me a beer and a shot and then told me he had brought weed with him so we could smoke later. He seemed so relaxed and kept smiling at me and telling me how happy he was that I came out to meet him. My heart was beating like crazy as I looked around to see if anyone I knew was there, but I didn't recognize anyone.

"So, where's the guy who gave you the ring tonight?" he asked.

"My husband? Do you have something against using the word *husband* or something?" I laughed. The longer I was with him, the better I felt.

"I would rather imagine you without a husband; that's all," he answered, with a smile.

"You must be imagining some interesting things."

"Is that bad?" he asked and looked in my eyes.

And with that I knew that I wasn't misreading any of his signals, and he wanted to be with me the same way I wanted to be with him. The metaphorical door was open, and I practically lunged through. "I must admit that I was pretty intrigued by you when I met you."

"Really?" His smiled broadened, and he looked slightly embarrassed.

"Yep. Not sure why because you really aren't my type, but there is something there." I smiled back and took a long drink of my beer.

"Not your type? Why?" he asked, moving closer to my side.

"I don't know—the beard for one thing and the toe shoes, of course!"

"You don't like beards?" he asked.

"I've never been with anyone with a beard before." I reached out and stroked his face tentatively and wanted to lean forward and kiss him, but I didn't.

"The toe shoes can come off, but the beard is another story." He moved a little closer to me.

I laughed. "OK, I can live with that."

We stood next to each other drinking beers and slowly being pushed closer and closer by the crowd as the night wore on. My body tingled with excitement every time his arm brushed mine or his thigh rested against mine, and as the music got louder, we leaned closer and closer, shouting into each other's ears. I could see the soft hairs on the back of his neck and feel his beard on my cheek.

He told me about living in San Diego and learning to surf in La Jolla and driving the Pacific Coast Highway with his family, and I told him about the Sleeping Bear sand dunes and working in a strip club and being a writer. He was laid-back and laughed at everything and put his hand over the top of mine on the bar when-ever he wanted to make a point.

I forgot that there was a wedding ring on my hand or that I was standing mere miles from my house and could be seen intertwined with a strange man by any number of people. I took Justin's hand and let him lead me out of the bar and into the parking lot, so we could smoke. He pushed me up against the door of his car and kissed me softly until my lips parted, and I took his tongue in my mouth, and he began to kiss me harder and harder. I could feel how hard he was against my leg as I kissed him back with equal passion.

He managed to pop the back door open, and we fell across the back seat and continued making out, our hands exploring each other's bodies. I could hear the muffled music coming out of the bar, cars coming and going, and strips of conversation as people drifted past, but mostly I could hear my heart pounding and Justin's breath as he worked his hands up my shirt and down my pants.

I opened his pants and grasped his warm, hard penis, and he moaned loudly. "I want this in me," I said, as if I could not control myself.

He pushed his jeans down and helped me work my jeans and shoes off my feet and onto the floor of the car. I knew anyone who looked in the windows would be able to see us, but I didn't care. I looked into his beautiful blue eyes and pulled him into me.

"Wow." He smiled at me. "That feels amazing."

"Oh yeah, keep going. I want more." I breathed and grabbed his ass and let the orgasm that had been building since I had walked into the bar come. His pace quickened, and I drew my legs up to take him deeper inside me, and I could feel his body respond as his own orgasm built.

He cupped the back of my head with one hand as he kissed me, creating a buffer between my head and the car door while we thrust against each other. I don't know whether it took two minutes or ten minutes, but I came again as soon as I felt him start to come. He collapsed on top of me in the back seat, and I wrapped my arms around him and hugged him.

"Damn, baby. Damn, baby. Goddamn," was all he said while he continued to kiss me lightly on the mouth and face.

I could feel our mingled juices running down my butt and onto the car seat as logic started to return to my brain. "Do you have napkins or Kleenex?"

"Yeah, I'm sure I do." He sat up and pulled his jeans back on and looked at the bottom half of my body lying there exposed and gave a low whistle. "Goddamn, baby, I mean to tell you."

A wave of modesty caught me, and I used my hand to try to cover myself.

"You're silly," he said and leaned over the front seat to look in the glove box. He handed me a wad of old McDonald's napkins, and I used them to clean up while he found my underwear and jeans on the floor and turned them right side out for me. After I was dressed and got my shoes back on, I sat back on the seat next to him and noticed the fog that had formed on the inside of the windows and laughed.

Justin laughed along with me and took my hand and started kissing me again. "You wanna smoke now?" he asked.

"Why not? I'm going to hell anyway," I said.

"I seriously doubt that!" He produced a small plastic bag, took a long, thin joint and a lighter out, lit it, and took a long drag before handing it to me.

The harsh smoke bit into the back of my throat, and I coughed until tears ran down my face before taking another puff and handing it back.

"Rookie," he said, jokingly.

I laughed. "Yeah, I don't smoke too much these days. Being married has really cut into my smoking-weed and sleeping-with-strange-guys time."

"Am I strange?" he said seriously.

"Not weird strange—unknown strange," I explained.

"Oh yeah, but you know me now, so I'm not strange anymore." He leaned over and kissed me on the lips.

"Since I can still feel your cum inside me, I guess saying that I don't know you makes me look bad at this point."

"You're high," he declared.

"I am high. I can feel it already. Can we not talk about anything serious because I know I'm gonna say something stupid, and I don't think I can think anymore?" The words floated around my brain, and I wasn't sure they were coming out in the correct order. I wondered if that was how people with Alzheimer's felt.

I looked at Justin sitting next me, gazing out the windshield as his hand slowly stroked the inside of my thigh. He looked at me and smiled and then held his finger up to his lips and whispered, "No talking," and immediately began to giggle.

"I said about nothing serious!" I giggled along with him.

"Oh, OK, so we can't talk about the trade deficit with China, but we can talk about puppies and butterflies?"

I laughed harder. "Stop; you are killing me. Stop making me laugh!"

"You're so high. What a rookie," he kidded. "Come on, let's go get another beer and listen to the jams."

We climbed out of the car and into the surprising fresh, cool air outside. "Your car smells like sex now," I whispered as we linked arms and walked back to the bar.

"Just how I like it!" he shouted and gave a loud yell into the sky.

The rest of the night floated by me in disjointed bits of loud music, people dancing, the taste of lukewarm beer, and the smell of people vaping. I hadn't intended to stay out so late, but the next thing I knew, the bartender was saying "Last call!" and Justin was requesting an Uber.

We left Justin's car in the parking lot and sat in the back of the Uber with our arms around each other until the driver dropped him off at the big house, and then I was alone in the back seat while we drove to my house. I figured it was a fifty-fifty shot that Craig was still up, and I rehearsed the casual way that I was going to say hello and the excuses I was going to use to explain why I was taking a shower. I decided that I would sleep on the couch and just say that I had bed spins or fell asleep watching a movie, and that way I could avoid having to lie next to him.

The house was dark and quiet when I got home, and Craig was asleep. I breathed a sigh of relief and stripped off my clothes and put them in the bottom of the hamper and jumped in the shower in the guest bathroom to rinse off.

When I was done, I fished a T-shirt and shorts out of my gym bag and flopped down on the couch and flipped through the channels until I found a movie I had seen a thousand times. I was lying there thinking back on my night with Justin, trying to remember how he smelled and how he felt inside of me when my phone buzzed with a text.

Great night. Had fun.

I smiled. *Me too.*

Want to C U again. Like that.

Me too. I knew I shouldn't, but I knew I would.

Good. Nite.

Nite. I made sure to delete all the messages off my phone and turned it off.

CHAPTER THIRTEEN

When I arrived at the redbrick house in Plymouth, Mr. Strumble was outside in the front yard throwing a large plastic ball to a young boy who I assumed was his grandson. Another man sat on the porch steps watching them, and based on his features, I knew this was his son, Mike.

"Hello!" I called cheerfully. I walked to Mike and shook his hand. "I'm Megan; I'm writing a piece on Alzheimer's."

"Yes, my mom told us you would be here today. Nice to meet you." He pushed himself off the step to shake my hand and then sat back down.

"Mr. Strumble, nice to see you again." I walked onto the grass to shake his hand.

He turned and greeted me with a warm smile. "Hello! Hello! How are you today?"

"Good, and who is this?" I gestured to the boy, who now stood behind his grandfather's legs in an attempt to hide.

"This is Ian," Mr. Strumble said proudly, "and he is my grandson." He shifted slightly and attempted to steer the boy forward.

"Hi, Ian. I'm Megan. How old are you?" I asked, bending down to talk to him.

Ian studied his fingers intently, folding them up and down several times before presenting me with four fingers.

"Four? Oh boy, you are getting big, aren't you?" I said enthusiastically.

He smiled and darted behind his grandfather's legs again.

I turned my attention back to Mr. Strumble. "Do you remember me from last week?"

"Yes, we met last week, yes. How are you?" I could tell that he didn't remember me, but he covered it well.

"I'm wonderful. Such a beautiful day today, eh?"

"Yes, yes. My grandson came to play here today. He likes our yard." Larry patted the boy on the top of the head.

Ian held his arms out as far as he could. "Big yard and big trees!" he yelled gleefully and ran off to get the ball.

"Well, don't let me interrupt your game," I said and went to sit next to Mike on the steps.

"Game?" Larry said and looked at Mike in confusion. Before Mike had a chance to say anything, Ian ran up and pushed the ball into the back of his grandfather's legs and darted away. Larry looked down in surprise and then seemed to remember that he was playing ball with Ian. The boy bounced the ball to him, and he made an attempt at catching it but missed and had to collect the ball from under a shrub before he could bounce it back to Ian.

"He is very cute. Do you have any other children?" I asked Mike.

"Yes, we have a daughter who is seven. She's in school today. Ian and I will go pick her up later on." He was a good-looking guy with thick dark-brown hair that he wore a bit long, but it looked good on him. He wore jeans and a navy pullover, and I noticed that he had an old scar across one of his eyebrows that left a strip of hair missing.

"How is your dad doing today?"

"Good. Today seems like a pretty good day. He doesn't like it when my mom's gone, so I bring Ian over to help keep his mind occupied while she shops."

"That sounds like a good plan," I said.

"Yes, you've got to have a lot of plans. I like to try to get him outside as much as possible."

"When did you first notice that something was wrong? What were the first signs?" I asked.

"Oh man." He shifted slightly to face me. "I don't know—I guess it was just a bunch of little things like forgetting words and losing his place in the conversation. He used to talk and tell stories, and then he started being quiet. I didn't think much of it at first, but then I started watching him a little closer, and I could see that something was off. It was like he couldn't follow what people were saying. I would ask him a direct question about something we were all talking about, and he couldn't answer."

"How long ago was that?"

He thought for a moment. "Three or four years ago, I guess."

"Did your mom know by then?" I asked.

"She was in denial. I brought it up, and she said I was crazy and to wait until I get older and see what happens to my brain. It took a while before she admitted it, which was weird because he would get short with her or lose patience with her when she was trying to explain something, and that wasn't like him at all."

Mr. Strumble and his grandson left the ball in the grass and were now walking around the yard looking at the trees and birds.

"Anyway, it was a process, but once he was diagnosed, everything made sense. I mean, made sense to us. I'm not sure anything really makes sense to him anymore. I mean, he knows he has it, but he doesn't talk about it anymore. He doesn't really talk about himself anymore. He can talk about knickknacks or movies or something that he is eating, but he has a hard time telling you how he

YWNfNnZf

Tracy Nadeau

feels or what he thinks about anything, you know? It's like he's not aware of himself as a person anymore."

"That's very interesting," I said.

"Are you going to write all this down?" he asked suddenly, as if he had just remembered why I was there.

"Probably not everything, bits and pieces," I explained. "It's an article on four different families, so I won't be able to fit in everything."

"I work with writers sometimes. I'm a videographer," he offered.

"Did you get that scar playing hockey?" I wasn't sure why I asked, but I did.

He reached up and ran his thumb along the scar and laughed. "Yeah, I did. How did you guess?"

"Looks like a stick to the head to me." I shrugged. "I won't include that in the article. I was just curious."

"Oops, here we go." Mike stood up and called to his father. "Dad, where are you going?" Ian had his grandfather by the hand and was leading him down the sidewalk. "Ian, don't leave the yard, please," he instructed, but the two kept walking. "Ian?" he called again.

"We're going for a walk," Ian yelled back.

"No, not outside the yard. Remember what I said." Mike walked toward the twosome.

"Just down to the brown dog and back," Ian insisted. Mr. Strumble looked from Mike to Ian and back, waiting to see who would win the argument. I hopped up and followed Mike over to the sidewalk.

"Later, Ian. We have company now," he said.

"We can all go. I don't mind," I offered.

Mike thought about it for a moment and then relented. "OK, down to the brown dog and back, OK?"

Ian let out a whoop of joy and again began leading his grandfather down the sidewalk, with us walking a short distance behind. I

104

could hear Ian chattering away to his grandfather about finding a frog in his yard but how his mother wouldn't let him keep it.

"So we are going to visit a brown dog, I take it?" I asked Mike.

"It's this big brown Labrador that lives down at the end of the street. Ian loves to visit him, but he's always too afraid to pet him. It's a thing with him now that he has to do every time we come over."

"That's cute," I said.

"I'd like to get a dog so he gets comfortable with them. I don't like him being afraid of dogs, but my wife is on a different page with that right now. I guess we have enough going on anyway. Still, a dog would be nice."

"Yeah, dogs are nice," I offered.

As we walked down the block, Ian would stop and point out the cracks and pieces of buckled cement to his grandfather and us, and I thought about what it would be like to have kids of my own and be walking down the street with Craig like this someday. I couldn't imagine having a little person who was with me all the time. The idea was totally foreign to me. I could imagine Craig with a son, carrying him on his back and playing ball with him in the yard. He was centered and patient, and he would be a good father.

Then I thought about Justin and being with him in the car just a few nights ago. Did I want to be the person walking down the street with my husband and son or the person fogging up the windows of a car in a public parking lot with a near stranger?

I forced those thoughts out of my head and reminded myself that I needed to concentrate on observing the family dynamic in front of me. Ian was now talking about whether or not he was going to pet the dog. He went back and forth on the subject while Mr. Strumble nodded and agreed with everything he said.

Before we reached the fenced-in yard, the dog began barking, and Ian let out an excited shriek. We all stopped at the corner of the fence, and Ian danced around the three of us. The brown lab wagged his tail and ran up and down the fence line, pausing to sniff us.

Mr. Strumble smiled at Ian, but he now had an uneasy look in his eyes, and I could see him looking up and down the street. I wasn't sure whether he was searching for his wife or he was lost, but it was clear that he was getting uncomfortable.

Mike went up and reached over to pet the dog that now stood on his hind legs with his paws on top of the fence. Ian watched his dad in awe and reached one hand up to pet the dog's paw. The dog saw the hand coming and licked it as soon as it was close enough, and Ian squealed and clutched his hand to his chest in delight.

"Pet him, Grandpa! Pet him!" Ian insisted, pushing his grandfather closer to the fence.

Mr. Strumble complied and gave the dog a few pats on the head but then turned toward the street and resumed looking back and forth.

"You pet him! Lady, pet him!" Ian said to me.

"You got it!" I happily walked over and petted the dog. I could see his dog tag, and his name was Buddy. "Do you know what this dog's name is?" I asked Ian.

"Big brown dog," he said confidently.

"No, that's what he is, but his name is Buddy."

"Buddy. Buddy. Buddy," he repeated and ran up and down the fence while Buddy followed him.

"I don't like this," Mr. Strumble announced suddenly, to no one in particular.

"OK, Dad, we'll go back now. Ian, it is time to go back. Take Grandpa's hand again, and let's go back."

"I don't like this," he said again.

Ian bounced up to his grandfather and took his hand and started to pull him back in the direction from which we had come.

Mr. Strumble resisted and looked at Mike for reassurance; Mike put his hand on his father's back and steered him forward, and we all began strolling up the street. It was a little moment, just a few glances and some body language that most people wouldn't notice, but it spoke volumes about what life with Mr. Strumble was like on a daily basis.

Once we were back at the house, Ian attempted to resume the game of catch with his grandfather, but Mr. Strumble insisted on going inside. He called out for his wife several times while he walked from room to room looking for her.

"Mom will back in a few minutes, Dad," Mike said, helping him out of his coat and hat. "What do you say we put a movie on while we wait?" He steered him toward the TV room, and Ian and I followed.

"OK, but she has been gone a long while. Are you sure she isn't back yet?" Mr. Strumble asked with concern.

"No, Dad, she's only been gone for a little while. I know it seems longer, but it's not. She'll be home very soon, and she'll have those mustard pretzels that you like, remember?" We all sat down, and Mike inserted a DVD into the player and started the movie. Instead of *Midway*, it was *Bridge on the River Kwai* this time.

"Yuck," Ian said. "I don't like this one."

"I know, buddy; we'll get your bag, and you can play with the toys you brought over," Mike offered, and Ian jumped up and ran into the other room.

Mr. Strumble sat in his chair, tapping his foot nervously on the ground and looking from the movie to the doorway.

"We watched *Midway* last time I was here, but I'm not very familiar with this one, Mr. Strumble. What's it about?" I asked, in an attempt to take his mind off things.

"Oh, this one is…" He started to speak and then lost his place as Ian bounced into the room with a red fabric bag and dumped the contents onto the floor in front of his father.

"I'm gonna find my tigers," Ian announced and began going through the pile of assorted toys.

"Go ahead, Mr. Strumble. You were going to tell me about the movie?" I prompted.

Mr. Strumble looked at me and struggled to find the words.

"It's in Burma, right?" I offered.

"Yes, Burma," he said, his face brightening a bit. "It was supposed to connect Bangkok and Rangoon."

"I don't like this one," Ian announced again and went back to playing.

"Ian, play with your tigers," his father directed.

"They killed a lot of men over there, thirteen thousand POWs and ten times that many civilians. That's a lot for one damn bridge, if you ask me," Mr. Strumble said thoughtfully.

"It sure is," I agreed.

The noise of the back door opening as Mrs. Strumble returned home caught everyone's attention, and Mike jumped up to help her carry the grocery bags.

"Oh, she's back, she's back," Mr. Strumble said with relief.

Mrs. Strumble came through the doorway and rushed over to her husband to give him a hug and reassure him. "How was your morning? Did you have fun playing with Ian?"

"Grandma, we went and saw the big brown dog!" Ian yelled and danced over to his grandmother for a hug.

"You did? How much fun was that? Did you pet him this time?"

"Almost. He kissed me on the hand!" He held up his hand and pointed to the spot where the dog had licked him.

"Oh my, that is progress!" she said.

Mr. Strumble looked a little lost in all the commotion but seemed calmer now that his wife was home. He wasn't tapping his foot any longer, and his attention drifted over to the TV to watch the movie.

"Well, I think I'll get out of your way," I announced and gathered my stuff to leave. "Thanks for including me in your walk today," I said to both Mr. Strumble and Ian.

"K," Ian answered and sat back down on the floor to play.

"I'll see you next week, OK, Mr. Strumble?"

"OK, you're going now. Drive safely. Goodbye," he said and seemed glad to get rid of me.

Mike was in the kitchen unloading grocery bags with his mother, and I thanked them both and left through the garage.

On my way down the street, I passed the big brown dog sitting in his yard and yelled, "Hi, Buddy!" from my car window.

CHAPTER FOURTEEN

I found the Phillips house much as I had left it the week before, very quiet and depressing. Mrs. Phillips was sitting up in the bed when I arrived. Her eyes flickered over to me when I came in but then settled on some distant point that only she could see.

Mr. Phillips placed a folding chair for me across from his recliner, and the three of us sat there like the world's most awkward tea party.

Mrs. Phillips twisted and turned in the bed, struggling to move her legs and arms over to the side without success. There was a look of fear in her eyes today, and she moved like she was trying to get away from something unseen on the opposite side of the bed. She moaned and said a few words of gibberish. I thought I heard her say no several times.

"She's restless today," Mr. Phillips said, getting up to reposition her on her back and straighten the covers. "It's OK, Melly; it's OK, it's OK," he said over and over as he did it. "There's nothing in the bed to hurt you; just lie back and relax." He managed to calm her for a few moments, and he held a cup of liquid with a straw up so she could take a drink. Her mouth seemed to obey out of reflex, and she sipped a little.

He sat back down. "She used to think there were animals or bugs or something trying to get her," he whispered to me.

"Really? So she has delusions? Is that something recent, or did it start a while ago?" I asked.

"Oh, it started a year ago or so. I think it started before she told me about it, and she tried to hide it because she knew it was all in her mind." He tapped his head with his finger. "She used to see our old dog, Muffin, when we were at the old house. She would stare into the corner and try to whistle and clap to get him to come over, and she kept asking me why he wouldn't come."

"What did you say?"

"At first I told her that Muffin was gone and that she was seeing things. Later on I just said that he was a silly dog, and he would come over later. You can't spend your whole day convincing someone of something that they will never remember. She would nod and seem like she got it, but five minutes later, she was back at it."

"Did she only see old pets or animals that she knew before?"

"No, eventually she saw every damn thing you can think of. Bugs and snakes, lots of bugs and snakes because she used to see them in the garden all the time, I guess."

As if on cue, Mrs. Phillips began to writhe and moan in the bed again, and I tried to imagine what she thought she saw. Snakes crawling up and down her bed? Huge beetles swarming all over her body? What must it be like to be convinced that you are being attacked, and you can't escape, and no one can help you? It would be pure hell, I decided; it would be like being trapped in your own personal hell with no way to escape.

Her eyes told the story of the terror she felt as she flayed her arms and legs uselessly against the side of the bed. "Is there anything that you can give her to help her?"

"They gave me some pills to help relax her, but I don't like to give them to her this early in the day. They don't work real well anymore. I suppose I should get the doctor to write me a prescription for something new." He got up and again eased her back into a comfortable position. "I could fill the back of a dump truck with half-empty bottles of pills. I'll show you." He went into the kitchen and opened the door to the pantry and removed four shoe boxes that were overflowing with orange prescription pill bottles and put them on the counter. I couldn't help but notice that the only other things in the pantry were a box of instant mashed potatoes and a jar of pickles.

"Wow," I said, getting up to inspect the boxes. "That's amazing."

"There's got to be about ten thousand dollars' worth of pills that are all useless to us now." He picked through the bottles, pausing to read a label here and there. "Insurance paid for most of it, of course, but it is still a damn waste if you ask me."

"None of these are any good anymore?"

"Not to us. I keep the current stuff in the refrigerator." He went over and opened the door and pointed to half a dozen bottles on the shelf. Besides the bottles, there wasn't much else in the refrigerator, and I wanted to ask him what he ate. I wanted to open the freezer to see if it was stacked with frozen dinners but couldn't think of an excuse that would make it appropriate.

He placed the shoe boxes back in the pantry and closed the door and returned to his spot on the recliner. Mrs. Phillips shifted on the bed, struggling against her unseen opponent. Her eyes darted around the room, and her mouth moved as if she were trying to form words, but only more unintelligible moans came out.

"How long do these episodes usually last?" I asked.

He shrugged. "Sometimes a few minutes and sometimes all day. I need to get her up and move her into the chair, and that might break the train of thought she's trapped in right now. Maybe not."

He got up and moved the wheelchair over to the side of the bed and locked the wheels.

"Can I help?" I asked, moving my chair over.

"You said you wanted to see how we do it, right?" he asked, looking at me with a serious look, and I knew that he wanted me to witness what he went through, so I nodded and sat back down.

He carefully rolled the blankets down to uncover his wife's body, and she began to move with more purpose in anticipation. The pink nightgown she wore had twisted itself around her waist, revealing incredibly thin legs covered with gray skin that looked paper-thin. He pulled the nightgown down as well as he could and used the remote to raise the back of the bed up as far as possible while he held her in place on the bed.

He eased her legs over the side of the bed and allowed her upper body to rest against him as he pulled her into a standing position. I wasn't sure if the full weight of her body ever hit the floor before he rotated her over to the wheelchair and folded her onto it.

After he fastened a safety belt around her and attached a tray to the front of the wheelchair, he turned to me and held his hands up and said, "And that's how that's done."

"You've really got that down," I said, truly admiring his skill at handling her, especially at his age.

"No choice in the matter," he said dryly and rolled her into the living room.

He placed her next to the couch and held the plastic cup and straw up so she could take a drink.

I moved the folding chair into the living room with them and sat down. "You told me your wife likes to garden. Can you tell me some other things about her?" I asked.

"Oh sure, I guess. Let's see." He reached over and took her hand in his while he spoke. "She played tennis when she was younger. She came from a big family, and she and her sisters all took tennis lessons when they were coming up. The sisters used to play before everyone started having kids and moving away. She belonged to some club in Birmingham up until a few years ago."

"How many siblings does she have?"

"Oh boy, it was a big family. Four sisters and three brothers. She still has a sister in Saint Louis, but all the others are gone."

"Did any of them have Alzheimer's?"

"Oh yeah, her father had it, but they didn't call it that back then; they called it dementia. I remember her telling me they used to tie him to the bed to keep him down at night. Her sister Sarah had it for sure, and I think her sister Bonnie had it, but she died of some kind of female cancer before she got too sick. They lived in California, so we never saw too much of them."

"That's interesting."

Mrs. Phillips seemed more comfortable and no longer looked afraid, but her eyes continued to move around the room as if she were searching for something, and she occasionally tried to talk.

"She played bridge, and she used to knit and crochet in wintertime. There are blankets around here somewhere—just haven't gotten around to unpacking yet," he said, looking around at the various boxes and bags stacked against the walls. "Oh, a picture. I know you wanted to see some pictures, and I think I know which box they're in. I'll try to have some out next time you come by."

"That would be very nice. Thank you," I said. "How about you? How many siblings do you have?"

"There were three of us brothers. Me and Ted and Allen—in that order, all about a year apart. They lived in Michigan. I outlived 'em both. Ted's wife lives in an assisted-living home in Grand Rapids now. At least I think she's still alive. Neither of them had Alzheimer's. Nobody in my family did, as far as I know."

I was again struck by how isolated Mr. and Mrs. Phillips were in their little condo. The whole world existed just outside the door and down the block, but it might as well have been a million miles away. They were marooned on an island, and no one even knew they were missing. No one was going to come looking for them. There was a feeling of hopelessness that permeated their situation.

In an effort to remain objective, I had to consider that the decisions they made contributed to their plight. There were resources they could have used to get more help, and Mr. Phillips could have chosen to move his wife to an assisted-living home. Surely they had insurance or Medicaid or savings or money from the sale of their home. This condo couldn't have cost much more than a hundred thousand, at the most, so why not spend some of that money to have a visiting nurse come every day?

I suspected that Mr. Phillips was suffering from depression and wondered if he was on any medication. In the end, I had to acknowledge that this might be the way they wanted to face the end. I thought of a careful way to ask the question and finally said, "Did you and your wife discuss a plan for her extended care?"

He snorted. "A plan? Well, I don't know that you'd call it a plan, but I promised to stay with her until the end. That's the way it's supposed to be, you know?"

"Yes, it is." I smiled and nodded.

"I know she wouldn't have wanted to be like this." He reached over and smoothed her thin gray hair against her head. "She always did things on her own, and she was the one who always took care of everything, and she wouldn't have wanted to be like this," he said firmly.

I choked back my own tears. "Yes, I imagine it is very difficult to see her this way."

He was silent for a few minutes. I started to gather my stuff up to leave.

"I'll find you some pictures for next time. There's one of her and her sisters in tennis dresses that used to be in the den that you should see." He smiled at the thought of the picture and got up to walk me the few steps to the door.

"Thanks again for your time. Goodbye, Mrs. Phillips; have a good week, and I'll see you next Wednesday, OK?" I walked over and touched the top of her hand and turned and shook Mr. Phillips's hand, and he nodded and waved as I left.

It was bright and breezy outside, and the birds were singing. I could hear traffic and the sound of a lawn mower, and I took several deep breaths as I walked to my car, glad to be back in the world.

CHAPTER FIFTEEN

Linda was outside planting flowers in the large pots that lined the sidewalk up to the door when I arrived. She gave me a hearty wave and went back to digging.

"Hello, Linda, how are you today?" I asked.

"Another day in paradise. At least it's warm out today, and I can get this planting done." There were several flats of flowers of various kinds scattered on the grass.

"Pretty flowers. I haven't planted anything yet. I guess I should get to it before the season slips past me." I made a mental note to buy some flowers and put them around the deck.

"You do anything besides write?" she asked, and I immediately wanted to answer, "Cheat on my husband," but instead I said, "No, not right now."

"How about kids? You got kids?"

Where was she going with this? "Nope, none yet."

"I never had any either. Never wanted them with that idiot I married." She shook her head from side to side slowly. "They're inside, if you wanna go on in through that door. I'm gonna finish this pot and then drive Dad over and come back and finish the rest this afternoon."

"Sounds good," I said and went into the house. I gave a loud hello as I walked through the kitchen. I could hear that the TV was on just as loud as the last time I was here.

"Hello! Hello!" Mr. Norman called out to me as I entered the room. "How are you?" He was standing behind the couch.

His wife sat in the same chair, and I noticed that she wore the same clothes as my last visit. She had a book of crossword puzzles on her lap today instead of the paper. I noticed a word-search book on the table next to her as well.

"I'm great, Mr. Norman; how are you?" I yelled over the sound of the TV. "And how are you today?" I asked Mrs. Norman.

"What's your name again?" she asked me, in a tone that told me she wasn't entirely happy that I was there again. Perhaps she didn't remember that I knew the tough answer for last week's puzzle.

"Megan."

"Yes, Megan. I know your face but not the title," Mr. Norman said as he walked over to me to shake my hand. I was very impressed that he recognized me.

"It's great to see you again, sir. You look wonderful." And he did look good, dressed in clean khakis with a blue-checked shirt and a blue sweater.

"You're not flirting with me, are you?" He laughed loudly and slapped me on the arm a little harder than I expected. "I think she is flirting with me! You'd better watch out!" he said to his wife with a laugh and went back to pacing behind the couch.

"Oh, Larry, you think everyone is flirting with you." She looked at me and shook her head in exasperation. "You're an old man, and you don't know who you are half the time, so believe me: nobody is flirting with you."

"Oh, listen, you don't know what you don't know in time to say it out loud," he said back.

"OK, OK, don't get all riled up. You're leaving soon anyway," she said, in a softer tone.

"Leaving soon anyway," he repeated. "Leaving soon…*soon.*" He pronounced the word very slowly, turning it over in his mouth again and again. "*Soon. Soon. Soon.* Is that right? Is that the right word? It doesn't sound right."

"Yes, it is right," she said to him and then turned to me. "He gets stuck on words sometimes now."

I could see him mumbling the word over and over as he paced.

"Larry, would you please keep still? I'm trying to watch this," she said, turning her attention to a talk show on TV with a panel of doctors discussing plastic surgery.

"Did you already finish the crossword from the paper today?" I asked, when a commercial came on.

"This morning. Larry is having a good day, so he knew all the answers. You're having a good day today, right?" she yelled at him, over her shoulder.

"Every day aboveground is a good day," he said and began laughing almost before he finished saying it.

Linda came in the back door and washed her hands in the sink and then stood drying them in the archway. "You almost ready, Dad? Did you go to the bathroom?"

"I went. I'm ready," he announced.

"No, you haven't gone lately, Larry. Go now," his wife directed.

"Stop talking about it in front of company. I went," he said tersely, smiling at me with a slightly embarrassed expression.

"Go. Now!" his wife yelled, and Larry went down the hallway and into the bathroom.

I collected my recorder and notes.

"You driving separate or in the Buick?" Linda asked me.

"Oh, I'll go separately and head out from there. Nice seeing you again, Mrs. Norman." I extended my hand, and she grasped just my fingertips and gave them a quick shake and went back to watching TV again.

I sat in my car and waited until the garage door opened and a burgundy-colored Buick backed out. I followed them during the ten-minute ride over to the Hope Memory Care Center. I thought it was ironic that all nursing homes had such hopeful and opti-mistic names and yet were filled with people who would never be cured and would mostly likely die within their walls.

This one was an old three-story brick building that used to be a middle school when I was a kid. What used to be the baseball field was now a large tree-lined garden with benches, paths, and a fountain. You could see the leaves and buds starting to fill in, and I imagined it was a very pretty place to be in the summer.

I met Linda and her father in the parking lot and walked a few paces behind them as they entered a bright reception area with tan striped walls and tan tile on the floor. There were three women behind a tall granite counter, and one of them, a heavy-set woman in a dark-blue sweater, said, "Well, hello, Charles," as he passed. He was clearly excited and didn't want to stop, but he paused and said hello to her before rushing down the hallway to the right.

The woman, whose name was Pam, according to her name tag, turned her attention to us. "Hello, Linda." She looked at me and said, "And…"

"Megan. Hello."

"She's the writer that I told you about," Linda explained while she filled out information on a clipboard.

A look of agitation crossed her face. "I remember, but you know that I can't have you in here," she said directly to me. "We would have to get permission from every single person in here in order for you to be interviewing them, and we just can't do that."

I was annoyed, but I also understood. No one wanted to take the chance of getting caught up in a lawsuit. I gave her a big smile. "I do understand. Not a problem. Is it OK if I just peek my head in and see what the room looks like before I go?"

I could tell that she wanted to say no.

"Just a quick peek to give me an idea of how Mr. Norman spends his afternoons, so when I ask him about it, I'll have a frame of reference? And do you have any literature about the program that I can take, or is there a website that I can access?"

"Well, OK, you can look through the window, but you can't talk with anyone or take any pictures. That OK?" she asked.

"Yes, perfect," I said.

"I'll walk her down there and back, Pam," Linda offered.

"I need to get out from behind this desk anyway. I'll go, too." And with that Pam disappeared through a doorway behind the reception desk. As we waited, I noticed other people being dropped off and escorted down the hallways to the right and left. It was a bit like watching kids being dropped off at school; some walked with purpose, and some stood still, full of uncertainty until someone guided them. One woman in a wheelchair pushed herself past me with surprising speed. When she paused to wait for the automatic door to swing open, I noticed that both her legs were gone below the knees. She noticed me noticing her, and she rearranged the blanket that sat on her lap before disappearing through the doorway.

Pam appeared through another door down the hallway, keys attached to a rubber spiral bracelet on her right wrist. She wore a navy skirt and tights and navy-blue nurses' shoes. The shoes were so well worn that they took on the shape of the feet that were stuffed inside them. Her chubby ankles spilled out over the tops of the shoes like bread baking over the side of a pan.

She waved us forward and began moving her bulk down a wide carpeted hallway. We passed several windows and doors before she stopped in front of a large window that looked into the café area. The venetian blinds were down but cranked open so that we could see through the slats. Tile floor and metal tables and chairs, with people scattered around. The back of the room was a large buffet area that was busy with people getting food, many of them being assisted by caregivers.

"Dad's over here," Linda said, pointing to the right.

I could see her father sitting at a table across from a gray-haired woman who had her back to us. She was slim and sat with her hands folded on her lap and her legs crossed at the ankle. She reminded me of a little girl sitting in just the way her mother had taught her at a school dance or church. Charles was leaned toward her smiling and telling her a story with a great deal of animation in his face.

"What do they talk about?" I asked Linda.

She shrugged. "I don't know. All kinds of things, I guess. A lot about the old days and the old neighborhood. Sometimes just about how the sherbet tastes today."

"How does your mom feel about this?"

"Oh, Mom doesn't say too much about it anymore. I know it probably bothers her, but she knows there's not much she can do about it, so she accepts it. It's not like they really have a life together anymore." Linda turned toward me. "You know how old couples who have been together forever are just together, like they don't really even notice the other one anymore? Like two parts of the same unit? They never yelled or touched or got annoyed with each other—I certainly could never imagine anything physical going on, if you know what I mean."

I nodded and smiled. "Who does he think Sophia is? To him, I mean?" As we talked, Charles got up from the table and got two glasses of milk and brought them to the table.

"It varies: sometimes his wife, sometimes his mother, sometimes a teacher from school, or his landlord." Linda exhaled. "He just seems to accept that she exists and doesn't really put too much thought into figuring out who she is. I told you it's a real hoot, didn't I?"

"You did." I turned to Pam. "If people with Alzheimer's can't make new memories, and he just met her at this day care group a few months ago, how come he can remember her from week to week?"

"Mr. Norman is still at a stage where he can make new memories. It's more how he processes the new memories. He knows that we have a salad bar with blue-cheese dressing, for instance, because he complained last week when we ran out of blue-cheese dressing, but he doesn't fully comprehend that this is a care facility. Rosalind is from his old neighborhood, so that has triggered something in him, and he remembers her, but he almost never remembers any of the other patients' names."

Charles made a plate of food and brought it over and set it in front of Rosalind and then returned to the buffet to make a plate of food for himself.

"He is losing the ability to keep his memories in any real order. He knows everything he knew before, but he can't always access the information when he wants it. It's a perplexing disease to deal with, even for us. He's lucky his wife is so understanding. Some people think their spouse is faking it so they can cheat on them, but we see it happen from time to time, and it's real."

"Does anyone ever have sex?" I asked, thinking the answer would be no.

"They sure do." Pam shook her head and muffled a laugh. "Yes, ma'am, they sure do. Everyone assumes people lose their desire after a certain age, but for some of them, it amplifies it. Oh my, yes. Sometimes patients act out sexually—with one another or with themselves—in public because they don't remember that it is inappropriate. Sometimes they will physically touch one of the staff or expose themselves, that kind of thing."

I was more than a little surprised. "Really? I had no idea."

"Oh, it doesn't happen a lot, but it happens. Believe you me." She nodded her head slowly up and down to underscore her point. "We just correct them and move on with our day. The folks that come for the day care program usually aren't an issue because they aren't at that stage of the illness yet, but some of our full-time patients act out occasionally. Of course, Mr. Norman is a perfect gentleman." She winked at Linda over my shoulder.

Charles returned with his plate of food and sat down. Rosalind picked up her fork, and the two began to eat while they chatted.

"I understand there is music after lunch?" I asked Pam.

"Yes, we have a piano player who comes in and plays for forty-five minutes, and then we have a group meeting where those who want to talk can talk and we make announcements, and then we have craft hour, and then we have free time until the program ends at four and those who are outpatient go home, and those who are inpatient can stay in the common areas or go back to their rooms or outside or whatever they want before dinner."

"That sounds wonderful," I said.

"It is a really nice program. There aren't many day programs for those with dementia around this area. We are hoping that other facilities will adopt programs like this since the number of people with Alzheimer's is growing, and more and more people are suffering from early onset so they will be living longer and needing more help along the way."

A short, round man with a round face and bald head hurried past us and into the cafeteria. "That's William, the piano player," Pam said. "He comes early to eat before he plays."

"Is that part of his pay?" I joked as I watched William make a heaping plate of food from the buffet.

"Oh, he doesn't get paid. His wife used to be here. She had dementia, too, but she passed on about two or three years ago now, I think." Pam scratched her head with one of her chubby hands and let the keys jingle against her hair. "Maybe even four by now. Time does fly. Anyway, he used to play for her, and the other patients liked it, so he kept coming back even after she was gone. Nice man."

"That is very nice," I said, and Linda nodded in affirmation.

"You know, if you like, there's a bench against that back wall." Pam pointed through the window to a green wooden bench with fake ficus trees on either side of it. "You can go sit there and watch while they play the music. If you like."

"Oh yes, that would be wonderful. I promise that I won't talk to anyone, just watch." I put my hand over my heart to demonstrate my sincerity.

"OK then, go ahead. I've got some things to attend to before lunch. Just leave back down this hallway when you're ready." She started to leave and turned back abruptly. "You're not filming or taking pictures or anything, right?"

"No, ma'am, just watching."

"OK. I don't want to get into any trouble over this," she muttered and left.

"Thanks, Pam," I called to her. "Are you going to stay, too?" I asked Linda, hoping she wasn't.

"No, I've got to get back to my planting to get it done before he comes home. It's nothing I haven't seen before."

"OK, see you next week then?" I extended my hand, and she shook it.

"Yes, sounds good." She turned to leave, and I went into the cafeteria and sat on the green bench.

I counted a total of thirteen patients and the piano player. A few were being fed by nurses, but the others were eating on their own with varying levels of success. One tall, thin man ate green beans with his fingers, pushing them into his mouth one at a time. He sat at a table with another man, who had no trouble using a fork.

I noticed another man who was dressed in a dark-gray suit with a white shirt and a pale-pink tie. He sat very erect with his napkin in his lap and his elbows off the table. He looked like someone you might find at high tea on the *Titanic.* He cut his food into small pieces and wiped his mouth in between each bite. He sat with a woman in a coral-color jogging suit and tennis shoes with silver sparkles on them. I watched them for a while before I realized that he was the one with dementia, and she was his wife, who was there to have lunch with him. There was something about the way she moved, a quickness and a confidence that you don't see in people with dementia.

I looked from the people with the disease to those in the room without it again and again, trying to notice the little differences. People with the disease moved a little slower and seemed unsure, as if they were questioning their own actions. Some repeated movements over and over again, and some barely moved at all. Their interactions were at a superficial level, as if they were living on the world but not in the world.

In contrast, the caregivers moved with a purpose and seemed connected to all the things around them in a tangible way. It was as if those with the disease were fading out of a photograph and everything else around them was staying sharp and clear.

An argument erupted between two women over a card game, with one accusing the other of taking two turns in a row. The other kept trying to count the cards in her hand but kept losing count after four or five. She finally tossed the cards into a pile on the table and folded her arms in disgust. The other woman collected all the cards, shuffled them, and dealt a new hand. She coaxed the other woman to pick up her cards and start playing again. I imagined that this argument was a daily, if not hourly, occurrence.

A round of applause broke out as the piano player arranged himself behind an upright piano that looked like it could have been the one my second-grade music teacher used. As he began to play, people pulled chairs across the floor, and caregivers rolled people in wheelchairs over and created a semicircle.

Larry stood up and offered his hand to Rosalind, and she smiled and took it and followed him to the dance floor. She was a very attractive woman, and when they danced, they made for a very attractive couple. His manic pacing was replaced by an elegant grace as he held the small of her back and cupped her hand in his and moved around the middle of the semicircle.

The man in the suit and his wife joined them on the makeshift dance floor for the second song. Some people clapped or sang along to the music. Two women sitting next to each other in wheelchairs held hands and swung them to the melody. The women playing cards seemed annoyed at the noise. One man looked upset and kept putting his hands over his ears. Some others didn't seem to notice or care about the music or dancing and sat locked in their own world.

I wondered if people like Mr. Norman, who were in the early stages of the disease, looked at those in the room in the later stages of the disease and made the connection that that was their future. It was an inescapable fact that they would all lose the ability to interact, dance, walk, eat, and ultimately breathe at some point in the not-too-distant future. They were all told those facts when they were diagnosed years ago, and all had to find a way to continue to live as best as they could knowing that they were fighting a losing battle.

The man who was upset looked like he was filled with fear and confusion. He was clearly overwhelmed by his surroundings, and he couldn't find joy in the music or pleasure in his companions or a way to escape his situation. I couldn't decide whether he was totally unaware or he was totally aware and unable to express or control himself.

To be unaware would be a confusing jumble of sights and sounds with no way to process or organize them. Time would lose all meaning, social cues would be lost, and a routine of any kind would be nonexistent. Something as simple as the process of getting up in the morning and putting on clothes would no longer be second nature; it would be a struggle to understand.

To be aware would be to know that your brain was now working against you, and you had no way to control it. Words, feelings, and thoughts would float just out of reach, and you would be left with the knowledge that you could never regain what you lost.

After a few songs, I slipped out and waved to Pam behind the desk as I left.

Later that night, I was sautéing onions and sipping red wine in the kitchen before Craig got home from work. I would see Justin again the next day, and I could feel a ball of nerves in my stomach building. I was excited but at the same time saw the impending disaster that my actions were going to bring to the rest of my life.

I debated whether or not I should sleep with him again. Just thinking about it was getting me excited, but I knew it was wrong. I also knew that I wouldn't be able to help myself. I had already opened the door; did it matter if I slept with him once or a hundred times? I tried to imagine Craig's reaction to finding out. He would be hurt, and that, for the first time, made me feel guilty. I didn't want to hurt him; he didn't deserve it.

And then the thought struck me that Justin might not even be there when I arrived tomorrow. Maybe he regretted hooking up with me and didn't want to see me again. Maybe it was just a typical guy thing of taking the opportunity to fuck when it fell in your lap—literally—and then moving on to the next girl. I imagined standing at the door and having Sam explain that Justin was out and me having to pretend that I was OK with that and not in the least bit hurt.

I added steak to the pan and poured another glass of red and tried to wrap my mind around the fact that someone I had known for only a week could hurt me. *How ridiculous,* I thought. What in God's name was wrong with me that I would leave the safety of my marriage and invite a stranger who could hurt me into my world? I realized that even as a happily married adult with a successful career and loving family, my self-destructive streak still followed me.

I heard the familiar sound of the garage door opening as Craig pulled up. He would park and walk down to the mailbox and come back through the garage and close the door and pop in through the back door and say hello and put the mail on the counter and look at what I was cooking and go upstairs to change.

Just then my phone chirped with a text message, and I looked down to see Justin's name across the screen. I grabbed it, almost tossing it into the pan with the steak by accident, and read: *Hey— just wanted to confirm that you'll be here at one tomorrow?*

I typed, *Yes. Does that work?*

You bet. Dinner tomorrow?

I jammed the phone into my pocket as Craig appeared through the back door.

"Hi," he said as he tossed the mail on the counter.

"Hey, you," I said, hoping that my face looked normal.

"What's up with you?" he said, pausing to look at me.

"What do you mean?" I could feel sweat break out on my face. I concentrated on turning the steak in the pan as he circled around me.

"Ah, red today, eh?" He took a drink out of my glass of wine and set it back on the counter. "Your face is flushed from the wine." He pinched one of my cheeks and left the kitchen to go upstairs.

I felt a huge surge of relief pass through me, and I took another gulp of my wine and a few deep breaths before I took the phone back out of my pocket. I reread the texts from Justin and typed, *Dinner's tough. See you at one.*

He answered almost immediately. *So looking forward to it...*

I deleted the texts off my phone and jammed it back into my pocket. I couldn't help but smile because I knew not only that he would be there but that he wanted to see me again.

CHAPTER SIXTEEN

I drove over to the Dittmer house, filled with anticipation and nervous energy. I thought of all the different ways that I could avoid sleeping with Justin again. I practiced my speech about being married and having made a mistake last Saturday night. I would admit to giving in to temptation once but explain why I could not do that again. I would make sure he understood that I was really attracted to him but that I loved my husband and had no intention of leaving him at this point. Justin was a nice guy, and he would understand, I reasoned. And if all else failed, I would tell him that I had my period.

At the same time, I had to acknowledge that I had worn my faded jeans that made my ass look the best and my green button-down shirt that allowed just the right amount of my cleavage to pop out. I was freshly shaven—everywhere—and I put perfume in all the right places.

I got out of the car and tried to calm my breathing as I walked to the door and knocked. I was sure that my face was flushed, and I could feel a light sweat break out all over my body. The door swung open, and Justin stood on the other side with a huge grin on his face.

"Well, hello there." I couldn't help but grin back. Just seeing him again—his eyes, his beard, and his smile—knocked my resolve completely out of my head. Husband? What husband?

"Happy Thursday, and welcome back." He reached out and took my hand and pulled me inside and shut the door.

"Thank you."

"I want to hug you. Is it OK if I hug you, or is that weird?" he asked, standing just a few inches from me.

"I…I don't know what to do. I'm actually nervous," I admitted.

"Really?"

"Yeah, I am."

"Then I'm going to hug you until you aren't nervous anymore." And with that he wrapped his arms around me and gave me a long hug.

I wrapped my arms around him and melted into his body. I couldn't believe how good he felt and smelled and how hungry I was to have him again.

"Better?" He gave me a light kiss on the cheek and stepped away from me.

"Yes, thank you, Dr. Justin," I said, smoothing my shirt and struggling to keep my mind on my assignment. I looked down and noticed his toe shoes. "Oh my gosh, another pair? How many pairs of those things do you have?"

"So many pairs, and I hit up Amazon the other day, so more are on the way," he said proudly.

"They are just so bad," I said.

"Oh, come on. They drive you crazy, and you know it!" He laughed.

"For sure. Anyway, how's your grandma today?"

"She's good. Sam has her out on the patio to enjoy the sunshine. You wanna go out there?"

"Yes, let's get down to business," I said and followed him through the house and out the sliding-glass doors. I couldn't help but notice how nice his butt and legs looked in his jeans. I wanted to reach out and grab him.

The large patio was made of brick pavers and lined with a short brick wall that was topped with neatly trimmed hedges. There were two seating areas made up of matching metal tables and chairs, and Mrs. Dittmer sat at one of the tables in her wheelchair. Although she was sitting in the sunshine, she was bundled in blankets.

Sam sat at the table leafing through a magazine. "Hello, Ms. Megan." He got up and came over to shake my hand.

"Hi, Sam, it's nice to see you again." I wondered if he knew that I had slept with Justin. I wondered if he and Justin discussed personal things.

"It is a lovely day, isn't it?" he asked me.

"Yes, it's beautiful. Hello, Mrs. Dittmer, so nice to see you outside enjoying the sunshine today." I put my hand on her wrist gently as I spoke, and her body moved almost imperceptibly toward me. "I don't know if you remember me, but I'm Megan, and I'm here to visit you for a little while today." Her eyes flickered up for a moment and then over to Sam and Justin and then back down.

"Would you like some lemonade?" Sam asked me.

"Sure, that sounds nice," I said, sitting in one of the chairs near Mrs. Dittmer.

"I'll grab it, Sam," Justin said, and he disappeared into the house.

"How long have you been a caregiver?" I asked Sam as he sat back down.

"A long time, about twenty years now," he said.

"What's the longest you've ever been with a family?"

"Oh my, that is a good question." He looked off into the backyard as he thought for a few minutes. "I was with one gentleman for about five years. That's the longest so far."

"That's a long time," I said, impressed.

"Yes—Mr. Benjamin. He lived not far from here actually. He had a stroke and lost the use of his left side, so he needed constant care. At first he couldn't talk very well either, but he regained most of his speech, and we used to sit and talk for hours. He was a very well-traveled man. Very interesting to talk with, very interesting indeed."

Justin reemerged with three glasses of lemonade on a small green tray shaped like a fish and joined us at the table. He handed out the lemonade and sat down.

"Have you cared for someone with Alzheimer's before caring for Mrs. Dittmer?" I asked.

"Oh yes, oh yes indeed. The last two families I worked with actually. Of course, you are the sweetest woman I have ever worked with, Mrs. Dittmer." He reached over and stroked her back reassuringly.

I took a drink of lemonade and immediately detected vodka. I shot Justin a look of exasperation: *Really? Really?*

What? What? He tried to look innocent but broke into a giggle and took a long drink from his glass.

"What is going on?" Sam asked.

"Oh, nothing, just someone spiking someone else's lemonade when that someone knows that work has to be done," I said accusingly and pushed the lemonade over to the side.

"Oh my, it is early for such things, isn't it?" Sam laughed and sniffed his lemonade.

"Don't worry, Sam. Yours is fine. Someone has to be in charge." Justin laughed again and pushed my glass back toward me.

"Let's try to maintain some kind of decorum in front of your grandma, for Pete's sake," I said.

"Oh, she would have approved. Right, Grandma?" Justin said. "She used to love to come out here in the summertime and have a cocktail in the late afternoon. She would come out here and read a book, and when I got home from school, she would have me make us martinis or open a bottle of wine, and we would just enjoy the birds and squirrels and the warm weather. My grandpa Ron was a fan of cocktail hour, too, so you can't blame me."

I looked around at the trees and hedges and beautiful green grass that covered the backyard and could feel how peaceful it was here. In the middle of the yard, two bronze statues, one of a boy and one of a girl, stood frozen in a game of catch. "Did I miss music hour?"

"Never. That's one of the perks of having Alzheimer's: you can have music hour four times a day because it's impossible to get sick of something you can't remember," Justin joked. "I can play now if you want me to."

"Oh, don't do anything based on me. Just do what you do."

"There is so much I want to do," he said, raising his eyebrows at me and grinning.

I saw Sam look from him to me and back to him again, and I could tell that he was picking up the vibe between us.

My face flushed again, and I took another drink of spiked lemonade and tried to make myself remember that I was not going to sleep with Justin again. "Tell me more stories about your grandma," I demanded, "and I would love to see some old photos, if you have any to show me."

"Yeah, of course, whatever you want." Justin leaned back and stared into the blue sky while he thought for a moment. "I don't know that much. I guess that's kind of sad, eh? I was in California most of the time, but I know my grandpa had money, and they used to have a yacht and they used to play golf and tennis and country-club shit like that. Oh yeah, and she used to breed standard poodles, too. My mom always complained about how the dogs bit her and her sister sometimes. She never had dogs when I lived here, but I guess there used to be a kennel out in the backyard. Too bad. It would have been cool to have doggies to play with in this big yard."

"Sounds like a nice life," I agreed. I couldn't help but reflect on the cruelty of the disease that left Mrs. Dittmer sitting in the middle of the American dream with all the money she would ever need and no ability to enjoy it. But she'd had a long life; the disease didn't catch up to her until she was in her late eighties, so was I wrong to feel so bad for her?

"She still played golf a couple of times a week in the summer when I first moved here. She tried to get me to play, but I don't have the patience for it, I guess."

"Or they don't make toe golf shoes, so you refused."

He laughed. "You got me on that one!"

"If you'll excuse me, I'm going to move Mrs. Dittmer in now," Sam said as he began to wheel her across the deck and into the house through the sliding-glass door.

I stood up and gathered my stuff as well. "I guess we should go in, too."

"We can sit out here a little longer, if you want. I can make us a few more drinks," Justin suggested.

He looked very comfortable leaning back in his chair, and I wanted to walk over and sit in his lap and kiss him. "Probably not a good idea. You and I need supervision, or bad things will happen," I said, mustering all the strength I could.

He leaned up with a serious look on his face. "Bad things? I don't remember anything being bad. Was something bad for you?"

"Besides cheating on my husband, you mean? That is a bad thing to do. Generally frowned upon in this culture. Even the word *cheating* has a negative connotation."

He leaned back with a look of relief on his face. "Oh, that."

"Yes, *that*. It is a big deal, ya know?" I whispered.

"Really? It didn't seem like a big deal to you when we were fucking the other night."

His statement annoyed me a little, and I wasn't quite sure what to say, so I said nothing. He sensed he had crossed the line and leaned over, wrapped his hands around my thigh, and put his head against the side of my hip.

"OK, OK, I get it. I shouldn't assume it's such an easy thing for you, I guess. How long you been married?"

I liked the way his hands felt on my leg, and I wanted him to slide them up and feel me. His head was so close to my crotch, and I wanted him to move it down and taste me. "Eleven years."

"That's a long time." As if he could sense my desire, he turned my body to face him but remained seated in front of me. "Is this the first time you cheated?"

I thought about lying because I knew the truth would make me look bad, but I didn't. "No. I slept with someone else a long time ago. A one-night stand in the Keys." I could feel myself getting wet just looking at him sitting in front of me.

"Oh really." That piece of information seemed to please him, and he stood up to face me, his ever-present smile playing at his lips. "You wanna know what I think?"

"Of course," I breathed. There was something about the way he looked into my eyes, as if he was trying to cast a spell on me. My whole body tingled.

"I think you like being bad; that's what I think."

"You took the easy way out. How disappointing," I teased and pushed him back a few paces.

"Disappointing?" he said, surprised.

"Yes, that was a disappointing answer. Everyone likes being bad. I thought you were going to come up with something clever," I challenged. "Something deep to explain human behavior."

He grinned and moved back in front me and put his hands around my waist. "You're something else; you know that?"

"Yes, I am aware." I put my hands on his arms in an effort to try to hold him back, but all I wanted to do was kiss him.

"Something clever? Something deep?" he repeated. "I'll have to contemplate that. How do you explain it?"

"Well, that's not fair because I already have all the answers."

"I have no doubt about that. And the answers are?"

"I have a self-destructive streak down me a mile wide, a problem with alcohol, and an inability to ignore how much I want to kiss you." I leaned forward and kissed him. His mouth opened immediately, and our tongues met as we pushed against each other.

I don't know how long we stood on the patio kissing; I just remember the softness of his mouth and the feeling of his hands all over me and the sound of his breathing. Nothing else in my life existed except Justin, and when he took my hand and led me through the house and up to his bedroom, I followed eagerly. I forgot I was there to write an article; I forgot to feel embarrassed when we passed Sam; I forgot that I was married and promised myself that I wasn't going to do this again.

With an entire king-size bed at our disposal, we stripped off our clothes and devoured each other. I let orgasm after orgasm wash over me as he entered me from every possible angle. He was more aggressive and forceful than I would have guessed, and that only turned me on more. When we were finally done, we lay next to each other, covered in sweat and holding hands. I didn't want to stop touching him for even a second.

Slowly, reality began to drift back into my mind, and I reluctantly looked around for a clock. It was 4:23, and that piece of information stunned me. I felt like I had been in this house, in this bed, my whole life, but it had been only a few hours. *Could this possibly still be the same day?* I asked myself.

Justin rolled over against me. "Hey, everything OK?"

I stroked the little hairs on the back of his neck and breathed in his scent and wondered if he would possibly be up for a third round this quickly. "Yes, I'm just realizing that I never want to leave this bed again."

He moaned deeply and snuggled against me tighter. "Fine by me."

It would have been so perfect to stay in this alternate world, but then I thought about Craig and the fact that I wouldn't have dinner ready when he got home again, and my stomach knotted up. This was such a stupid thing to do, and I knew that I should leave this house and never return. I should call my editor and tell him that I couldn't use Mrs. Dittmer, or I should just use the information that I already had and finish the story that way. I pushed myself away from Justin and off the bed and began to look for my clothes.

"Can't you stay for dinner? Tell the hubs that's part of the research or something?" he said, in a sleepy voice. "We can smoke and have a cocktail."

"I can't. I'm sorry. I want to stay with you, but I've got this whole other life thing. Oh God, what a mess!" I said in frustration, pulling on my clothes.

"It's OK, babe. I get it. You can use my shower to rinse off, if you want," he offered.

"I do smell, don't I?" I asked, sniffing my arms.

"After what we just did?" He popped off the bed and hugged me. "I kissed and licked and sucked and fucked every square inch of you. Yeah, I would guess that you smell." He nuzzled my neck and breathed into my ear.

I hugged his naked body against me, and we started kissing again before I pulled away. "Stop; stop kissing me, for God's sake, or we will never stop!" I looked down and saw that he had a partial erection. "Oh my God! You're amazing, but I have to go! Put it away!" I went into the bathroom and shut the door and turned on the shower.

I undressed again and jumped in before the water even got warm; I figured that discomfort was part of my penance. As I washed, it struck me that now I would smell like strange soap and the ends of my hair would be wet, and I didn't have a way to explain those things either. I wanted to kick myself for being so stupid. I wondered if I secretly wanted to be caught.

While I was trying to think of good explanations for coming home freshly showered, Justin came in the bathroom and joined me in the shower, his partial erection still intact. "I can't help it; you're so fucking hot," he said as he began kissing me again.

Our quickie in the shower moved out to the sink before ending up on the soft white throw rug that barely cushioned the tile floor.

"Oh crap, now it's got to be almost six." I pushed myself up off the floor and pulled my clothes on. "You have to stop touching me!" I warned Justin, moving away from him.

"I promise that I won't touch you anymore," he panted. "I think I need a nap now."

"Yes, you need to take a nap. Good idea. Holy fuck, I can't believe I did this again!" I left the bathroom and began to frantically search for my shoes on his bedroom floor.

Justin was still lying on the bathroom floor when I stuck my head back in. "I've got to bolt." I didn't know what to say next, so I gave him a lame wave.

"See you, babe," I heard him call as I left.

Once I got down the street, I pulled over and tried to figure out what excuse to text Craig. I knew that I absolutely could not see him right now, and I wasn't sure I could talk to him either. I needed to put space in between my affair and my husband or he would know for sure that something was up. Usually I showed up late or missed dinner after meeting one of my friends for lunch that turned into happy hour that turned into me taking an Uber home and sleeping on the bathroom floor. For once I wished that I had a gym membership so I could say I decided to take a spin class or something that sounded healthy and good for me. I really needed to make some changes, and I promised myself that if I got through this night, I would start first thing tomorrow.

First I texted Paula: *You working tonight?*

It took a few minutes, but then I saw the text bubble appear. *Yeah, just got here. You need some cookies?*

Cookies was our code name for cocaine, and I doubled down on my promise to make some changes. I couldn't believe this was actually my life. *No, thanks, stopping for a drink on my way home. See you in a few.*

Cool beans.

Next I texted Craig: *Hey honey—got caught up with Paula and lost track of time. Sorry. Worst wife ever, I know!!! I'll be home in a few.*

I started driving to the Pink Pony while I waited for his response. I knew he wasn't going to be happy; he thought I drank too much as it was, and he wasn't a fan of me hanging out in strip clubs, but that was what made the lie so perfect. He would be angry, and that would deflect his mind away from thinking that I might be having an affair.

I pulled into the parking lot and gave my car to the valet. The bright-pink building was beyond obnoxious, and I had no doubt you could see it from the surface of the moon. I walked down the glass block hallway and said hello to Rick, the doorman, as I entered and allowed my eyes to get used to the dark interior before I went to the bar and sat down in front of Paula.

The after-work crowd was slowly filing in, and most sat facing the stage and watching the dancers with the same blank stares on their faces that I had gotten used to when I worked there.

"Hey, girl," Paula said. "What brings you by today?"

"Oh my God, you wouldn't believe me if I told you. I need a big drink and a shot, pronto." I rested my head in my hands and tried to wrap my mind around what I had done and what I was doing.

Paula placed a tall cranberry and vodka in front of me, along with a shot glass of clear liquid and a lime. "Tequila blanco, at your service," she said.

"Perfect," I said and eagerly drank the shot and let the tequila burn its way down my throat before I bit the lime.

I heard a guy next to me say, "All right, time to party," as I did it, but I ignored him. I didn't need to make any more friends.

"You're not having one?" I asked Paula.

"I'll catch you on the next one. I'm trying to cut back before I have to buy new clothes," she said, patting her belly. "So what's the haps?"

I sat shaking my head and letting the tequila do its job and trying to figure out the right words to use to tell her what I had gotten myself into and finally said, "Oh, fuck it. I'm banging this guy who is the subject of one of my articles. Can you believe that?"

Paula blinked a few times and leaned in closer. "Really? You? How long you been seeing him?"

"Oh God, I've only know him for two weeks. This just happened. I mean, I'm coming from there right now, and I can't go home yet because Craig will know."

Just then, I realized that I hadn't heard back from Craig yet, and I checked my phone. There was a text from him, and it read, *Great.* Oh boy, a one-word answer. That meant he was pissed. I took a sip of my drink and reasoned that I didn't deserve anything else from him. In fact, it was the least I should expect given the circumstances.

"Who's the guy?"

"Grandson of an Alzheimer's patient that I'm writing about." Even as I said it out loud, I knew how ridiculous it sounded.

"Eh, I thought you were going to tell me you were writing about guys with big dicks or something." Paula worked her way down the bar and served a few guys who had just walked in. As soon as they got a good look at Paula, who was very blond and very pretty and had her enormous fake boobs on display under a low-cut top, the guys lost interest in the dancers and started flirting with her. She laughed and bent over extra low as she put ice in their glasses to let them look down her top. Although I didn't have her body, it was a game I knew well and had played when I worked there.

She flirted back with them for a few minutes and then worked her way back down the bar to me. "How long you and Craig been having troubles?"

"That's just it: we aren't having troubles. We're the same as always, ya know? Fuck me, I don't know how this happened."

"Don't beat yourself up. It's not natural for people to be with the same person all the time. Just look around you. Every one of these guys has a girl somewhere. You gonna tell Craig?"

"Hell to the no! Are you kidding? I need to stop this immediately and take it to the grave, which means you have to take it to the grave—right?" I demanded.

"Of course, of course. Pinkie swear." She held her little finger up and waited for me to link mine with hers. "You know I won't tell anyone. Shot time." Paula poured two shots of tequila and set them on the bar along with two limes.

"So anyway," I said, holding my shot up and waiting for Paula to hold hers up as well. "You are my alibi for today because I told Craig that I was drinking with you and lost track of time." We clinked our glasses together and both did our shots.

"Fine by me; he hates me anyway," she said simply.

"He doesn't hate you, but he does hate me hanging out with you," I admitted.

"He's such an old lady. I still have a hard time seeing you with him, but if he makes you happy, then more power to you. Hey, see the chick on center stage?"

I turned and looked as a very tall brunette took the steps up to the main stage and started slowly grinding her ass against the pole while she massaged her breasts. "Yeah, is she new?"

"Yeah, started a few weeks back. I'm telling you that she has nailed almost every girl in here already and half the bouncers. She is the Charlie Sheen of the Pony."

"Really?" I looked at her again. She was very attractive. "Has she gotten a taste of any of that?" I asked, pointing to Paula's crotch.

"Don't be a dick! No, but the way the other girls are talking about her, I should probably let her have me. No kidding. Since you're cheating on Craig already, you might as well go all the way to hell," she joked.

"Stop! I've gone this long without eating pussy; I think I can make it the rest of my life." I drank my drink and watched the new girl crawl across the stage while guys leaned forward and put dollar bills in her G-string.

"What's the new guy like anyway? Boyfriend material?" Paula asked.

"I don't know. He's so cute I could just eat him alive. I just lose my mind around him. You know how you were with Alex? That's how I am with him," I explained.

"Oh God, I was a total idiot around Alex. Do you not remember how that ended? He took out a restraining order against me because he made me so crazy."

"I don't think I'm that crazy about Justin, but I feel so damn happy when I'm around him." Just thinking about him made me giddy inside.

"Oh God, look at the smile on your face!" Paula exclaimed and tossed an ice cube at me. "Craig never made you smile like that, by the way."

"Stop. I love Craig; you know that. He levels me out," I said, feeling suddenly defensive about my husband.

"What did you say? 'He bums me out'? Is that what I just heard?" she teased.

"If it weren't for him, I would be trading pussy for crack; you know that. I would have hooked up with another degenerate alcoholic like myself, and I would be working the third shift at the tool-and-die shop, for Christ's sake."

We both laughed, and Paula poured two more shots of tequila for us and said, "You be you, boo."

"Love you, sister," I said, and we drank. I could really feel the effects of the alcohol on me, and all my dilemmas began to drift away. "OK, I think I smell boozy enough that I can go home and pretend to be drunk, and he'll be pissed and leave me alone, and then I can wash Justin off of me and go to bed and start this whole life over again tomorrow."

"Are you sure? You can hang at my apartment if you want," she offered.

"I'm sure. Thanks for everything, girl. You know I love you." I tossed forty bucks on the bar and leaned over to hug her, ignoring a couple of hoots and a call for us to kiss that came from two guys down the bar.

"Here, this is too much. Take your fucking money," Paula said as she shoved one of the twenties down my blouse.

When I got home, Craig was sitting in the TV room watching a police show that I recognized but didn't watch myself. I could see from the dirty pans on the stove that he had cooked pancakes and eggs for dinner. I pretended to be upbeat and a little drunker than I actually was as I bounced into the room. "Ah, breakfast for dinner. Nice."

He looked up at me and nodded and went back to watching the TV.

"Uh-oh, the silent treatment. You're mad, eh?" I said, and he didn't respond. I knew that meant he was really mad, and I felt bad, even though I was hoping the whole way home that he would be mad and not want anything to do with me so I could hide my true crime.

"Well, sorry. I don't blame you. I know we talked about it before, and I know you hate it when I drink during the day and when I leave you hanging for dinner like this and—"

"Stop it, please. I don't want to deal with you right now, OK?" he said, without looking at me.

"Got it. I'm gonna grab a shower." I backed out of the room and escaped to the bedroom with a huge pit in my stomach. I had gotten everything that I wanted that day: I'd had amazing sex with Justin and cooked up a plan to cover my tracks with my husband,

and it all worked. I didn't feel happy or relieved or even excited about my conquest. I just felt buzzed and numb and promised myself to do better starting tomorrow.

CHAPTER SEVENTEEN

B y the third week of my assignment, I was exhausted just think-ing about visiting everyone again. It was beginning to dawn on me that taking care of someone with dementia was an inescapable responsibility for these families. Caregivers performed an unre-lenting series of tasks for people who were seldom happy with the results or aware enough to appreciate the scope of their demands.

The fact that the disease lasts for so long before finally tak-ing the person's life is another cruel irony that locks everyone in-volved in an awkward dance for what can be a decade or more. I was surprised that more people didn't commit suicide in the early stages—or did they, and it was just one of those dirty little secrets that hospitals kept because they understood the alternative?

The alternative is to allow people who have lost their minds to go on living because their physical bodies continue to live. At what point do the scales tip and the life that is left is no life at all? If a person doesn't recognize his or her spouse or children or neigh-borhood but still enjoys watching *Wheel of Fortune*, is that enough to justify that life?

I thought of my subjects one by one. Mr. Strumble still ate, watched movies, played with his grandson, and could quote statistics off the top of his head, but he didn't seem to be happy. He didn't seem to be enjoying the experiences. He seemed to be fighting to hold on to each piece of the puzzle at every moment, afraid that if he let go, he would never get it back. You could feel his constant anxiety when you were with him, and I wondered how his wife was able to relax.

Mrs. Phillips was so far gone that I didn't think she was able to enjoy anything. On the contrary, she was filled with fear and suffering from delusions. She no longer ate or seemed to be aware of much of anything around her, and even her husband seemed resigned to her fate.

Mr. Norman was an interesting mix because when he was home, he was lost and restless and confused. But in the course of his disease, he had actually developed a whole other life where, for a few hours a day, he was peaceful and had a girlfriend and danced every afternoon like in an old movie on TV.

Mrs. Dittmer was at the end stages of her disease, but she still responded to music and the sunshine on her face. It was impossible to put a value on how much enjoyment was enough to justify the effort it took to keep someone alive.

And then there were the caregivers themselves, clinging on to the last remnants that made up their family members, taking comfort in the small familiar gestures and physical presence that reminded them of the past. They were faced with losing their loved ones a piece at a time and then losing them again in death. It was an overwhelming situation for everyone involved.

I wondered what I would do if Craig were sick and needed that kind of twenty-four/seven care. I tried to imagine myself staying home with him all day, changing him, talking to him, reassuring him, and answering the same questions over and over again with the same patience that I had seen the caregivers in my story have day after day. I know that when people are faced with an unexpected challenge, they adapt and push themselves beyond what they even thought they were capable of, but I just couldn't imagine it.

Just the thought of Craig and me together in our old age was difficult for me to grasp. I married him with the intention of dying with him, but now, eleven years down the road, I didn't feel the same connection, yet I couldn't imagine not being with him.

The thought of being with Justin made me giddy inside, but I refused to allow myself to believe there was anything real between us. I had decided Justin was a symbol of my restlessness or my need to destroy everything good in my life. I had gotten away with two indiscretions, and although I promised myself that I would not sleep with him again, I ended up having spirited text sex with him after my husband went to bed on Saturday. We weren't really touching, so what could it hurt at this point? I reasoned.

I ran different scenarios of how this was all going to end in my head while I drove the hour to Plymouth, but I wasn't any closer to knowing what I wanted or what I was going to do by the time I arrived. I sat in my car and read through my notes to put myself in the right frame of mind before I went in.

Mrs. Strumble ushered me back to the TV room, where I found Mr. Strumble in his chair, working on a puzzle on the tray table in front of him while *Bridge on the River Kwai* played on the TV. His tiny wife was busy moving from room to room taking the curtains down to wash them as a part of her spring-cleaning routine.

"I'm sorry to leave you alone, but I have to get the rest of these sheers down today," she explained, dragging a stepladder behind her.

"It's not a problem, really," I assured her and sat in my usual spot on the love seat.

"How are you today?" I asked Mr. Strumble.

"Fine, fine. I'm strong like a horse. It's up here that isn't," he said, tapping his head.

"I know. I'm sorry about that, but you seem to be doing well. I went for a walk with you last week. Do you remember?"

"This is a nice neighborhood for a walk," he said.

"Your son, Mike, was here with your grandson, Ian, and we walked down to pet the dog at the end of the street."

"That Mike loves that dog...no, I don't mean Mike...I mean... my grandson." I could see he was struggling to remember the name.

"Ian," I said. "He's a handsome boy."

"Yes, gets that blond hair from his mother. Mike had a head full of black hair when he was a boy."

"Really? That's nice."

"I don't think they're coming today. What day is it?" he asked.

"It's Monday."

"Monday? No, he comes on Tuesdays." He brightened up at the thought. "When he's here, his mother leaves to visit her sister. Her sister is not doing well these days."

"Well, that's nice; it gives you something to look forward to. What's the puzzle of?" I asked.

He reached down and brought up a box from the floor next to his chair and held it up for me. It was a picture of two red foxes sitting in the snow.

"Foxes, nice. But I bet the background is hard to do with all that snow, eh?"

"I don't know if I've ever done this one before," he said and looked down at the pieces spread out in front of him. Part of one fox was together so far. He picked up a piece and traced the edges with his finger and then tried to put it in several places before giving up and setting it back in the pile and selecting another piece.

I got up and walked over to take a closer look at the photos on the entertainment center. "These old photos are great," I said and picked up the one of him at his daughter's wedding and carried it over to him so he could see it. "Is this from your daughter's wedding?"

He took the framed photo from me and studied it with a smile on his face. "Yes, yes, that was Bev's wedding at Cranbrook. That's me right there, and then there's my wife and Beverly and her husband, Ken." He pointed to each person as he said the names.

"It's a lovely photo. How long ago was that?"

"Oh, it's got to be...I don't know...let's see..." He stared at the photo intently as he tried to remember. "Not a big time and not a short time." He looked around the room and out the doorway before yelling, "Carol?"

"Oh, that's OK. You don't have to get your wife. I was just wondering," I said, taking the photo back from him and placing it back on the shelf.

I heard her making her way back to the TV room, the creaking of the old wood floor calling out each of her steps. She popped her head into the room. "Yes? How we doing in here?"

"She's got a question about that picture."

"I was just wondering when the picture at your daughter's wedding was taken," I said.

"About eighteen years ago," she answered.

"Eighteen years ago!" Mr. Strumble exclaimed in surprise. "It couldn't have been that long ago!"

"Well, it was. Did you see this one?" She walked over and took an old photo of a couple standing together on their wedding day in front of the wooden doors of a church and showed it to me.

"This has to be you two, right?" She looked even smaller in a tea-length dress and huge veil and long white formal gloves. Mr. Strumble looked dapper in his suit and tie with a head full of greased-back jet-black hair.

"That's us all right." She smiled and moved over to show the picture to her husband. "Right, Larry?"

He studied the photo for a moment. "We took that picture right when we came out of church after the ceremony. That's the first picture of us as man and wife."

"That's right." She put the photo back.

"It's wonderful; you two look very happy," I said and envied the fact that they had been together for so long.

"OK, back to the curtains while you watch the movie and work the puzzle, and then we'll have lunch."

He nodded and looked at me and back to her and said, "I want you to stay during the tests. I don't like it when they make you leave the room."

It took his wife a moment to realize what he was saying. "Oh, the tests are next week, dear. Not today."

"She's from Dr. Burton's office?" he said, pointing to me.

"Yes, but Megan doesn't do the tests; she just comes to visit." She then said to me, "They do a whole series of tests every year to measure his progress, or rather, the progress of...it on him, and they start next week."

"Yes, I am familiar with those. They take several days, don't they?"

"It is an exhausting process," she admitted.

"So you don't do the tests?" he asked me.

"No, but I've seen them done and read about them. Lots of puzzles and things you have to remember like lists of words and pictures," I said.

"Oh, they go on and on and ask so many questions, and I don't think I could have answered them when I was twenty-five!" Mr. Strumble exclaimed.

"Well, don't worry about it now. That's a problem for next week," Mrs. Strumble said and left to return to her work.

"Do you want any help with that puzzle?" I asked.

"All I can get," he answered with a wink. I sat in the chair next to him, and he pushed the tray table over so it was between us. I did my best to help, but I was honestly more interested in seeing how Mr. Strumble's mind worked as he picked up piece after piece and tried to find a place for them. I could sometimes see that he had made a match in his mind, but by the time he picked up the piece and looked back at the puzzle, the connection had disappeared, leaving him to start the process anew over and over again.

He also seemed to have a hard time comprehending the contrast in the color between the red fox fur and the white snow. Even when I would hand him a piece and point to the space where it belonged, he had difficulty turning the piece the correct way to match the colors and only managed to get it to fit by trial and error.

We passed the next hour working the puzzle and watching William Holden and Alec Guinness argue with Japanese soldiers. Mr. Strumble stopped to tell me facts about the war or the movie from time to time, and I marveled at his ability to remember details from so long ago when I knew he probably wouldn't remember that I was there at all after I left.

"Sometimes I think I see it, but then I lose it," he said, returning another unused puzzle piece to the pile.

"This is a hard puzzle," I admitted, and I meant it. "I've only gotten a few pieces in myself, and that's mostly because of the grass sticking through the snow on this side."

"One more for you is one less I have to see, so that's OK," he said with a smile.

"Do you like to play cards or any other games?" I asked.

"Let's see; I don't think so. Not anymore. I can't keep up like I used to." He tapped his head again.

"Lunchtime," his wife called out as she entered the room. "I'll just move this table out of the way and move the other one over so I don't mess up the puzzle."

I followed her lead and moved one of the other tray tables in front of him once the puzzle had been moved to the side and then followed her to the kitchen to help her carry the sandwiches and milk. It was funny how natural it felt to eat lunch with them after only three weeks.

"How long have you been married, Megan?" Mrs. Strumble asked me in between bites.

"Eleven years," I answered.

"Oh, eleven, is that right?" Mr. Strumble said.

"You must have gotten married young, like we did. Were you high school sweethearts?" Mrs. Strumble asked.

"No, I met him a few years after high school, but we got married when we were still in college, so I guess we were young."

"How many children do you have?" she asked.

I dreaded this question and the ones that always followed it. "None. No kids yet."

"Really?" She didn't try to hide her surprise, and I could see her trying to work it out in her head before she said, "Lots of couples wait these days, I guess."

"Yeah, we do talk about it but just haven't gotten around to it yet," I said, hoping that would be the end of it.

"Well, don't wait too long because it goes by faster than you think. I feel like it was just yesterday that we bought this house and started our family, and forty years went by in the blink of an eye." She smiled at her husband and looked at me, and I had the feeling she was trying to tell me that it's over before you know it. I realized that her old life and whatever plans they had made together before his illness were over and this life was what was left, and once he was gone, she would start another life.

And that's what life really is, a series of lives that grow and develop before they fade away and new ones take their place. My life up until high school gave way to my life with Craig, and now that life might be ending so I could start a life with Justin, or Justin would just end up being a small pothole in my life with Craig that I would reflect on while I was nursing Craig's children and picking out preschools years from now. A feeling of peace came over me as I realized that no matter what happened, I would be OK, and life would keep replacing itself until the end.

I helped Mrs. Strumble clean up the dishes and carried the tray with the puzzle back over to Mr. Strumble before I left.

CHAPTER EIGHTEEN

I answered my phone, and it was Don Felder, the editor from *Michigan Leisure*. "Hey, Meg, how's it going?" he asked, in a tone that told me his question was just a formality.

"Fine, Don, just fine. You got something for me?" I got right to the point.

"Yes, if you're available. I need a quick piece on a new place in Saugatuck."

"Ah, Saugatuck in the springtime. A little chilly this time of year, but the trees are blooming so it should be nice."

"And this place is right up your alley; it's some kind of a microbrewery combined with a B and B or something like that. I don't know. It's a friend of Steve's, and he wants us to do him a solid and get a few hundred words in for him, and you know how that goes. So can you do it in the next week?"

"Yeah, yeah, I'm working on a longer piece right now, but I can pop up there for a night. You got room budget, or are they comping it?"

"Comp. I'll e-mail you with all the information. Can you get it to me by Monday? And take some decent pictures, please? The ones he e-mailed me look like they were taken from an airplane."

"Gotcha. Consider it done."

"Thanks, Meg." And with that he hung up.

My mind immediately began to race. I wanted Justin to go to Saugatuck with me, and that meant figuring out a way to go without Craig. He used to tag along on some of my assignments when we were first married, but he grew impatient with the short nature of most of my trips, complaining that we spent more time flying than we did at the location. That wasn't really true, but it wasn't far off either.

But Saugatuck was barely a three-hour drive away, and he would go with me if I went on the weekend. I had to go on Thursday. Craig would never miss work for something like this, I reasoned.

I texted Justin, *Hey, want to go on an adventure on Thursday?*

I saw the dot bubble appear almost immediately. *Hmmm. Mysterious. What do u have in mind?*

I have to write a quick piece about a place in Saugatuck. Go Thurs and come back Fri. Wanna cum?

Hee-hee-hee. You are a wild one. Fuck yeah.

My heart felt like it was going to burst out of my chest. *I'll come over at my usual time, and we'll leave right after. About a three-hour drive.*

K. What do I need to bring?

I couldn't resist: *Your gorgeous blue eyes and that beautiful cock.*

Wow. I'm hard just thinking about it.

Me too.

And I was. I wanted to drive over to his house and fuck him. I contemplated suggesting it. I looked at the time and thought about excuses I could tell Craig to explain my absence. I wondered how I could so easily and thoughtlessly cheat on Craig. Shouldn't I feel bad? Deep remorse? Pure guilt? What was wrong with me that I was so willing to risk my marriage? I felt like I was possessed and had no power to stop myself.

I checked my e-mail and saw one from Don with all the information. I called my contact, a guy named Ray, who I quickly surmised was gay from the sound of his voice and his exuberant response to my call. I explained that I wanted to come on Thursday because I already had commitments this weekend, and he gladly accommodated me. I told him that I would be bringing a friend and would prefer a king bed in a quiet part of the house, and he sounded delighted.

After the call ended, my stomach did a little flip-flop. This was taking things to a whole different level, and I knew it. I practiced a few versions of what I would say to Craig in my head and wondered when he would be home before I realized that it was racquetball night and he wouldn't be home until later. And he would want to have sex. My body was already humming at the thought of going away with Justin, and I began to look forward to seeing Craig with great anticipation.

CHAPTER NINETEEN

O f all the subjects in my piece, the Phillipses were the ones that I found myself thinking of the most. Their situation was the most isolated and depressing and, frankly, hopeless. As close to the end as she was, I knew from my research that Mrs. Phillips could easily last another year or more. I wanted to intervene on their behalf and send in the cavalry, but it wasn't my place, and even if I did, I knew it was likely that Mr. Phillips would refuse any help that came his way.

I couldn't figure out if he was stubborn or trying to be strong or embarrassed to ask for help and decided it was probably a combination. I knew Mr. Phillips liked to read, so I stopped at the Alzheimer's Association offices and gathered up some literature and printed off a list of resources in the community and bundled it in a pack that I planned to "forget" on the coffee table.

I was surprised to see Mrs. Phillips dressed in khaki sweatpants, a button-down shirt, and a pink sweater when I arrived. Her hair was freshly combed back and in the loose ponytail I was used to seeing.

"Wow, you're all dressed up today!" I exclaimed to her, reaching out to pat her hands.

She looked at me and then over to her husband and back again before exhaling deeply. She seemed slightly more animated today but without the fear that I had seen on my last visit.

"Yes, I wanted you to know that she can still dress up sometimes; it's not just pajamas and housecoats around here," Mr. Phillips said, smiling. He was more upbeat today, and I noticed that some of the moving boxes had been opened and moved. I took this as a good sign that he was feeling more positive and wanted to make the condo a bit homier.

I took out my recorder and notebook and the pack of information that I had brought over. "Oh, this is for you," I said, placing the packet on the table. "Just some information that I put together for everyone participating in the article," I lied.

"That's very nice of you," he said, glancing at the stack for a moment before he went over and picked up one of the moving boxes and carried it over to the couch. "I found some old photos for you."

"Oh, that's great!"

He sat on the couch with the box on the floor in front of him and took out a framed photo of himself and his wife standing on either side of his son at a military ceremony. "This was his graduation day in San Diego. We flew out for the ceremony."

In the photo, Mrs. Phillips had long brown hair and wore it in the same low ponytail. She looked very much the same, and I looked from her face in the photo to her face sitting in front of me over and over, trying to discern the differences. "You still look just as beautiful, Mrs. Phillips," I said, with a smile.

Mr. Phillips was a little harder to recognize because he seemed so much taller in the photograph than he did in real life, and he must have broken his nose somewhere along the line because the man in the photo had a sharp, smooth nose while the man in front of me had a stubby nose that turned to the left. "You look pretty much the same, too," I said to him.

"Yeah, I bet!" he scoffed.

"Your son was very handsome." And he was. He looked strong and confident in his dress blues, his steely eyes starting out from under the brim of his white dress hat.

"That's for sure. He could have been a movie star with his face. The girls used to follow him home even when he was a little boy." Mr. Phillips chuckled. He took the picture from me and held it in front of his wife. "See, Melly? It's the photo from graduation, remember?"

She glanced at it several times but never seemed to connect with it, and he put it back on the table and took out another framed photograph.

"This is the one I was telling you about, of Melly and her sisters. It says 1961 on the back."

In the photograph, all four sisters stood in a row, slightly sideways to the camera, dressed in white tennis skirts and pastel tops and holding tennis rackets. They all looked to be in their teens or early twenties. They were laughing, as if someone had said something very funny just before the picture was taken. The laughter and joy on their faces was infectious and made me smile just looking at it. "What a great picture! Which one is Mrs. Phillips?" I asked.

"This one," he said, pointing to the girl the second from the right. "They're in order of age. They always stood that way. Isabel is the oldest; then came Andrea and then Melly and then Sandra. Andrea is the one who lives in Saint Louis." He again took the photo and held it up for his wife to see. "Remember this one? You and your sisters? Remember it used to hang on the wall in the den?"

This time, her eyes locked on the photo, and she did not look away. Some part of her connected with it, and she raised her hand and tapped the frame.

"That's right; that's you and your sisters, Melly," he said to her enthusiastically.

"She recognizes it; that's for sure," I said, astonished at her sudden focus. "Have you showed her these pictures lately?"

"Not since we moved. They've been packed away." He held the photo in her lap and let her look at it and touch it with her unsteady hand until she lost interest, and then he laid it on the table with the other one.

The next photo was from their wedding in 1964 and showed the two of them flanked by seven bridesmaids in baby-blue dresses and seven groomsmen in black tuxes. Mr. Phillips wore a white tuxedo jacket, and Mrs. Phillips wore horn-rimmed glasses with her white satin dress.

"Wow! That is a lot of people to have standing up in a wedding," I exclaimed.

"Did you ever hear of the movie *Seven Brides for Seven Brothers*? You're probably too young."

"I've heard of it. I think I probably saw it when I was younger, but I can't quite remember it."

"Well, it was one of Melly's favorites, so that's why you see that army of people standing next to us." He rolled his eyes and chuckled and held it up for Mrs. Phillips to see.

She looked at it briefly but didn't seem to connect with it like she did the last photograph.

"This was on our wedding day, Mel; do you remember? This is me, and this is you," he said, pointing.

"Was that picture hanging in the house as well?" I asked.

"This one? No, not for a while. It used to be on the bureau in our bedroom, but she took it down a long time ago."

"I wonder if that's why she isn't reacting in the same way as with the one of her and her sisters that was hanging up in the den," I wondered out loud.

"Could be. Who knows? Don't worry, Mel; I won't take it personally." He kidded her and placed the photo on the table.

"I'm just thinking that she saw the photo in the den on a daily basis, so it imprinted on her brain in a different way than the wedding picture. What about the one with your son? Where was that one kept?"

"That was in the den, too, for a long time, but after we lost him, we moved it up into his room, or what used to be his room. It was hard for us to look at for a while, I guess," he said apologetically.

"Understandable. It's interesting, though, because she didn't see that photo every day, either." I took pictures of the photographs on the table. "May I take her photo today, too?" I asked.

"Yes, I think that would be OK," he said.

"She looks so pretty, all dressed up," I said and snapped a photo of both of them and then one of just Mrs. Phillips.

"Thank you so much for digging these out for me," I said, rising to shake Mr. Phillips's hand before I left. "It was wonderful to be able to see a bit of your family history."

"It was my pleasure. This is how she should be remembered," he said, sweeping his hand across the photos on the table. "It's how we all should be remembered."

"That would be nice," I admitted, "but unfortunately time has other plans for us, eh? Not much you can do about that." I placed my hand on top of Mrs. Phillips's hands again. "It was nice seeing you and looking through your old photos, Mrs. Phillips. You look very nice today."

Her eyes drifted upward to my face and held for a second, and I thought I could see a slight smile play at her lips, but I wasn't sure whether I was reading too much into it because it had been such a pleasant day.

"Thanks for coming over today," Mr. Phillips said, walking me to the door.

"Of course. I'll see you next week for the final visit, and then I'll drop by with a copy of the article as soon as it's edited so you have it to read. I can bring more than one copy if you would like to give it to anyone else?" I offered.

"No, one should be fine," he said.

"OK then, have a good week," I said and left.

I drove home with a smile on my face, shocked at how much better I felt since that morning. Today had been a good day for the Phillipses, and although I knew good days were very hit-and-miss, it lightened my heart to know that it was still possible for them.

CHAPTER TWENTY

Mr. Norman was engaged in a heated argument with his wife when I arrived for my third visit. Linda shook her head and rolled her eyes and said, "You want to experience what it's like? Well, this is what it is like," she said and pointed me toward the living room.

Mr. Norman and his wife stood over the dining-room table, looking at a pad of paper.

"You write it down here, and Linda will get it for you. That's how it works!" she yelled at him.

"I can get it myself!" he yelled back.

"How? How? You can't drive anymore. End of discussion. You write it down, and Linda will bring it for you." She pushed the pad of paper and pen over in front of him.

"I don't need anyone to bring me my things. I want to get them myself!" He pushed the pad across the table. "I want to go to the store myself! You need to give me my money, so I can go!"

"Stop it, Charles! You are not being reasonable, and I'm tired of explaining it to you. You have to accept what I say, just like the doctor told you."

Mr. Norman looked around with exasperation and noticed me in the room. "You, you need to help me!" he yelled at me. "They took all my goddamn money, and they won't let me go to the store!"

"I'm sorry, Mr. Norman. I'm sure they're doing their best to take care of you," I offered, unsure of how to defuse the situation.

"They stole my money! They stole my car! They won't let me go to the store, and they won't tell me why!" he yelled, smacking one hand in the palm of the other with each point.

"You have Alzheimer's; that's why!" his wife said, and then, pausing between each word, "You. Are. Sick!"

"You don't know what you know. You people won't tell me what's going on here, and I won't stand for it anymore!" He stomped off down the hallway, disappeared into one of the bedrooms, and slammed the door.

Mrs. Norman braced herself against the back of one of the dining-room chairs and exhaled, blowing her bangs off her forehead in the process.

"He's having a hard day today for some reason," Linda explained from the kitchen.

"More and more hard days now, if you ask me." Mrs. Norman moved over to her chair and sat down heavily.

"Is there something that triggered him today?" I asked.

"Who knows? You just got the tail end of it; he's been arguing for a good twenty minutes. It's exhausting," Linda said.

I listened for a minute and could hear movement and the sound of drawers opening and closing coming from down the hallway. "What is he doing now? Is he OK alone?"

"He's packing," Mrs. Norman answered.

"Packing?"

"He does it every time he gets frustrated. It's nothing new," she said flatly.

Linda went down the hallway and opened the door. "Dad, stop packing, or we won't be able to go to the club this afternoon," she warned.

"Get out of my room!" he yelled. "I can go to the club if I want to, and you cannot stop me, little girl!"

Linda backed out and shut the door and joined us back in the living room. "The biggest pain the ass is that if I don't put his clothes back, they will end up all over the place because he can't remember where anything goes."

"So what happens now?" I asked.

"He'll work his way out of it eventually," Linda said. "Something else will catch his attention, and he'll forget that he was mad or why he was mad. Sometimes he stays angry, but when I ask him why he's mad at me, he can't answer me and just says that I must have done something bad."

"He's always mad at me," Mrs. Norman said, and I noticed that she was back working on a crossword puzzle. "You wanna hear a funny story?"

"Yes, of course," I answered.

"He had this white Chevrolet car that he loved back in the day. Must have been a seventy-two or seventy-three, I think. Anyway, he wouldn't let me drive it for the first year or so he had it, but then finally, he let me start driving it, and one day when I was visiting my friend Joy, I was backing out of her driveway, and I scraped the side along this chain-link fence. It left these horrible gouges, and of course I knew Charles was going to be mad—and he was, but he got over it eventually."

"I was little, but I remember that," Linda chimed in.

"So life goes on, ya know? Years go by, and he forgets all about it until his mind starts playing tricks a few years back, and suddenly he's mad at me all over again." She laughed. "I'm watching TV one day, and he just starts yelling at me about scratching his white

Chevrolet! It took me a while to even remember what the hell he was talking about."

"That's amazing. Does he still bring it up?" I asked.

"It's been a month or two now, I guess," she said, still chuckling.

"Last time we all went in the car together to the doctor, he said not to let her drive because she scratched his car," Linda said.

Just then, Mr. Norman stomped back into the room with a duffel bag in his hand and dropped it on the floor. He had changed his clothes and now wore gray sweatpants with a tan and brown sweater that was far too heavy for the weather outside.

"I didn't ask for any of this, you know," he declared in frustration. "I didn't ask to have to deal with this thing."

"We know, Dad. Neither did we. We're all doing the best we can. It's OK."

"Just relax, Charles. You know that getting angry doesn't help you sort things out. It just makes it worse. Sit down now," Mrs. Norman said sympathetically.

"Well, it's getting worse, and those doctors can't do a thing about it." He stayed standing and stared off into the distance.

"We'll get through it, Dad," Linda offered.

"You'll get through it. I'll end up…" He pointed to the ground.

"We all end up there," Mrs. Norman said simply.

"Are all the ones you study like this?" he asked me, holding his arms out.

"Everyone is different—in different stages, I mean. You are actually doing very well from what I can see," I said and then tried to divert his attention. "I saw you dance last week, and you were wonderful."

"I like the…" He paused, searching for the word. "The sound… the playing…music," he said, finally finding the word he wanted.

"Dad, you aren't going to wear sweatpants to the club today, are you?" Linda asked.

He looked down at his outfit and back at her. "No one cares what I wear," he shot back.

"Rosalind will care," she said in a calm voice. "You know that she'll be dressed up, so don't you think you should have proper pants on?"

"You don't have to take me. I can take myself," he said, but I could tell his anger was wearing off.

"My car is in the driveway anyway. Might as well take it, eh?"

Mr. Norman walked to the window and looked out at the driveway for several minutes. He came back and sat on the couch, his long legs sticking up awkwardly.

"How about if I go and lay your clothes out on the bed for you so when you are ready to go, you can change?" Mrs. Norman said, getting up.

"I don't want to wear those navy-blue pants. I don't like them."

"OK, no navy blue. Got it." And she went down the hallway.

"You want some juice, Dad? You've got to be thirsty," Linda offered.

He nodded at her and began watching *The Price Is Right* on TV. Linda returned with a big glass of apple juice and handed it to him. After he took it, she quietly picked up the duffel bag and carried it back to the bedroom and left it for her mother to unpack. Mr. Norman either didn't notice or didn't care.

CHAPTER TWENTY-ONE

My eyes popped open at a little after four in the morning, and I lay quietly in the bed listening to Craig's breathing and thinking about going out of town with Justin later that day. I knew it was the wrong thing to do, but I didn't care and couldn't figure why. Craig was a good husband, a nice guy, and a good provider who loved me. Our sex life had always been good, if a little predictable, so it wasn't like my base needs were being denied. He had even been patient with me about having kids. He had everything you were supposed to want in a mate, and I knew that I was lucky to have him, but I couldn't stop myself from wanting Justin.

I wondered if he had ever cheated or even thought about cheating on me. It would have made me feel better to know that he had some of the same urges. There was a girl at his office I met at one of the Christmas parties whom I caught a vibe off of while we were talking. She was pretty hot for an IT girl, and she knew it. She wore a supershort skirt and high leather boots, and I could see all the guys in their khaki pants, brown loafers, and button-down shirts watching her as she crossed the room. Craig introduced us, and she called me the "lucky woman" for having managed to catch Craig and touched his arm repeatedly while she talked. I jokingly accused Craig of having an affair with her on the way home and referred to her as his "office wife" whenever she came up in conversation. He would just look at me with exasperation and tell me to stop being ridiculous.

Although anything was possible, I couldn't come up with any scenario that put Craig in the back of a car with a stranger at any point in our marriage, and I had to accept the fact that I was the only guilty party in this bed. I decided that I would take this trip to Saugatuck with Justin and then end it. It would be my last fling, and then I would buckle down and get serious about getting pregnant. Once I gave Craig a child, I would be absolved of all my sins, I figured.

I drifted in and out of sleep for the next few hours and then got up before Craig left to remind him that I wouldn't be home that night. I promised to leave him dinner in the refrigerator, and he kissed me on the forehead on the way out.

I did some yoga, took a quick run, and made a batch of chicken carbonara that I left in the refrigerator with a Post-it note saying "Miss you" in a heart stuck on the foil. I wasn't a bad wife; I just wasn't a very good one either.

I showered and shaved every inch of my body and put my favorite underwear and push-up bra on under my jeans and turquoise top that was just low-cut enough. I packed my light-purple, lacy thong underwear and bra and the K-Y Jelly along with a fresh pair of blue jeans and shirt for tomorrow into a small duffel bag and left for the Dittmer house.

Justin greeted me at the door with a big hug and immediately asked, "Are we still going?"

"Oh yeah, can't wait," I answered and kissed his neck.

"Fab." He reached back and carefully pulled the hair tie out of my hair and let my hair fall on my shoulders.

"Why did you do that?" I asked as he handed me the hair tie.

"'Cause that's how I like it best." He ran his hands through my hair, and I wondered if I could even wait to get to Saugatuck before I fucked him again.

"Does that mean I can make you take off those awful toe shoes?" I joked.

He laughed. "Trying to get me undressed already, eh? I see how you work."

"Come on, let's spend some time with your grandma before we leave, so I can pretend that I'm doing my job."

"I've got lots of 'jobs' for you," he said mischievously.

"Wow, you are really in a mood today, aren't you?" I pulled away from him.

"Just very much looking forward to our trip; that's all." He took my hand, and we went into his grandmother's room.

Mrs. Dittmer was back in the kitchen, sitting in her wheelchair next to the door that led out onto the patio. Sam was at the counter making lunch.

"Hi, Gram-Gram!" Justin called loudly as we entered. "Megan is here to see you."

"Hello, Mrs. Dittmer," I said and then turned to Sam. "Hi, Sam."

"Hello and welcome, Ms. Megan," he said cheerfully.

Mrs. Dittmer looked up at us as we approached and then went back to looking outside. I noticed that she wore pants and a blouse with buttons and hard-soled shoes today.

"She likes to watch the birds in the garden," Sam explained.

"You're dressed up today, Mrs. Dittmer. You look so nice!" I exclaimed, and then I asked Sam, "Does she have a doctor's appointment today?"

"No, no, I like to dress her properly sometimes. A housecoat or nightgown is easier, but that is no way to go through life. I think she feels better when she has proper clothes on," he explained.

"That's nice. Do you notice a difference in her when you do that?" I asked.

"Yes, sometimes," he said, smiling.

I could see how skinny her legs were through the fabric of her pants and how thin her wrists looked sticking out of the cuffs of her blouse.

"Gram-Gram, have you seen any blue jays today?" Justin asked, kneeling in front of her. "Blue jays are her favorites," he said to me. "We used to have a whole family of them that hung out on the patio. They were mean as shit…sorry, Gram…crap. They used to chase all the other little birds around and steal their bread crumbs."

Mrs. Dittmer looked at Justin and nodded and looked at me and nodded and then looked back outside.

"How long until lunch, Sam?" Justin asked.

"Oh, about ten or fifteen minutes. Will you be having lunch before you go?" he asked, and I felt a little embarrassed that Sam knew we were going away together but realized that Justin would have had to tell them his whereabouts.

"Yes, we'll have lunch, and then I'll play for a while before we go," he said and then looked at me. "Sound good?"

"Sounds great." I pulled a dining-room chair over to sit next to Mrs. Dittmer. I stared out into the backyard and watched the birds come and go from the shrubs and trees while Justin made us turkey sandwiches and Sam finished making lunch for Mrs. Dittmer and himself, and then we all sat around the table and ate together.

Mrs. Dittmer ate in the same mechanical way that I had seen other patients eat before: muscle memory seemed to take over once the meal began, and she ate each mouthful without protest until Sam got to the green beans. Once she saw them on the fork, she turned her head away and raised her hand.

"Oh, what's wrong? You don't like green beans today?" Sam asked.

She shifted away again and made a soft groan.

"But you like green beans. You do."

Mrs. Dittmer stared at Sam with an intensity I hadn't seen before, her eyes trying to speak the words she could not say. Her breath came out in sharp bursts as she stared at him.

Sam finally gave up and dumped the green beans back on the plate. "OK, for you, no green beans today, m'lady."

Mrs. Dittmer examined the next forkful of mashed potatoes carefully before eating it.

"She does like green beans, most of the time," Sam said to me, "but you can never tell from day to day."

"I understand. I feel the same way about green beans, Mrs. Dittmer," I said.

"Not me. I hate them all the time. I am very consistent," Justin said proudly.

We finished eating and moved into the living room so Justin could play the piano. I was getting impatient to be with him, and I could tell he felt the same way. Just as before, Mrs. Dittmer became more animated when he played, and she tapped her fingers along with the music. It was such a beautiful thing to watch that I began to feel guilty about wanting to take Justin away so quickly, and I urged him to play song after song until he finally refused to play anymore.

He knelt down in front of her and said, "I am going away for a little while, just a night, Gram-Gram, but I will come back tomorrow in time to play again before dinner, OK?"

She stared at him without responding, and he stood up and hugged her and kissed her on the cheek, and I couldn't help but fall for him a little more.

"Goodbye, Mrs. Dittmer. I'll see you again next week," I said and gave her hand a little shake. She looked up and seemed to study my face for a few moments, as if she were trying to figure something out, before looking back down.

Justin took my hand, and instead of leading me out to the front door, he led me to the back of the kitchen and down a short hallway. "One quick stop first," he said and opened a door that revealed a staircase down to the basement.

"The basement? Mysterious. Is this the part where you kidnap me and make me your slave?" I whispered, and then the unmistakable smell of weed hit me. "Oh my" was all I could say.

"You are already my slave; didn't you know that?" he joked and kissed me before leading me down the stairs.

"We're going to your grow room, I take it from the smell?" I asked.

"Yeah. It is delightfully pungent down here, isn't it?" he said and walked me past a rec room with a bar and pool table and through another door to reveal a room filled with plants and lights. Some plants were on the floor, some were on racks, and there were a couple of aisles that allowed you to navigate the room. The smell in this room was incredible, and I felt like I was getting high just standing there.

"Oh my God!" I exclaimed. "This is outrageous. You have hundreds of plants down here! When the fuck did you put all this equipment down here, and how do Sam and his sisters not know about it?"

Justin smiled and worked his way down one of the aisles to a cleaning table in the back of the room. "It took some time. I started with just a few plants for myself a while ago. Gram-Gram never really came down here, and this was a storage room that was mostly empty, so I appropriated a corner and then another corner and so on, and before you know it—"

"Old MacDonald had a farm!" I finished.

"Yep. I just want to grab some to take with us," he said, and I watched as he cleaned some buds of the leaves and seeds and put them in a ziplock baggie. "OK, let's bolt." He gave me another quick kiss and led me back out of the basement.

"So, does Sam know about this?" I whispered as we reentered the kitchen.

"I'm sure he does. He knows I smoke because he has seen me do it about a hundred times, but he doesn't care. I've never gone out of my way to point it out to him or anything."

We crossed back through the kitchen and waved to Sam, who was sitting outside with Mrs. Dittmer.

"You two enjoy yourselves; we'll be fine here," Sam called as we left.

"Thanks, Sam. Call if anything happens," Justin said, and we left to begin our adventure.

The B and B was a white carriage-style house with a black roof and black trim that looked like something out of the Revolutionary War. A circular driveway constructed from brick pavers wound under an overhang and to the front door. We parked in the small parking lot off to the side. In the distance, you could see a large barn also painted in white and black, with the words *Ashcroft B and B and Brewery*, along with the logo, on the side.

Ray met us on the sidewalk as we walked up to the front doors. "Hello and hello and welcome!" he sang out. He was very tall and slim and wore red jeans with a red-and-green-checked shirt and red tennis shoes. At first glance, I thought he was bald, but he had very thin close-cropped blond hair.

"Hi!" I tried to match his enthusiasm. "I'm Megan, and this is Justin."

"Excellent. I am Ray." He shook each of our hands. "Any trouble finding the place?"

"No, we did good," I answered.

"I keep telling Brad that we need to put a sign on the corner of Center Street because people are just going to blast by us and never even know we're here."

"Maybe. Yes, that's a good idea. I mean, we didn't have a problem, but there isn't much traffic today, so we took our time," I explained. I noticed Ray noticing my wedding ring. His eyes then moved to Justin's hand. He looked from me to Justin and back to me as he tried to work things out in his head.

"Well, let's go inside, and I'll show you around and get you settled, and then we can go out and meet Brad and tour the brewery. Sound good?" he said, but it was more a statement than a question, and we nodded in agreement.

Inside, the house was warm and welcoming. Dark-stained hardwood floors were covered in period runners, and high-back chairs with tea tables sat on both sides of the reception desk in the foyer. Ray reached behind the desk and grabbed an old-fashioned metal key attached to a key ring with a wooden circle.

He started down a narrow hallway. "The kitchen and dining areas are back here."

There were old pictures of people from various time periods along the walls. "Are these family photos?" I asked.

"Yes, but don't ask me whose families." Ray chuckled. "When we first started renovations, we put up a Facebook post asking people to send us old photos, and we got a shit ton! I mean to tell you, I could fill a room with all the pictures people sent or dropped off. It was a blast looking through them. We've got a storage room in case we want to change them out or if any get broken. You know, it's our way of saying that the inn belongs to everyone. Very kumbaya."

"Nice," Justin said as we stepped into a dining room that was furnished with several small white tables and chairs. A large banquet ran along one wall. There was a large flower centerpiece, two coffee urns, and a plate of wrapped pound cake.

"So, this is where we serve breakfast every morning, and you can always come to the kitchen for coffee and snacks. We always have a selection of Danish and pound cakes or cookies and fruit out for guests." Ray paused to allow us to take a look at the room and then gestured for us to follow him. "And the kitchen is back here if you need a cold beverage. There's also a small seating area around the bay window."

"Really charming," I commented.

"We worked really hard on it. It's so nice to have it completed. We can't wait for people to start enjoying it. Come on, I'll show you to your room so you can freshen up. Did you want to see all the rooms now?"

I considered it for a moment. Justin grabbed my hand and squeezed, and I flushed. "No, I think I'll wait until tomorrow morning so the light will be as bright as possible for the pictures."

"Oh, you're good. See, I wouldn't have thought of that. Good thinking." He tapped his head with his fingers.

We followed him down another hallway to a corridor and up a staircase to a landing. Ray turned and handed the key to me. "End of the hallway on the right. It's the Peach Suite, our quietest room, and it does have its own bathroom."

I took the key. "Sounds great. Thanks so much."

"You are the only guests for tonight, so we can go over to the brewery as soon as you're ready, but we should go before it gets dark so you can see the grounds. What time would you like to meet in the reception area?"

"Umm." I looked at the time on my phone and at Justin, who just smiled back at me. I could see from the look in his eyes that we were on the same page. "I think a half hour oughta do it. Sound good?"

"We aim to please. See you in the lobby in thirty." With that Ray turned and went back down the stairs.

Once we got into our room and shut the door, the anticipation built up over the three-hour car ride took over, and we tossed our bags on the floor and kissed while we worked our way over to the bed. I was vaguely aware of pushing the thick peach and white comforter and fluffy pillows onto the floor as I pulled Justin on top of me. I was so turned on that I came as soon as I felt him enter me.

He pulled back and smiled at me. "Well, that didn't take long."

"I'm surprised I didn't cum while I was walking up the stairs." I smiled back and leaned up to kiss him again. "Don't worry; that's just round one for me."

"Oh yeah," he moaned and continued moving into me.

Afterward, we lay on the bed on our backs holding hands while our breathing returned to normal. We both still had our shirts on, and I noted that we had ten minutes before we had to meet Ray downstairs. There was no way he wouldn't know that we'd had sex. We would still be flushed, and our eyes would still be dreamy with postsex satisfaction. I actually didn't want to stop; I was still turned on, and I wanted to fuck Justin in every position possible without stopping until I was forced to return to reality.

I reminded myself to text my husband that I had arrived at the inn OK so he wouldn't worry.

"We have to go back downstairs," I said, finally letting go of Justin's hand and sitting up.

"You have to go; you're the writer. I'm just a bed warmer you brought along."

I loved how playful he was. "Two words for you: brewery tour."

He opened his eyes wide and jumped out of the bed and searched for his pants and shoes. "Brewery tour! Brewery tour! Brewery tour!" he chanted.

We both laughed and re-dressed and went downstairs.

"Refreshed?" The look on Ray's face told me that he knew we'd had sex.

"Oh yeah, refreshed and ready to go!" I said back enthusiastically.

Justin chanted, "Brewery tour! Brewery tour!"

I felt fantastic; my whole body was humming, and I was giggling and practically skipping alongside Justin as we followed Ray outside and along a well-manicured path out to the barn. I took advantage of the golden light of twilight and stopped to take photos along the way. I could smell the flowers on the magnolia trees and see the large buds on the rhododendrons that lined the walkway.

We were met at the door by Ray's partner, Brad. He was as tall and slim as Ray but with a mop of dark hair on his head. He wore an apron over khaki pants, a blue-checked shirt, and hiking boots.

"Well, hello, hello, hello!" he called as we approached. "I am Brad." He extended his hand.

"Hi, I'm Megan, and this is Justin. It's so nice to meet you!" We both shook his hand and followed him into the barn.

"Welcome to our brewery in a barn!" he said, swinging around to face us and extending his arms out to present the copper vats that were before us.

It was impressive. On the cement barn floor were four large round copper vats with copper pipes running up into the rafters of the barn. Wooden tables and chairs sat in front of a long bar. The barstools were carved in the shape of horses' rear ends and legs.

"Nice!" I said.

"Very nice! I'm thirsty already," Justin said.

"And I hope you are hungry, too, because we fired up the oven and have some munchies to go along with the beer so you can get a sense of what guests can expect. Would you prefer a table or seats at the bar?" Brad said, gesturing to each of our options.

"I think we're bar people," I said, glancing at Justin to see if he agreed. It occurred to me that I didn't know a thing about his likes or dislikes, but I had an idea that he was open to everything.

"We are bar people!" he exclaimed and took my hand as we crossed the room behind Brad and chose two horse-bottom stools in the middle of the bar. Ray disappeared behind the bar and busied himself on the workbench in front of a set of double pizza ovens.

The back of the bar was a sea of liquor bottles and serving glasses set against a large mirror. A mix of old-fashioned kitchen utensils and outdoor tools hung on the walls and from the rafters. Taylor Swift–style country music was in the background.

"Now, I want to take you through a traditional tasting of our house beers, and then we'll bring on the munchies, and then you can drink whatever you want after that. Hopefully it will be one of our own brews, but if you want a cosmopolitan or a dirty martini, I can go there, too!"

"Great," we both said in unison. I took out my camera and snapped a couple of shots of Brad filling our glasses and Ray assembling pizzas. "I'll want a couple of you guys behind the bar together and standing in front of the beer vats, please. You'll have to help me remember once you get me drunk," I joked.

I noticed several old-fashioned photos of men brewing beer that looked like they were from the 1800s or 1900s. "Did people donate those photos, too?" I asked.

"Oh no, we got those off Amazon. They look real, don't they? The frames came from this funky old junk shop in Homestead, Florida. If you want stuff that looks wonderfully old-fashioned, go to Florida. God's waiting room, ya know? Everything down there is old as dirt and covered in mildew."

"And you wanted to open the brewery there. Remember?" Ray called over sarcastically.

Brad looked at us and rolled his eyes. "Not in Homestead. In Islamorada. Big difference." He looked over at Ray. "And we wouldn't have had to shovel snow off the driveway there."

"Well, we won't have to here, either, because we will be so successful that we'll be on the beach all winter long." He looked at us. "That's the plan."

"That's everybody's plan in Michigan," I called back, with a smile.

Brad snorted in agreement and presented two wooden trays with the B-and-B logo branded on them, each with four mini beer glasses in various shades of amber sitting in four precut circles. "OK, here we go!" he announced, before launching into a detailed history of the property and his beer-brewing history.

We drank each small glass with enthusiasm, allowing the beer to run over our tongues and savoring the different flavors. Brad took a great amount of pride in his brewing skills, and it showed. He was a delightful guide, and I could imagine the inn at the height of the season with all the tables filled and people sitting at the bar laughing and enjoying his conversation after a day spent hiking or boating on the lake.

Justin and I sat next to each other with our thighs touching, laughing and enjoying the beer and Brad and Ray's conversation. It was as if a completely new universe had opened up and I had left my old life behind. None of it existed to me; I wasn't married in this world. All my successes and failures were meaningless. There were no sick people or exhausted caregivers here. Where I had been and where I was going didn't matter.

I leaned over and kissed Justin, tasting the beer in his mouth. I wanted to climb on top of him and straddle him.

Brad smiled. "Oh, watch out, Ray, second honeymoon! How long have you two been married?" he asked.

I looked at him and shook my head back and forth slowly. Justin simply smiled.

I watched as realization crossed over Brad's face. "Ah, no wonder you two are so happy." He smiled and shot a quick look over to Ray, who also smiled.

"Yes, I am apparently a whore," I said lightly and downed the last of my beer and planted another kiss on Justin.

"Oh, honey, no! We are all whores. What happens at the B and B stays at the B and B. Now, no more sippy cups. It's time for adult-size glasses. Which was your favorite one?"

"The blond," I answered.

"I'll go with the honey wheat," Justin said.

Two full beers appeared, along with small plates and silverware and a basket of soft pretzel sticks with melted cheese for dipping. That was followed with a small goat-cheese, spinach, and ricotta pizza. I forced Justin to leave everything alone until I took photos, and then we dug into the feast.

Brad and Ray poured themselves beers and sat down next to us with another large spinach and ricotta pizza. The food was fantastic. My beer glass never seemed to be empty. The next thing I knew, Justin and I and Brad and Ray were slow dancing to some Lady Antebellum song. I was completely at peace in this new universe.

Several beers later, both couples made it back to the main house laughing and leaning heavily on one another for support. Brad and Ray wished us a good night, and we stumbled up the stairs and to our room and directly into the bed.

The next morning, I woke up in a tangle of sheets and pillows and gazed out the window at the maple and magnolia trees for several seconds before I remembered where I was and turned to find Justin. He was lying next to me with his eyes open and the same slightly confused expression that I assumed was on my face. We smiled at each other, and he reached over and put his hand on my stomach. I put my hand on top of his and let the sleep drift slowly out of my head while I waited to feel guilty. But that feeling didn't come. Instead, I could feel the excitement starting to build between my legs.

I lay on my back and tried to discern exactly what he smelled like: sweet and musty, a mixture of sweat from last night's sex, and soap or body spray of some kind that had almost completely worn off. He smelled good to me, and smelling him made me want to kiss him and taste him, but all I could taste was stale beer and morning breath in my mouth, so I lay still and stared at the white ceiling fan above the bed. I felt the soft skin on his hand and the soft hairs that ran up his forearm. I wrapped my fingers around his thumb and caressed the tip suggestively.

Justin, it seemed, was on the same page because he rolled onto his side and slipped his other hand under my shirt and started to rub my breasts. "I wanna fuck," he breathed. "Are you good to go or do you want to hit the bathroom first?"

"Fuck first," I said and pulled my shirt off and rolled onto my side, presenting my back to him.

"Oh yeah," he breathed and tucked himself in behind me, his hand already probing between my legs.

I could feel his cock pushing against me as he rubbed my clit and inserted his fingers inside me. He groaned loudly as soon as he felt how wet I was already. I shifted my legs apart for him and eased back as he fed his cock into me and began to thrust. He grabbed both of my breasts and squeezed hard as he used them to pull me into him.

I pushed against the softness of the bed with my hands, shoving pillows and blankets off the side and onto the floor as I climaxed. Justin kissed the back of my neck and ears and moaned in approval. My climax only made me want him more, and I shifted over onto my stomach and slowly worked my way up onto my hands and knees. He followed my movements, and I felt a renewed sense of desire to have him in every way possible.

As if sensing my thoughts, he grabbed my hips and began to thrust harder and faster. "Oh yeah, is this what you want?" I moaned loudly in response, and he gripped me even harder. "Fuck yeah, you are so hot."

"Keep giving it to me. Make me take it all," I breathed, feeling another orgasm building.

Justin kept going, moaning, "Oh man, oh God, oh man," as he neared his orgasm.

"No, keep going. I'm almost there again; keep giving it to me," I begged.

"Oh fuck yeah, come with me, baby, come with me. I'm so close."

I could feel his cock get even harder as his fingertips gripped my flesh, and that was all I needed. "Now!" I screamed as I came.

With several more hard thrusts, Justin came, too, and we both collapsed back down on the bed, his penis gently slipping out of me as it softened.

We lay like that for several minutes before I got up and went into the bathroom to wash up. I just wanted to toss my jeans back on but felt that, after having sex multiple times over the past twenty-four hours, I needed a shower.

"Taking a shower," I called out the door. "Jump in if you want."

"I can't shower with you. I'll just want to fuck you again," he called back.

That made me smile. I washed my hair with the complimentary shampoo and conditioner, smelling the strong fragrance of coconut. I ran my hands between my legs and into my vagina, feeling the mixture of Justin and my juices in my fingers. It would all just wash away like it never happened. It was just skin on skin, I reasoned.

While Justin showered, I took the camera and went around the property taking pictures that captured its essence. It really was a nice place; I wouldn't have to fake a glowing review like I'd had to in the past, and that made me happy. I sat on a bench outside the barn and thought about how ironic it was that I was cheating on my husband and didn't feel bad about it but fudging a review about a B and B in Nowheresville, Michigan, bothered me. Well, I guess I still had some standards.

We drank strong coffee and ate warm blueberry muffins and quiche with Ray and Brad in the nook in the kitchen. The sun glowed through the windows and made the whole room warm and cozy, and we listened as they told us stories about the challenges they faced during the building renovation and how they had navigated several near disasters before being able to open. They were the kind of couple that seemed to function as one unit when they were together, and I could not imagine them ever being apart. We left with a few recommendations from them for lunch on the way back and drove down the winding driveway and back into reality.

CHAPTER TWENTY-TWO

Craig was already home when I got back from my trip, and I did my best to avoid touching him. As crazy as it sounds, I didn't want to wash Justin off me, but Craig was in a playful mood, and he followed me up to our room when I went up to unpack my duffel bag.

"So, how was the resort or B-and-B thing or whatever it was?" he asked, hugging me from behind.

My heart was running a mile a minute, and I couldn't believe he couldn't smell Justin on me. "Very quaint. You would have liked it. They have a brewery on premises, too." I turned and hugged him quickly and then broke away and hung my blouse in the closet. "I took pictures, if you want see?"

"So, I missed hotel sex, eh?" He plopped down on the bed.

My mind raced as I tried to figure out how to avoid having sex with him. I counted back in my head and calculated that I'd had sex with Justin about seven hours earlier. "You're in a mood, eh?" I said.

"Come find out," he lay back and stroked himself through his shorts.

"Oh boy, let me jump in the shower first, OK?"

"No, come here. I want you dirty."

I cursed myself for letting myself get into this situation and tried to figure a way out of it, but I had never turned down sex with Craig and was afraid that doing so now would only raise suspicion. "Shower first," I said sternly. "This is not 'good' dirty. Stop rubbing yourself. You'll get too far ahead of me." I grabbed my towel off the rack and retreated into the bathroom, closing the door behind me.

Once I was in the shower, I realized that my phone was out on the nightstand, and I was struck with terror at the thought that Justin might text me, and Craig might see it. I then wondered if Craig would ever look through my calls or texts and tried to remember the last time I deleted my history. I washed as quickly as possible and opened the door while I dried myself off.

Craig was still lying in the same position but with his pants off now. He was watching me and smiling, and I was filled with remorse. My head was pounding, my stomach was nauseated, and I was filled with anxiety. I couldn't understand how people had affairs without completely losing their minds.

"All cleaned up now?" he said in his low, sexy voice.

"Good to go," I said and joined him on the bed.

Once the initial awkwardness passed and it was clear that he couldn't detect Justin on me, I relaxed, and the sex was actually quite good. I was now a person who could have sex with more than one guy in the same day, I realized. I couldn't figure out if that made me really smart or really stupid. This could not go on. I needed to end the affair with Justin, or I needed to end my marriage with Craig.

I looked at him as he lay next to me dozing and tried to imagine my life without him, but it was impossible. Was I really contemplating leaving him for Justin? The thought seemed ridiculous. Justin was fun and exciting, but he never asked about my marriage, never pushed to spend more time with me or brought up the future. So why was I risking everything to be with him?

I got out of bed and dressed, aware that I had gone through this same ritual several times in the last twenty-four hours. Craig stirred and made a move like he was going to get up.

"I'm gonna start dinner," I said.

"I got us Tom Petty tickets for tomorrow night," he said.

"Really? That's a nice surprise!" I exclaimed, feeling even lower. "Just us or what?"

"Sarah and Tom are going, too, and Len and Becca, but they aren't sitting with us." He sat up and swung his legs over the side of the bed.

"Great. We're going to dinner first then, right?" I asked.

"That's up to you ladies to figure out. Just tell me when, and I'll be ready. Not Fiddler's though. I hate that place."

"I know, I know. OK, I'll get with them and figure it out." And just like that, I was back to being a married woman, doing married-woman things with my married friends.

CHAPTER TWENTY-THREE

T he weather was finally turning warm enough to leave the windows open, and I lay in bed and listened to the birds for a while after I woke up. I could also hear the sounds of a soccer game coming from the middle school down the street. Coaches yelling directions, a referee blowing a whistle, and kids cheering every so often. The proximity of the school was one of the reasons we had bought this house, but now it just reminded me that we didn't have kids yet. It was an ever-present item on my list of things to do that somehow never got done.

I began thinking about Justin and wished that it was Thursday already so I could see him again. I grabbed my phone and texted him *Hey*.

Happy Monday, he texted back after a few minutes. *What U up two?*

Thinking about U…

Really? Nice Nasty thoughts, I hope?

It's the only kind I have. Flirting with him made me feel so happy.

Coming by? he asked. My mind began building scenarios that would make that possible. I had to go to Plymouth and visit the Strumbles and run some errands, and it was Monday, so Craig would be expecting sex after racquetball. *Can't today. Just wanted to say hi,* I typed.

K. Up 2 U. BTW—wish we had spent the whole weekend in bed in Saugatuck, he typed.

I was so delighted by his text that I kissed my phone screen and hugged it to my chest and then typed, *Me too.*

I practically danced out of bed. I put on my workout clothes and went downstairs to go for a bike ride. The whole way around my neighborhood, I thought about our time together and tried to figure out whether I could go and see him before Thursday. Craig had now become an obstacle that I had to navigate in order to be with Justin.

Then it occurred to me that this was the final week of interviews and after this Thursday I wouldn't really have an excuse to see Justin, and my heart sank a little. Now the relationship would go from a tryst of convenience to an actual affair. I wasn't sure that made any real difference from a moral point of view, but for some reason, it weighed heavier on me.

Now each meeting would have to be planned, and I would have to openly lie about my whereabouts and actions. I wasn't even sure whether Justin wanted to pursue anything with me, so I would have to figure that out as well. How long could it last, anyway? A few more weeks or six months? Would I be sneaking off to see him on Christmas Eve while Craig built the fire in the family room and carved the turkey? And Craig was really starting to push for me to stop taking the pill, so we could get pregnant, but that was out of the question with Justin in the picture. By the end of the bike ride, it all seemed very complicated, and I was filled with dread.

I showered and did some laundry and took some chicken out of the freezer to defrost for dinner before leaving for the Strumble house. On the drive over, I decided that Monday was Married Monday and I would live the entire day present in my married life with Craig. I would not talk or text with Justin, and I would try my hardest not to think about him. I would instead concentrate on the things that I had been working toward all these years: my career and marriage and home. In my mind, this was a fair arrangement.

Mrs. Strumble greeted me with her usual refined sweetness and then stepped out on the porch with me and said, "Just so you know, Larry had a fall a few days ago, so he's a little banged up right now, but he'll be OK."

"Oh no, that's terrible. Do you want me to come back later in the week?" I offered.

"No, no, it's fine. I just didn't want you to be caught off guard. Come on in; he's in the kitchen with me now." Mrs. Strumble led me into the house and back to the kitchen.

Mr. Strumble sat in a wheelchair in front of the table. He had a large square white bandage on the side of his head. I could see that his left elbow and forearm were badly bruised, and there was an ACE bandage on his right wrist.

"Oh my, Mr. Strumble, you had a little accident, eh?" I said, approaching him and gently taking his left hand in mine.

"Yeah, I sure did!" he exclaimed. "I smacked myself up pretty good; I did."

"What happened?" I asked.

"Well, my legs just don't work so well on some days, I guess. I get off...the floor is moved...where my feet can't find a spot..." He looked at his wife while he struggled to express himself.

"Balance. Your balance is off, honey," she said, filling in the blank for him.

"Yes, I get off-balance—that's the word I wanted," he said, with relief.

"Oh, that's terrible. I see you're really bruised here. Did you have to get any stitches on your head?" I asked.

"Oh, I don't know. Did I get stitches, Carol?" he asked.

"No stiches, just a deep scrape." She started rinsing off fruit in a colander in the sink.

"Just a scrape," he repeated to me.

"So how did it happen?" I asked.

"I fell on the newspapers," he said simply. "Wish I could say that an elephant ran through the room and knocked me down, but I fell on newspapers."

"Really?" I looked to his wife to see if there was more of an explanation.

"He was helping me clean up by picking up the newspapers off the floor in the TV room," she explained. "All the bending down and back up must have made him a little light-headed, and he lost his balance and fell against the entertainment center."

"Oh no, that sounds horrible, Mr. Strumble!" I exclaimed.

"Yes, she knows," he said, pointing at his wife and nodding in agreement.

"Thank God Mike was home and could help me get him to the hospital. I'm not strong enough to get him up by myself. If he hadn't been here, I would have had to call an ambulance," she said.

"They put me in this thing, but I don't have to stay in it," he said, indicating his wheelchair.

"Is your balance better now?" I asked.

"Oh, sometimes I can walk just fine, but sometimes can't," he said.

Mrs. Strumble looked over at me and shook her head solemnly. "The chair will be good for you, Larry. Our biggest problem is that it doesn't fit through all the doors. This is a pretty old house, so we have to decide if we can widen the doorways in some of the rooms. And we'll have to put a ramp out front. Mike is working on getting bids for that for us."

I realized that I was looking at the next stage of his disease unfolding in front of me. His steady decline had now taken another turn, and all the adapting Mrs. Strumble had done now had to be redone to accommodate this new phase. I watched her tiny frame rinse fruit and pat it dry and separate it in containers on the counter, and marveled at her strength.

"You see those tiles there?" Mr. Strumble said to me, pointing at the backsplash.

Among the rows of white tiles, there were tiles with red-and-green bunches of grapes that ran the length of the kitchen. "Yes, the grapes?" I answered.

"Yes, the grapes. I bought those in California and brought them home, and we designed the whole kitchen around them, didn't we, Carol?" he said proudly.

She smiled back at him. "Yes, we did. Spent a small fortune trying to match thirty dollars' worth of tiles!"

"I laid all of this tile myself. Hung the cupboards, too."

"Really? It's beautiful. Your whole house is beautiful," I said.

"Thank you, dear, thank you," he said.

I imagined Ian pushing his grandpa in the wheelchair down to see the brown dog on his next visit, but my assignment was over, and I would have to miss it and everything else that came after it. I had grown attached to each family in one way or another, and I wanted to keep in touch, but I also knew that it would be easier to drift away and not have to see what was next. It would never get any better; it would only get worse, and I would be spared a front-row seat.

"Well, my assignment is done, so I won't be seeing you every week, but I will drop by with a few copies of the magazine for you once it's published."

"Yes, I like to read. I have a hard time following the words sometimes now, but I can if I read them slowly," he said, seemingly unaware that he was the subject of the article.

"Thank you; we would appreciate that very much," Mrs. Strumble said, wiping her hands dry and coming to walk me out.

I stood up, took Mr. Strumble's hand again, and said, "Goodbye, Mr. Strumble. I hope you feel better soon. Be careful now, OK?"

"Yes, goodbye, dear. I'll see you later. Thanks for visiting." He shook my hand and let it go and waved to me.

I hugged Mrs. Strumble at the door. "Good luck with everything. You are a very strong woman, and Mr. Strumble is lucky to have you to take care of him."

"I do the best I can; that's all any of us can do. No other choice, really," she said, shrugging.

"See you in a few weeks," I said and left the neat Craftsman house in Plymouth with the grape-leaf tiles in the backsplash.

CHAPTER TWENTY-FOUR

For my final visit to the Normans, I decided to go over after Mr. Norman came back from his afternoon visit at Hope Memory Care Center to see if he was as agitated as he usually is in the mornings. Linda wasn't back with her father yet, so Mrs. Norman let me in the back door, and I joined her in the TV room.

She was watching Dr. Phil with her ever-present crossword puzzles tucked next to her in the chair cushions.

"If you ask me, I think this guy is an idiot, but I do enjoy this show," she admitted.

"Yeah, he can be entertaining. Did you already finish the crossword for today?"

"Yeah, took care of the one in the paper this morning before Charles left."

"Do you ever go over to the center with him?" I asked, curious how she felt about her husband's relationship with Rosalind.

"Oh, every now and again. They have little parties for the families on the holidays, so I guess Christmas was probably the last time I went over."

"So you've met Rosalind?" I asked, unsure of how she would react.

"Oh yeah, I've met her. It doesn't bother me, if that's what you want to know," she said, cutting to the chase.

"Well, yes, I did wonder how you felt about it. It's such an odd situation to have to deal with on top of everything else."

"I guess it threw me at first, but Charles was already gone. That's what you have to understand: Charles has been gone for a while now." She said it in a very matter-of-fact way. "It's like being a widow and haunted by the ghost of your husband at the same time."

"That's an interesting way to put it," I said.

She laughed again. "Interesting or not, that's the best I can put it. Once I accepted that he wasn't coming back, it didn't bother me how he felt about Rosalind, and if that makes him happy and keeps him calm, then I've got to give him that, you know? It may be the last happiness that he gets before he really is gone."

What she said made such perfect sense, and I admired her for being able to sacrifice her feelings in favor of her husband's happiness. I was again struck by how sad and, at the same time, beautiful the journey was for these couples that had dedicated their lives to one another. "What was he like before?" I asked.

"Oh, Charles was Charles." She looked at me and laughed. "I guess that didn't answer your question, eh? Sorry, let me think." She leaned back in her chair and stared at the ceiling for a moment. "Charles was this bigger-than-life guy that I met when I worked at the Manufacturer's Bank downtown. He was in the navy, and he was so tall, and with his uniform, he looked like a movie star."

"I would love to see some pictures, if you have any?"

"Pictures? I've got some around here somewhere," she said and got up and started looking in the credenza that sat behind her chair. "Anyway, we dated and got married and bought this house and had Linda and did all the usual things you do."

"What kind of work did he do?"

"He managed a parts factory in Allen Park. Automotive parts. He did that for years until the company was bought out. He stayed for a little while, but the new owners didn't much like him and gave him an early retirement package to get rid of him." She dug through the contents of the credenza, piling books, puzzles, and large brown envelopes of papers on the floor.

"So, he's been retired for a long time? Did you get to travel or anything once he stopped working?"

"He stopped working for that company, but then he ended up working over at the school teaching an automotive-mechanics class to the kids."

"Really?" I was surprised. "He was a teacher? That's great."

"Oh, here we go," she said, holding up a manila envelope that was bulging with its contents. She came over, and instead of sitting in her chair, she sat next to me on the couch and dumped the folder across the top of the table. Pictures in black-and-white and color and in all different sizes spilled out, and Mrs. Norman used her hands to spread them out.

"Let me find one of him in his uniform," she said and sorted through them until she found the one she was looking for. "This one is of him and his buddies." It was a black-and-white shot of four young men in naval uniforms standing together at a formal gathering in a ballroom. Mr. Norman was clearly recognizable due to his height, and his face wasn't too dissimilar to how he looked now, just fuller and more robust.

"I think we were down at the Book Cadillac downtown. Do you know it?" she asked, handing me another photo from the same night with the same men, but each was now paired with a woman in a formal gown.

"Yes, I've actually written about the Book Cadillac before," I said, now recognizing the chandeliers in the photo that still hung in that ballroom. "What was the occasion?"

"I think it was New Year's Eve. God, don't ask me which year."

"And this is you?" I said, pointing to the beautiful young woman in the silver gown who stood next to Mr. Norman. "How beautiful!"

"Yeah, I was a looker back then. That dress was scandalous! Look at how you can see my cleavage. I can't believe my mother allowed me to dress that way. I don't even think I was twenty yet. Jezebel!" She laughed again, and this time I could see a little glimpse of the woman she used to be years before.

"I think you look great. Very glamorous. You all look like movie stars. And you can see everyone else's cleavage, too, so you fit right in with the style," I said and handed the photo back to her.

"I suppose. I never kept in touch with any of these girls. I wonder if any of them are still alive." She went back to sorting through the photos and pulled out one of Mr. Norman holding a tiny baby and handed it to me. "Here's Linda."

The juxtaposition of Mr. Norman's size and the tiny baby made the picture look distorted. "My God, look how little she looks!" I exclaimed.

"She was a little baby, came out just over six pounds. She didn't stay little for long. She takes after her dad's side of the family." She handed me a photo of her and her husband and Linda at Disney World when Linda was a toddler. The next photo was from Colonial Williamsburg and the next from the Grand Canyon.

I loved looking through the photos; it was like being a modern-day archaeologist and getting the opportunity to study the clothing, hairstyles, and lives of my subjects throughout the years. I heard the car pull up, and soon the back door banged open as Linda and her father returned from the center. They were arguing about something, and their voices filled the house as soon as they were inside.

"Oh Christ, what now?" Mrs. Norman said to me, shaking her head.

"You just had lunch. I know you had lunch, Dad. I don't know how much you ate, but I know you ate because you always do," Linda insisted.

"No, I don't think so. I think I would know if I had eaten," he shot back. "Do you think I'm stupid!"

"No, Dad, not stupid, but you're forgetful. You have Alzheimer's."

"You think I don't know when I'm hungry? If I feel hungry and I say I'm hungry, it is because I am hungry, and you can't say that I'm not hungry," he argued.

"Dad, please give me a break and sit down," she said as they both made their way through the archway and into the TV room. Linda looked at her mom. "All the way home. This has been going on all the way home."

As soon as he saw his wife, Mr. Norman renewed his pleading to her. "They wouldn't give me lunch, and I'm hungry, and she says she won't give me lunch."

"OK, sit down, Charles. Don't get all worked up. Sit down and look at the pictures, and I'll get you a snack." She stood up and patted the cushion and waited while her husband moved over and reluctantly sat down.

"I don't want a snack. I want a proper lunch like I was supposed to get!" he demanded.

"Stop your yelling, Charles. We have company, and besides, it's almost dinnertime, so you'll be eating dinner soon anyway. Stop your fussing about. Look at the photos with Megan," she directed and went into the kitchen.

"Who the hell are you?" he said.

I laughed out loud. I couldn't help it; there was something so pure in the way he said it to me. "I'm Megan. I've been visiting the last month to write about your experiences. I've met you a couple of times now, and I went to the center with you one day."

"If you say so," he said dismissively.

"I think you had meat loaf for lunch the day I was there. Is the meat loaf good?" I asked, trying to distract him.

He looked hard at me for a minute and then down at the photos before yelling, "Jim Crawley! I'll be damned; that's Jim Crawley!"

He held up the photo of the four men together and pointed to one of the men standing next to him. "Do you know him?" he asked me.

"No, I don't. Your wife was just showing me these old photos," I answered.

"Why do you have a photo of Jim Crawley?" he asked.

"I don't; these are your photos," I explained.

He looked at the photo and then at some of the others on the table before asking me, "Are you related to Jim Crawley?"

"No, I'm not. He was a friend of yours?"

"You bet your ass he's my friend! He lives in Toledo with his wife...his wife...What's Jim Crawley's wife's name?" he yelled into the kitchen.

Mrs. Norman came back into the room and handed her husband half of a cheese sandwich. "What?"

"Jim Crawley's wife—what's her name?"

"Donna. I think it was Donna."

"Yes! Jim and Donna live in Toledo. Donna. Donna and Jim," he said and looked at the sandwich.

"They don't live anywhere anymore because they're both gone now," his wife said.

Mr. Norman's head snapped around to face his wife, and he stood up so quickly that it startled me, and I expected him to be upset because he had forgotten that his friend and his wife were gone, but instead his booming voice yelled, "What the hell happened to the rest of this sandwich?"

"Charles, sit down," his wife directed, calmly. "It's a half sandwich."

"I can see it's a half sandwich! Where's the other half?" he demanded.

Linda came into the room. "What's going on now?"

"Where's the other half of this sandwich?" he demanded again.

"I only made half. It's a snack, Charles; calm down," his wife said.

"That doesn't make sense. You can't make half of something. You have to make it all and then just take half. You can't make half. Don't you understand?" He looked from his wife to his daughter to me with exasperation. None of us knew what to say. He sat back down and took a bite of the half sandwich in his hand.

I stared at the TV and wondered what Dr. Phil would have said in this situation.

"Don't worry, Dad; I'm making pork chops for dinner, so you'll have plenty to eat tonight. I'm baking them just like you like, OK?" Linda said and went into the kitchen.

"You can't make a half," he mumbled under his breath, and for some reason, it made me laugh. There was just something very pure about his logic, and it reminded me of a child's logic that was empirically correct and unarguable.

"How was the music today, Mr. Norman?" I asked, in another attempt at distraction.

"Fine, fine, the music was fine today," he said, munching away.

"Look at this picture, Charles. Do you remember it?" His wife handed him a photo out of the pile of the three of them standing in front of a statue of a moose.

"Of course. That's Alaska. That was a long time ago—ten years?" he asked her. "Twenty years?"

"Look at how little Linda is," his wife pointed out. "Try more like thirty years ago."

"Thirty years? Oh no, that can't be right. Really?" He studied the photo intently before putting it down.

"I haven't looked at these in years. They're really bringing back memories," Mrs. Norman said. "I should sort them out properly so they're in order by date. I always meant to do it, but somehow, I never got around to it."

She handed photo after photo to her husband, and he looked at them and handed them to me, pointing out people and places as we went along. It was clear that he was missing a few details here and there, and his wife and Linda chimed in to fill in the missing pieces. His demeanor changed as he relaxed, and he once again became the gentle giant that I had seen on previous visits.

When Linda announced that the pork chops were done, I gathered my stuff and stood up to say goodbye. In her usual fashion, Mrs. Norman stayed seated and waved to me from her chair.

"Goodbye, Mr. Norman," I said. "I'll stop by again in a few weeks to say hello."

"OK, that will be fine," he said and stood up, my small hand disappearing into his larger one as he shook it.

Linda gave me a hug, and I could feel how solid she was. "This has been a much more pleasant experience than I thought it would be. I hope we were interesting enough for you," she said as she walked me out.

"Oh, you are interesting enough, all right." I laughed. "It's been a pleasure. You are doing a great job, Linda. I'll bring a copy of the article by in a week or two."

"With the grace of God, I'm doing my best. That's all I can do."

I smiled and nodded in agreement and left the little brick house.

CHAPTER TWENTY-FIVE

I took a quick run and did a series of stretches on my yoga mat before jumping in the shower and going to meet the Phillipses for their last interview. My last visit with them had been so nice that I looked forward to today's meeting, and I was determined to be in a good mood no matter what condition I found Mrs. Phillips in today.

But when my first knock at the door went unanswered, a feeling of dread settled over me, and my stomach went queasy. I knocked louder the second time and leaned a little closer to the door to see if I could hear any movement from within, but it was silent. I stood with the screen door propped open against my hip and waited, unsure of how long to wait before I gave up. I tried to remember if I had put Mr. Phillips's phone number in my phone or just written it in my notepad.

I decided to honor the three-strikes rule and knocked again, even more aggressively, just in case Mr. Phillips had fallen asleep.

"Hello there!"

I jumped at the sound of a voice close to me and turned to see a woman coming toward me up the sidewalk.

"Excuse me, hello. Hello!" A stocky gray-haired woman hurried up to the porch. She wore a teal-green jogging suit with two cats embroidered on the front in gold thread. It reminded me of something I would see in one of the Indian casinos up north.

"Hello," I said back, expecting her to tell me that they took Mrs. Phillips to the hospital.

"I've seen you here before. Are you the daughter?" she asked bluntly.

"No, I'm not related to the Phillipses. I'm—"

"Are you a nurse?"

"No, I'm—"

"I've seen you here before. I remember your car because my son has one like it." Her voice had a bit of a New Jersey accent.

"No, I'm working with them on a project," I said quickly, afraid of being cut off again.

"Well, do you know anything about the arrangements? I'm on the board, and we like to put the notices up in the clubhouse so folks can see them and pay respects, if they are so inclined. I can't find any relatives to contact. They're supposed to get the information when people move in, but somebody dropped the ball."

My heart dropped; she was gone. Even though I knew it was for the best, given her condition, I couldn't help but feel sad. Mr. Phillips would be alone now.

"Oh, she passed then? I didn't know. When did it happen?" I asked.

"They're both gone—don't you know that? The man and his wife," she said, annoyed.

I went numb. They were both gone. My mind struggled to make sense of what I was hearing. "I don't understand."

"Who are you? Maybe I shouldn't even be telling you this." She turned as if she were going to leave.

"I'm a writer, and I've been writing about them. Tell me what happened, please. This doesn't make any sense to me." I followed her down the sidewalk.

"Well, you can't make sense of a thing like this," she said flatly. "Writer?"

"They're both dead? How?" I pleaded.

"I can only tell you what Mrs. Schodowski told me. I don't want to be responsible for spreading rumors or saying things that aren't true."

The more this woman talked, the angrier I became. I wanted to grab her by the shoulders and shake her and force her to tell me what happened. "How?" I almost shouted.

"Are you a newspaper writer? You aren't putting this in the papers, are you?"

"How?" I shouted.

She rolled her eyes and began talking. "Well, Mrs. Schodowski lives there, you see." She pointed at the condo next door. "And she told me that when that colored woman who looks in on Mrs. Phillips came on Monday, she found them both passed, and they took them out on gurneys. Now," she said and leaned in closer to me and whispered, "she said that there were pill containers all over the kitchen. Empty pill containers."

Suddenly, everything fell into place. The boxes that never got unpacked, the pictures that were never hung, the empty refrigerator, the empty pantry, the condo that he had no intention of ever living in without his wife, and the shoe boxes of old pill bottles just waiting for the right time to be used.

I remembered how happy and peaceful he seemed during my last visit and remembered that some people who commit suicide go through a stage of euphoria once they have made their decision. In showing me the old family photos, he was celebrating their life one last time before the end. I sat back on the porch, the weight of everything that I had just realized pushing me down.

"You OK?" she asked, as if she were surprised at my reaction.

I wanted her to go away, so I nodded and waved her off. "Yes, yes, I'm fine, just surprised is all. Thank you for your help."

"You just gonna sit there?" she asked.

"For a moment, yes." I willed her to leave.

She stood and stared at me for a moment before turning and walking across the street to her condo.

I was running through my visits with the Phillipses in my head, trying desperately to figure out if I could have known or if I should have known. Now that it was too late, it was all so obvious to me. I had thought about trying to get them some help but never took action. I knew that I wasn't to blame and that I was just here to observe, yet I couldn't help but feel guilty. I was one of the very few people who even knew what was going on inside this house, so I was one of the few who could have helped.

I started thinking about my childhood friend Chelsea. Deep inside, I blamed myself for her death. I should have forgiven her, and if I had, she would still be alive. I knew that as sure as I knew the sun would rise tomorrow, but I also knew there was nothing I could do about it, so I stuffed it down and covered it with wine and weed and reckless behavior and hoped it would go away, but the feeling was always waiting for me.

I buried my head in my hands and tried to concentrate on taking deep breaths. My head was spinning, and I felt like I was going to explode out of my skin.

I imagined Mr. Phillips in the kitchen, crushing the pills together and mixing them with applesauce and then feeding the mixture to his wife. I imagined him holding her while she slipped away, and I wondered how long it took. Did it work the first time? Did she suffer, or did she just fall asleep? He would have been alone among his boxes, an entire life condensed into labeled cardboard and stacked neatly against the white walls.

Did he follow her immediately, or did he sit for a while? I decided that he probably took his pills as soon as she was gone. This was a well-thought-out plan, and he was ready. He had probably made this plan years ago; maybe they made this plan together before she got too sick.

Chelsea had slit her wrists—the long way. It wasn't a cry for help. She had meant to die that day, and she did. She did it in the bathtub and left a note apologizing for the mess she left behind. I wondered if Mr. Phillips had left a note, but I was overcome with sadness when I realized that he didn't really have anyone to leave a note for.

I pushed myself up and got in my car and turned it on with no idea of where I wanted to go. I could see the lady from across the street watch me leave through her curtains as I pulled out. I drove aimlessly and replayed conversations in my head as my mind flipped through memories of the Phillipses and Chelsea. I pulled in front of a bar and parked but decided I didn't want to be there and started home but then decided I didn't want to be there either. I wanted to talk to Justin.

When I got there, Sam opened the door to greet me, and I walked past him into the foyer.

"Ms. Megan, I didn't know you were coming today," he said, and his sister Dee peeked around the corner and gave me a wave.

"I didn't plan on it. I just decided to drop by," I said, my words sticking in my mouth.

"Oh, OK. Mrs. Dittmer is actually napping right now, but why don't you come in and sit? Can I get you something?"

"No, that's OK." I looked up the stairs, half expecting to see Justin bouncing down them, and when I looked back at Sam, I saw a look in his eyes that told me I wasn't supposed to be there, and I went cold. I knew that Justin was upstairs and that he wasn't alone.

My breath caught in my throat, and tears popped out of my eyes, and there was nothing I could do to stop it from happening.

"Maybe some water or juice would be nice?" Sam offered, clearly uncomfortable in this situation.

I plopped down in one of the chairs. "No, it's OK. Been a rough day today is all." I could hear a door upstairs open and Justin's familiar cadence as he came down the stairs.

"Hey, hey," he said, looking as uncomfortable as Sam did, and I noticed that his hair was messed up under his baseball cap, and he didn't have any shoes on, and I knew that he had been naked with whoever was upstairs just moments before. I felt sick and suddenly became aware that I had a crushing headache.

"Shit" was all I could say.

"I didn't realize you were coming by today," he began, and Sam drifted out of the room.

"I wasn't. I shouldn't have. I'm sorry. Something happened, and I wanted to see you, but I didn't think it through. I should have texted or something. Fuck."

He knelt in front of me. "Are you OK? What happened?"

"Apparently this really isn't the time to talk, so I'll take off. Sorry." I got up and went to the door, and he followed me, but I caught him sneaking a look upstairs.

"Yeah, I'll have some time later, if you want to call," he offered and opened the door. I could feel how badly he wanted me to leave. "I'll shoot you a text later."

I wanted so much to play it cool and be the girl who was evolved enough to not let it bother her, but too much had happened, and I didn't have the strength. "Who's up there, anyway?" I asked.

He looked down and took a deep breath. "I didn't know you were coming over today."

"Yeah, I get that part."

"Well, I...I know her from school; it's not a serious thing," he stammered.

"Don't worry about it. I am married, after all, so I have no right to expect exclusivity," I said and got in my car.

He came and stood next to me so I couldn't close the door. "I want to talk later, OK?"

"Whatever. I'm good," I lied.

"You seem upset."

"I am upset but not about this. This is just a cherry on top of a fucked day. You should go; she'll know we've got something going on if you keep standing there like that. Chicks pick up on the little things, you know?"

He stared at me and shook his head, and I could tell he wanted to say more, but he begrudgingly stepped back and allowed me to close the door. I pulled away without looking back and drove home.

CHAPTER TWENTY-SIX

T here was half a bottle of red on the kitchen counter, and I took the cork out and drank it straight out of the bottle while I stared at the backyard out the window. It was a beautiful spring day in Michigan; the grass was deep green, the trees were bursting with leaves, and it was warm and sunny. I looked at my postage-stamp backyard and wondered if I had been taking it all for granted these past few weeks. I ran my hands over the cool granite countertop and studied the tile backsplash that I had picked out and helped Craig put up with such excitement.

I got caught up in my affair and had become disconnected from my life. Or was I disconnected and then had an affair? I had everything you were supposed to want, so I should have been content, but I kept wanting something else.

I thought about the look on Justin's face as he stood in the driveway, and I let a few tears drift down my face. I felt ridiculous. I had allowed myself to get wrapped up in an actual relationship without ever even considering the implications or finding out if Justin even wanted a relationship. To be honest, I wasn't even thinking about asking for a divorce, so what right did I have to pull someone else into my life?

There wasn't any white wine in the refrigerator, so I took a warm bottle out of the pantry and grabbed an opener and a glass and went out onto the deck. I sat at the table and opened the wine, filled my glass to the top, and took a big drink. I heard my phone buzz with a text message. It was Justin: *Hey.*

Hey.

You OK?

I wanted to say, "Of course not. You're fucking another girl," but instead I typed, *No worries.*

K. Talk later?

See you tomorrow.

I watched as the typing bubble appeared and disappeared a few times before the message *K. Up 2 U* came through. I deleted the conversation and tossed the phone on the table. For the first time in the last month, I had no desire to communicate with him.

I sat on the deck looking at nothing in particular and letting the wine do its job on my mind and body. Slowly, the weight of everything began lifting off me and flowing away on my buzz. Chelsea had now been dead longer than she had been alive, and life had gone on. I had slept with a bartender, and life had gone on. Mr. and Mrs. Phillips had lost a son and now were both dead, and life would go on. I had a fling with a subject's nephew, and life would go on.

I heard Craig pull up and realized that, once again, I had not made anything for dinner and decided that I was officially the worst wife in the world. I listened as he walked through the house and waited until he discovered me out on the deck.

"Hey," he said, and I laughed because it was exactly what Justin had said.

"Hey back," I said, lifting my glass to salute his arrival.

"What's up with you?" He studied me hard. "Have you been crying or something?"

"Yes, crying or something is correct." I nodded.

"What's up?" He sat in one of the other chairs at the table. "I can tell from all the wine that you didn't find out you were pregnant today, so that's not it."

"Really? Did you just fucking say that to me?" I said in disbelief. Out of all the things that had gone wrong today, he had managed to bring up something else.

"Here we go," he shot back. "Megan drama time."

"No, no, not Megan drama time. You just fucking walked in. Why are you being such a shit?"

"Maybe I didn't have a good day either. The only difference is I can't just sit home and chug wine every time I get annoyed. I have to be an adult."

"So are you jealous of me or mad at me?" I challenged.

"I'm nothing. It's just that we talked about all the drinking and how it would be nice to have something to eat at least once in a while when I come home from my fucking twelve-hour day. It's not just all about you, you know?"

I sat stunned. I wanted to leave but knew that I had already drunk too much to drive, so I sat and tried to process what was happening.

Craig picked up the now-empty bottle and held it in front of me. "I saw the other one on the counter, so you've had two today already?"

"No! That other one wasn't full." I knew how lame it sounded as soon as it came out of my mouth.

"Oh, so you've only had one and a half bottles of wine? Congratulations." He tossed the empty bottle into the yard, and it landed in the soft grass and rolled under a hedge.

"Who said I'm done?" I drank all the wine that was left in my glass.

"By all means, keep going. Drink until you puke, for all I care. Lie in bed all day tomorrow with a headache. I don't really give a fuck." He stood up and took his car keys out of his pocket.

"You're leaving?" I asked incredulously.

"Well, I don't want to leave, but I do want to eat, so I guess I have to leave to fix that little problem."

"Are you coming right back?"

"Why do you give a fuck?" he asked and turned to leave.

"You're a dick. If you knew the day I had today!" I yelled. I was so angry I felt like I could explode.

"Whatever, Megan. Drink another bottle of wine; that'll fix everything!" he shouted back.

"Well, I wanted to talk to my husband about it, but I forgot that you're a dick."

"Hey, I don't have anything to do with all this." He waved his hands in front of my face. "This is all you, and I'd appreciate it if you just kept it to yourself." He stomped into the house, and I heard him go into the garage and drive off.

I sat in stunned silence. I was filled with adrenaline. My ears were ringing, and I could feel my heart pumping blood into every part of my body. My day had gone from bad to awful to unbelievable. I felt like a refugee with no safe place to hide. I felt like I did when I was a child, like I was floating on the surface of life but wasn't really a part of it. I was a puzzle piece that didn't fit into any picture.

I stood up on wobbly legs and went into the kitchen to get another bottle of wine. I had to do something to stop myself from feeling the way I felt. While opening the second bottle of wine, I pushed the corkscrew into the palm of my hand and cut it open. I stood crying while I watched blood fill up the gash and spill down my hand. It seemed I was incapable of doing anything right today. I was a danger to myself and to anyone around me.

I wrapped a paper towel around my hand and struggled to open the bottle. I ended up putting it on the ground between my feet and using my good hand to pull the cork out. I went back out onto the deck and filled my glass and stretched out on one of the chaise lounges. I was a mess of emotions, and my head was throbbing, and I was suddenly very tired. Random thoughts of Chelsea and the Phillipses and the other Alzheimer's families and Justin rolled through my head, but I wasn't capable of thinking coherently anymore, so I tried to ignore them and watch the leaves flutter in the breeze instead.

After an hour, I started waiting for the sound of Craig's car returning. It reminded me of when we were dating, and I would hear him pull up in front of the house to pick me up, and I was always so excited. It was in that uncertain period when you first start dating, and you aren't really sure how the other person feels, and you don't really know where you stand, but I would hear his car and know that I had him, at least for that night. I tried to remember the last time that I was excited to hear him come home.

I woke up sometime later, still on the chaise; the wine was gone, and there was a blanket on me. My head was pounding as I made my way into the house. It was a little after midnight, and there was a white carryout container on the counter with the words *turkey wrap* written on it. I opened it to find a turkey wrap along with a side of potato salad and a side of coleslaw.

I felt guilty immediately. Craig had gone out to eat at Kelly's Kitchen and brought my usual order back for me. I knew we had fought but struggled to remember who had started the argument or what we argued about. The sense of dread I felt told me that everything was my fault. But even though he was mad at me, he still was thoughtful enough to bring food home for me. I doubt that I would have done the same.

I was incredibly hungry and thirsty, and I stood over the sink with the blanket still wrapped around me and ate and washed it down with glass after glass of water. I remembered that the Phillipses were gone, and I remembered the awkward scene at

Justin's place, and it all felt like it had happened weeks ago instead of hours ago.

I couldn't eat all the food, so I put the rest in the refrigerator, took three aspirins, lay down on the couch, and let myself drift off to sleep wondering whether I should come clean and tell Craig about the affair with Justin.

CHAPTER TWENTY-SEVEN

I awoke to the sound of Craig making breakfast the next morning. The way he was banging the dishes around told me all was not forgiven. I sat up on the couch, and my stomach did a flip-flop, and I waited to see if I had to throw up. Craig looked at me but didn't say anything.

My stomach calmed down, and I knew I was safe. "Thanks for the food."

"Yeah, I figured that you hadn't eaten. You never do when you get like that." His tone was terse.

I watched him scramble eggs in a bowl with a fork and pour them into the frying pan.

"Should I be making you eggs, too?" he asked.

"No, no, thanks."

"It's early yet—six thirty or so—you should go up and go back to bed for a while," he suggested without looking at me.

"One of my subjects in the Alzheimer's piece killed his wife and himself. It happened over the weekend, but I just found out yesterday," I said, feeling the tears well up in my eyes.

Craig stopped what he was doing and looked at me and nod-ded slowly. "That's what you were upset about?"

I certainly couldn't tell him the rest of the reason I was upset. "Yeah."

Craig went back to cooking before stopping again and saying, "I get it—I really do—but this has got to stop. You can't fall off a cliff every time something goes wrong."

I felt my defenses going up. "You don't get it. I saw the signs—I could have helped—maybe even prevented it. I knew he was de-pressed, and I thought about doing something, but I didn't do anything."

"Their lives and their decisions don't have anything to do with you," he said, his voice rising. "You knew these people for a nano-second. You were nothing to them, and they should be nothing to you."

I shook my head and crossed my arms over my chest. "You don't get it. They didn't have anyone else around them. I was one of the few people who could have done something. You don't get it. There's more to it. The suicide just brought up all these old feel-ings that I have about Chelsea's suicide, and it was overwhelming. Can't you understand that?"

"No, you don't get it. That girl has been dead for over twenty years—move on. It didn't have anything to do with you either, and don't even bother telling me that sad-ass story again. She did what she did, and it had nothing to do with you." Before I could protest, he started again. "You have a life right here, right now, that you ignore. When are you going to start doing something about that? We are supposed to be raising a family right now, but you're stuck in this mode and can't move forward, and that's not OK anymore. Do you want to be here anymore or what?" he challenged.

"I had an affair."

Craig's face froze, and he stared at me without blinking for a few moments. He took the frying pan off the hot burner and turned the stove off and turned around so his back was to me. He was silent except for the sound of his breath going in and out through his nose. I felt all the muscles in my body loosen up as I realized that everything that had come before that sentence was now over and everything that would come after it would be different. A few tears spilled down my face as I waited.

Craig turned around slowly, his face red with emotion. His eyes flickered on me and then away from me to an imaginary spot over my shoulder. "When did this happen?"

"It's over now but over the last few weeks," I whispered back.

He nodded and took another deep breath. "So it didn't 'happen'; it is 'happening'?"

"No, it's not happening anymore," I answered.

"Was it 'happening' yesterday? Is that really why you're acting like this?"

I wasn't sure what to say; I felt the need to minimize the damage. "No, yesterday didn't have anything to do with him. I haven't been with him for a while."

"Who?" he asked calmly.

"Oh fuck, just some guy I met doing this article. He's the grandson of one of my subjects, and I don't know what is wrong with me. I just ended up with him one time, and then it happened again, and I don't know what is wrong with me." I tried to read Craig's face, but he was stoic. Now that I was down this road, I had no idea how to navigate myself back.

"Grandson? How old is he?" he asked.

"He's thirty-two or thirty-three," I said, realizing how much worse that made things.

"Are you serious? Really?" His head dropped back, and he stared at the ceiling. "Is that what this is about? Getting banged by some young guy?"

"No! Age has nothing to do with it. I don't know why. I don't know what's wrong with me or why I did it; I just did it."

He nodded and took all his dishes and piled them into the sink and used the washcloth to wipe down the counter.

I wanted him to yell at me and call me a slut and throw the dishes on the floor in a rage. I wanted anything but this silence that told me nothing about where I stood. "I'm sorry, Craig. I didn't mean to do it. I wasn't looking for it; it just happened."

He left the kitchen and walked past me without acknowledging me and went upstairs to the bedroom. I knew that it would be useless to follow him, so I sat on the couch and listened to him moving around upstairs for several minutes.

He had a duffel bag with him when he came downstairs, and he grabbed his computer bag and keys and stopped in front of the door and said, "I can't be here right now."

"I understand" was all I could get out.

"I just can't be here right now," he repeated, and he left.

I sat on the couch and tried to comprehend what had just happened, and then I went upstairs and took a sleeping pill and crawled into bed and waited for it to work.

CHAPTER TWENTY-EIGHT

The clock said 2:18, but the room was filled with sunlight. I struggled to make sense of this information. My dreams had been a chaotic mishmash of people and situations that all left me feeling like I had done something very wrong, and as the pieces of the puzzle floated back into my conscious mind, my stomach twisted. I went into the bathroom and threw up and then lay on the cool tile floor.

It was Thursday afternoon, and I was supposed to be at Mrs. Dittmer's house for the final interview. I tried to figure out where Craig was going to go and wondered if I should call him. I realized that I hadn't told him that I loved him this morning and felt bad; I should have made sure he knew that I loved him before he left. I regretted telling him the truth and wondered if I truly had a self-destructive streak. I could have lied and not told him, and he never would have found out, and married life would have rolled on status quo. But I imploded the whole thing, and now I had to live with the consequences.

I felt better and got up and went downstairs to find my phone. It was in the kitchen plugged into the charger, and I felt a pang of guilt as I realized that Craig must have done that last night when he came outside and put the blanket on me. I turned it on, and it immediately sprang to life with text messages and voice messages. They were all from Justin, the ones in the morning wanting to know if I was coming over and the ones in the afternoon assuming that I was mad and that was why I wasn't there already.

I actually did want to see him. I wanted to talk to someone who knew me but wouldn't judge me. I texted, *Sorry!! Took a sleeping pill and way overslept. On my way. That OK?*

He replied immediately. *Yes, of course. Can't wait to see you.*

Before I put the phone down, I texted Craig. *I'm truly sorry. I love you. I know you need time, but please talk to me when you can.* I didn't bother to wait for a reply because I knew he wouldn't text me back.

I brushed my teeth and jumped in the shower and put on clean clothes and drove over to the Dittmer house, wondering if I was still married.

Justin opened the door before I even had a chance to knock. "Hey, girl, I'm so happy to see you!" he said and gave me a big hug.

It felt so good to have his arms wrapped around me, and I'm ashamed to say that I started to get a little turned on. I held on to him tightly and kissed his cheek when he pulled back. He leaned forward and kissed my lips a little at first and then a little more, and I kissed him back before pulling away.

"Let's not get started with that," I said.

"OK. Up to you," he said and put his hands in his jeans pockets. "You OK?"

"Well, it's been a hell of a twenty-four hours; I'll tell you that!" I said and sat on the steps that led upstairs.

"Wanna go up?" he asked.

"I should see your grandmother first. This is the last interview day, and I really haven't spent much time with her because of you," I said and pushed him away playfully.

Justin smiled back, and I was again struck by how attracted I was to him.

"They're bathing her now anyway, so we've got time." And with that, I followed him upstairs.

"Beer?" he offered.

I dropped down on his couch and curled my knees up in front of me. "No, thanks. I'm still hungover from last night."

He sat next to me. "What happened? Tell me what happened yesterday."

"One of my other subjects, a couple named Phillips—she was pretty far gone, and he was depressed—I think I told you about them?"

"The ones in the condo with all the boxes?" he guessed.

"Yes, that's them. I went to visit them yesterday and found out that he killed her and then killed himself last weekend."

"No way! Really?" Justin said.

"Yep. I know, right? I was just shocked. Just—just freaked, you know?"

Justin reached over and put his hands on my knees and pulled me toward him. "I'm so sorry, hon. Wow, I can't imagine how crazy that is for you." He pulled my head into his shoulder and hugged me, and I moved into him and lay against him. "How did he do it? You didn't see them, did you?"

"No, no, I didn't see anything. A neighbor told me." I leaned back against the couch. "He used old pills he had hanging around."

"Wow." Justin leaned against my legs and held both my hands in his. "That's big stuff. Some of the green will make you feel better. Do you want me to get some?"

I shook my head. "I saw all the pills a couple of weeks ago. He had shoe boxes full of them," I explained.

"Really? Did you suspect what he was going to do?"

I started crying a little thinking about it. "I didn't, but I feel like I should have, you know?"

"Nah, don't do that to yourself. You can't control anyone but yourself, Megan; you know that." He kissed both my hands. "That's heavy stuff. I'm sorry you had to go through that, and I'm sorry I had company and couldn't be there for you."

I took my hands back. "Not your fault. Don't worry about it."

"She's not my girlfriend or anything. She lives in Saginaw, and she just comes down to hang once in a while."

"It's really none of my business." I felt awkward and really didn't want to talk about it.

"Don't be that way. I never thought about saying anything 'cause—I don't know—I didn't really know where this was going, you know?" He stood up and went to the refrigerator and got a beer. "Want one?"

"No, I'm still good."

He sat back down and opened his beer and took a long drink.

"I told my husband about the affair this morning," I admitted.

"About me?" he asked, surprised.

"Yes, about you. You are the only affair I am having, you know?"

"Of course. I just...wow! Wow, this is big stuff." He took his baseball cap off and ran his hands through his hair and put it back on. "OK, yeah, I get it. What did he...how did he take that news?"

"He packed a duffel bag and left. I haven't heard from him since." I shrugged.

"Fuck. That's rough. How are you doing with that?"

"Numb. I can't believe I told him. I could've just shut up and not said anything. I don't think he ever would have known."

"Why did you tell him?" He leaned over and put his hand on my leg and rubbed it gently.

"I don't know. Maybe I want it to be over?" The thought had never really occurred to me until I said it out loud. "I don't know. It wasn't bad or anything; I just met you, and one thing led to another. I really didn't plan on any of this happening."

"Me neither."

"It's like I'm possessed when I'm around you, and everything else just goes out the window, and the worst part is I don't even feel bad about it. I mean, I felt bad this morning, and I feel bad now because I didn't mean to hurt him, but I swear that I would run away to South America with you right now and never look back."

Justin laughed. "You're a crazy girl, you know that? That's what you want to do? Go to South America?"

"No, no, I don't. I just used that as example because you make me do things I shouldn't do."

He leaned over and kissed me softly, and I kissed him back. "Like that?" he said when we were done.

"Yes, exactly like that. How many girls do you 'hang with' anyway?"

"Oh boy, here we go." He chuckled and sat back on the couch. "I don't know—a couple of girls here and there, but I don't have anything serious going on."

"And that includes me? I'm just one of the girls you hang with sometimes?" I didn't want to know the answer, but I had to ask.

He was silent for a moment, and I could see him weighing his options before he answered. "This is one of those questions that does nothing but get you in trouble."

"No, it's not like that. Just say how you feel."

"K. I'm totally into you, but you are married, so I didn't really think about anything more; I just thought you wanted to hook up here and there. You know, casual stuff. But you're fantastic, and I love spending time with you."

"I bet you say that to all the girls," I said.

He smiled and shook his head. "No, not really. What did you want to happen?"

"I have no idea," I admitted. "I'm sorry I got you involved in something without really thinking it through."

"No, don't say that. I'm so glad that you didn't think it through. I dug you the moment I saw you, and I just would have been walking around with blue balls for the last month knowing that you existed and not being able to do anything about it."

"Gosh, you really know how to make a lady feel special," I joked and reached out and took his hand and held it tightly.

"Are you gonna get a divorce?"

"I have no fucking clue what's gonna happen. I never really considered it seriously before, but now it may be out of my hands. Craig may be sitting in a lawyer's office as we speak."

We both sat silently, contemplating our new reality. I didn't want to let his hand go; I wanted to touch him everywhere and feel him touch me.

"Well, do you want a divorce?" he asked.

"I don't know what I want." And it was true.

"I think you need to figure that out before you do anything else," he said.

"Yeah, I get that, but it's like my head is disconnected from my body right now."

"If I get a choice, can I have the body?" He laughed.

"Sorry, package deal." I leaned up and kissed him, and he slipped his hand around my head and held me tight as he kissed me back. My mind told me to stop, but when he put his hand on my breast, I put mine between his legs and grabbed his penis through his jeans. I wanted to feel him on top of me and inside me so bad that I didn't care about anything else, so I let him push me back on the couch and helped him off with his jeans and then mine and pulled him into me.

His skin was so soft, and he felt so wonderfully warm, and I wrapped my legs around him and thrust my hips up to meet him as I kissed him and felt the hair of his beard brush against my face. When he sensed my orgasm was near, he quickened his pace and thrust even deeper into me, and I gripped his back tightly as I came.

"Oh my God, I could feel that. You feel so good," he breathed into my ear when I was finished.

"You make me come so hard," I breathed back.

He got off me and pulled me to the end of the couch and knelt on the floor in front of me and entered me again. His penis felt twice as hard and big in this position, and I moaned loudly as my body exploded in pleasure. He grabbed my breasts and thrust into me deeply until I came again, and then he came, too. He left himself inside me and laid his upper body on top of me, and we stayed like that for a while, letting our sweat mingle as our breath returned to normal.

I wanted him to stay wrapped around me like that forever. I wanted to feel the weight of his body and smell his scent every day of my life. I slowly caressed the soft skin on the back of his neck, running my fingers through the little hairs of his hairline and feeling utterly content. That's the only way I could describe it. I was content in a way that I had never felt before, and I wondered what it was about this guy that made me feel that way.

"See, you make me crazy," I said as he got up and started picking up his clothes.

"You didn't seem confused to me. You seemed like you knew exactly what you wanted," Justin said, pulling his jeans back on. He walked over and handed me one of my socks. "Seriously, are you thinking that you shouldn't be doing it when we are doing it?"

I shook my head. "No way. All I'm thinking is how much I want you and how I never want it to stop."

He smiled at that and sat on the couch. "Well then, sounds like you have your answer."

"Yes, but then I have to walk out that door and back into the real world, and that's when it gets complicated," I explained.

"The real world is what you make it," he said simply.

"Very philosophical, Justin, but I still have a whole life that has to be dealt with out there. Houses, cars, my family, his family, everything that was planned for the future, and all that crap. I've been on a certain road for a long time, and it's not so easy to just change lanes, you know?"

"But you can if that's what you want," he countered.

"Are you saying you want to be with me?" I asked.

"Well, of course I want to keep seeing you, but it shouldn't be about me. You should do what makes you happy; it doesn't have anything to do with me."

And in that moment, I knew that I stood alone, that Justin wasn't going to be my life raft away from a mediocre marriage, and that I would have to make this decision alone. "Fair enough."

"Look, you're awesome—you know that—but you have to do what's right for you, you know?"

"Yep, I know. I should visit your grandma now. I've got to finish this piece this weekend, and now I'm not sure how to handle what happened with the Phillipses. My mind is spinning."

"You can stay here tonight if you want, you know. I'd love to have you," Justin offered.

"Thanks, but if my husband comes home and I'm not there, it's not going to help anything at this point."

"OK, but I want you to know that I'm here for you if you need anything. I don't want you to disappear from my life." He stood up and held me again.

"I won't disappear; I promise," I said, and we went downstairs and through the double doors and into Mrs. Dittmer's rooms.

It was dinnertime, and Sam and Mrs. Dittmer sat at the kitchen table. Dee was also in the kitchen, making some type of juice concoction from fresh fruit and vegetables. I always felt self-conscious about my relationship with Justin when I saw them, even though both had probably seen a lot worse in their years working in other people's houses.

"Hello, Ms. Megan." Sam greeted me in his booming voice.

"Hi, Sam. Hi, Dee."

"Hello, Ms. Megan," Dee answered.

"Hello, Mrs. Dittmer," I said and stroked her shoulder softly. She looked up at me quickly and back down at her plate of applesauce and something green that was also mashed up.

"How's dinner tonight, Gram-Gram?" Justin asked in an up-beat tone, and he sat down across from her at the table.

I watched as her gaze shifted up from the food to his face, and he waved at her enthusiastically. "Hi, Gram-Gram!" She looked over at Sam and smiled and lifted her hand slightly in a gesture that looked like she was pointing at Justin and then looked back at Justin. I could imagine her trying to say, "Look, Sam, my grandson Justin is here. Isn't he handsome?" But the words were trapped inside her.

"Let's see what you have tonight," Justin said, leaning over the table to inspect her dish. "Applesauce and mashed peas? Oh boy, what a feast!" he joked.

Her hair was still slightly damp from her bath, and I could smell lavender from whatever kind of soap or lotion had been used on her.

"There was some ham, too, but she already finished that. Didn't you, Mrs. Dittmer?" Sam said, holding a spoonful of mashed peas up to her mouth. As soon as she felt the spoon touch her lips, her mouth opened, and she chewed the food mechanically. I marveled at how the body could continue to function in order to preserve itself, even without the mind's participation.

Dee turned the blender on and created another pitcher of liquefied juice and poured it into a plastic cup, put the lid on it, and put it on the counter with three others that were already full.

"What are you making, Dee?" I asked.

"I like to do a variety for her, so she doesn't get bored," she said, in her thick Filipino accent. "This one is beets, carrots, and apples. Very simple. Very good for the brain. Very simple."

"Interesting," I said.

"And I do one with oranges, grapefruit, lime, cranberries, and some honey for a little sweetness. Very good for the brain, too."

"I like that one," Justin said.

"Yes, but the juice is for the missus, not you. The sir can make his own juices whenever he wants," she scolded, and she was clearly not kidding.

I laughed at Justin and said, "Tsk-tsk," and he rolled his eyes at me.

"I put some additional vitamins and zinc in with the juices, too. Many studies show that vitamins B_1 and E and B_{12} can be helpful, so I figure, why not?" Dee said proudly.

"That's great. Do you do your own research, or is there a source for caregivers?" I asked.

"I do my own research. There are blogs, too. I like to read on my own. There is so much time when the missus is asleep and I have nothing to do, so I like to read."

"You should write your own blog on your ideas for other caregivers," I suggested.

"Yes, maybe I will someday when I think that I have enough to say."

"Oh, photo albums," Justin said suddenly and got up from the table. "You wanted to see old photos, right?"

"Yeah."

Justin left the room and came back with two photo albums and put them on the table in front of me. "Here, I dug these out the other day."

"Fantastic! Thank you!" I said. The first one had a brown leather cover with a flower etched on the front in gold. The edges of the pages were also gold.

"Wait, she's done now, so let me move this stuff out of the way, and I'll move her over so she can see the photos," Sam said, clearing the dishes and place mat off the table. I scooted my chair a little closer to Mrs. Dittmer's and held the album in my lap at an angle that would allow her to see them. Justin and Sam stood behind me as I turned the pages.

The photos were black-and-white with white scalloped borders, and some had faded to a pale-yellow color. The first set was a family out for a picnic near a lake with kids playing badminton, a baby on a blanket in the grass, and a woman dressed in capri pants and a tank top.

"Is this your grandma?" I asked Justin.

"Yes, I think so. I think this is my mom, and that's her brother, and the baby on the blanket is my aunt Carol, who lives in Novi."

"Is this you, Mrs. Dittmer?" I asked her. Her eyes scanned the page but seemed to refuse to lock onto any of the photos. I tried again. "Looks like a family picnic. Are these your daughters and your son?" Again, she didn't respond.

I looked from the woman in the photo to the woman next to me and studied the similarities and the differences. The same face, now filled with lines and sagging. Her hair had once been full and dark and grown past her shoulders. The woman in the photo looked tall and robust, and the woman next to me was a fragile shadow.

The next set of photos was at a confirmation ceremony in front of a large stone church that I recognized but couldn't quite place. Then there were photos from a camping trip and then from Christmas and then a vacation on a beach somewhere tropical. The children in the photos got bigger, and Mrs. Dittmer's pageboy was bobbed and then turned into a bouffant and a shag before turning into a neat perm of brown and gray.

Her husband, Justin's grandfather, was tall and balding on top from the first photo to the last. He wasn't in many photos because, I assumed, he was the one taking the photos through the years, but when he was photographed, he always had a cigarette in his hand or mouth.

Photos of the family in the house we were now sitting in were in color, and the woman in the photos began to look a little more familiar. There was a section of photos for each child as they got

married and then photos of Mrs. Dittmer and her husband holding a succession of grandchildren.

"Tell me which one is you," I demanded, and Justin reluctantly pointed out his grandmother holding a crying baby at a
Thanksgiving dinner table.

"Figures!" I laughed, and Sam and Dee laughed with me.

"I was just crying 'cause I wasn't old enough to eat turkey," he
joked.

Mrs. Dittmer sat quietly for the most part. The photos didn't
seem to interest her at all until I got to the ones of her with her
dogs. I remembered Justin telling me that she had bred standard
poodles, and there were several photos of her in the backyard surrounded by several large black poodles. There were also photos of
her at dog shows, posing with a dog and holding a ribbon or tro-
phy. In a few photos, she sat on the ground surrounded by poodle
puppies as they tumbled over one another.

I heard Mrs. Dittmer moan softly, and then she reached out
and touched the edge of the album. I adjusted it and moved it into
her lap, and she put her hand over the photos and moaned again.

We all looked at one another in surprise, and Justin said, "Do
you remember your dogs, Gram-Gram? Those are your poodles."

She breathed in deeply and patted the page like you would pat
the top of a dog's head and then moved her hand to the next page
and did the same thing.

"They were beautiful dogs, Mrs. Dittmer," I said. "I know poodles are very smart dogs, and yours looked like they were well
trained."

She moaned again and looked up at me and then back down at
the photos again. I reached over and lifted her hand and turned
to the next page to reveal more dog photos, and she repeated the
petting gesture.

Justin knelt next to her. "Now, Gram-Gram, I think you liked
your dogs more than you liked us!" he joked and stroked her arm.

She looked at him and then moved her hand over and patted his arm before her gaze drifted off, and she seemed to lose the connection that had just formed.

Justin stood up, and I saw that he had tears in his eyes, and I stood up and hugged him.

"Sorry, it's just that she almost never does anything like that anymore. Touches me, I mean," he said, holding on to me and letting a few more tears fall.

"That was very nice," Sam said. "You could really see that she reacted to those photographs, and then she reacted to you. It's when those little windows open that you see the blessings that are still left." Sam took the album off her lap and prepared to move Mrs. Dittmer and then said to Dee, "I'll get her ready for bed before I leave," and moved her away from the table.

I let go of Justin and checked my phone and was surprised to see that it was 7:34. There were no messages from Craig. "I forgot how late I got over here today. I've got to go."

"OK." Justin took my hand and led me to the front door.

I looked at Justin's bearded face and slightly misty eyes under his beat-up baseball cap and wondered if I would ever see him again. "Thanks for everything. I guess I'll see you later," I said.

"Text me later on, and let me know if you're OK, OK?" he said.

"I will."

"You know you can stay or you can come back—whatever?" I could tell that he felt as awkward as I did.

"I know, thanks." I gave him a quick kiss on the lips and turned and left before I changed my mind.

CHAPTER TWENTY-NINE

There was no sign of Craig when I got home. Part of me was hoping he would be standing on the porch when I pulled up, even though I had no idea what to say to him. I tried calling him with no answer. I texted him, *Hey, are you OK? Where are you staying?* I stuck the phone in my pocket in case he responded and walked around the house aimlessly for a while. I looked at our furniture and photos and the knickknacks we had collected over the last eleven years as we built a life together and tried to figure out what it all meant and wondered if what I had done had erased all the meaning.

Craig still hadn't responded after an hour, and I tried to call again, but it went immediately to voice mail, so I texted again. *I know you're mad, and I'm sorry, but I need to know that you're OK. Come home if you want. I'll sleep in the spare room.*

I dropped down on the sofa and turned the TV on and began to click through the channels without really watching any of it. My phone beeped with a text message, and I grabbed it, hoping it was Craig, but it was Justin: *Hey—U OK?*

Yeah, I answered back.

U alone? he asked.

Yeah.

Can I do anything for U?

I pictured him sitting in the corner of his couch with his baseball hat on, sipping a beer, and I wanted to go to him and lie against his body and feel his hand on my shoulder while I fell asleep, but that wasn't the life I had made. *You're sweet, thanks. I'll be OK.*

K. Miss you. U R amazing, U know?

I smiled and let my heart fill up a little. Another text came through. *I'm in Naperville,* and I stared at it, trying to make sense of what it meant before I realized it wasn't from Justin; it was from Craig. He was at his brother's house in Naperville, Illinois. I broke into a sweat; I was texting my husband and lover at the same time. I sat momentarily paralyzed, trying to figure out who I should respond to first. I decided to end my conversation with Justin. *Glad you think so. Talk tomorrow.*

The implications of Craig's message were enormous; he was at his brother's, which meant that his brother knew about the affair, which meant that his sister-in-law knew about the affair and that news would continue through the family until everyone knew. My heart dropped because I knew there was no chance Craig would come walking through the door and we would hug it out and move on with our marriage.

I pictured Craig sitting on the beige couch in his brother's house with the cathedral ceilings while his brother and his wife looked at him in disbelief and counseled him to divorce me. They were the perfect couple, and they had followed the playbook step-by-step: they married right out of college, waited two years, and then had two children in quick succession, and to them, my actions would be unforgivable.

Craig's parents would never forgive me either; his mother had already let her disappointment over our lack of children drift into almost every conversation. The gravity of my situation began to sink in, and I kicked myself again for telling him about Justin. If I had only shut up, we would be sitting on the couch watching a movie together and planning a trip to Home Depot for Saturday morning.

I finally forced myself to respond, *Really? I was hoping you would come home so we could talk.*

It took him a few minutes to respond, but when he did, he typed, *You can't talk your way out of this one.*

My heart dropped again. *Didn't think I could. I know what I did was wrong. Want to move forward.*

He responded immediately. *Forward? There is no forward for us.*

I reread the words over and over and started to cry. My gut reaction was to fight for him, even though I wasn't sure what I was fighting for. I typed, *Don't say that.*

Not my fault was his response.

I know. Call me tomorrow? Please, I pleaded.

Maybe. Need time.

I know. Sorry. I do love you.

He didn't respond.

I went into the bathroom and washed my face and blew my nose and sat on the side of the tub for a while. I reached out and pulled open the drawer on his side of the vanity, and it was empty except for an old ChapStick and bottle of aftershave that he had once said made him break out. His hair dryer and chest shaver were gone. He had taken more than I realized. He was prepared to be gone for an extended period of time.

CHAPTER THIRTY

I spent most of Saturday morning on the phone with my editor; the decision had been made that I should take all mention of the Phillipses out of my article and just go with Strumble, Norman, and Dittmer for the final piece. I reluctantly agreed; it would make my assessment of the plight of the caregivers easier to write and give the story more continuity if the Phillipses weren't involved, but there was still so much to say. I successfully campaigned for them to allow me to write a second piece on the Phillipses. This would be an article that was more of a cautionary tale with some solid recommendations for getting help for anyone in a similar situation having similar thoughts.

I hung up, pleased with myself for being able to stay focused on my work while the rest of my life fell to pieces at my feet. I drank a Red Bull and pushed myself to rewrite my main article and add the final paragraphs. Thoughts of Craig and Chelsea and Justin and the Phillipses drifted in and out of my head, and I pushed them away. I concentrated on the one asset I had left that I hadn't managed to screw up yet and let the words flow through my fingers and out onto the page.

I sent the first article off to my editor and opened another Red Bull before I started into the second article. I checked my phone and saw a text from Justin reading, *Hey*, and one from Paula saying, *Catch me up*, and I didn't return either one. There were no calls or texts from Craig, and I imagined him at his brother's house out in the backyard in the sunshine, pushing his niece and nephew on the swings and wondering how he'd married such a terrible person. I pushed those images away and started in on some research for my article on the Phillipses.

The last part of the article was a call to action with advice for those pushed to the edge by caring for someone with Alzheimer's and for those who might recognize that in someone they know. It was easy to write the words, but I still felt guilty that I hadn't recognized the signs and taken action.

I knew I would never be able to forget what they looked like and sounded like and all the pills in the shoe boxes and empty refrigerator and the sight of him helping his wife out of bed so gently. He knew all along, the whole time he was talking to me, that he was going to do what he was going to do, and he showed me their life so I could witness it and record it. It occurred to me that he had placed a heavy burden on me, and I was angry at him.

Chelsea had placed a heavy burden on me, too; she had to know that I would blame myself. She had already made me suffer by sleeping with Jimmy, and then I made her suffer by refusing to forgive her, so was her suicide just another volley in that battle? She, of all people, knew that I could never forget what she did. My feelings were still raw over twenty years later, and I wondered if that was what she had been counting on.

And then it struck me that if she had lived, her feelings would be just as raw now, too. We had the same curse, after all. I allowed myself to think that she didn't kill herself to punish me but to escape the feelings that she knew she would never be able to escape. She would never be able to turn off the open frequency in her head that let every voice in unfiltered, and for her, it was too much to bear.

A lightness came over me, and as I sat there, I almost didn't notice the tears streaming down my face. I had found a way to deal with my busy brain, but I had to accept that not everyone could and that Chelsea had taken another way out. I hated it, and I hated my part in it, but that didn't mean I had to live it every day. I gave myself permission to put that burden down and to walk away from it for good.

Mr. Phillips had reached the end of his ability to cope, too, and in me he saw an opportunity to have someone to bear witness and to understand his struggle and perhaps, in his mind, his humanity. In this moment of clarity, I could see how all his actions were orchestrated to this end and that he could not conceive of any other way out, and my anger melted away. He needed me to tell his story, and that was what I would do, and I would move on. I would not pick this burden up.

I finished the piece and sent it off to the editor. It was after seven o'clock at night, and I could feel hunger through the nauseated feeling in my stomach. I checked my phone again and found another message from Justin. *You OK? Thinking abt U.* I stared at it for a long time, unsure of how I felt about him. I knew that Craig wouldn't be home and that I could go to Justin and spend the night, but I was emotionally drained and didn't want him to see me when I was this vulnerable.

I finally typed, *Sorry, been writing all day. I'm OK.*

His responded quickly. *U alone?*

Yes.

Come over. I'll take care of you.

I smiled for the first time all day and typed, *So sweet. You make me happy.*

Same. Coming over?

No, need to get myself together. Wanna see you soon. Keep in touch.

He sent a sad-face emoji back with the words *Miss you.*

I reread the texts and deleted them all and then opened a bottle of wine and drank it right from the bottle while I stood in front of the refrigerator and looked for something to eat. The refrigerator was a mess of old leftovers and containers of half-eaten carryout, and I pulled the garbage can over and started throwing it all out. The second bowl I grabbed was topped with foil and still had the Post-it note reading *Miss you* in a heart on it. It was the leftover chicken carbonara that I had made for Craig before I went to Saugatuck with Justin.

Time slid sideways to me as I realized that it was only a little over a week old. It didn't seem possible; that trip seemed like it had happened a year ago, to another person in another life. "Fuck me," I said out loud, and I took it over to the counter and put some on a plate and stuck it in the microwave. I ate it without really tasting it while sitting on the couch and drinking the rest of the wine out of the bottle. My busy brain slowly ground to a halt as the alcohol took effect, and I fell asleep without bothering to change out of my clothes.

CHAPTER THIRTY-ONE

I kept myself busy on Sunday cleaning the house and mowing the lawn and checking my phone for messages from Craig and Justin obsessively. I didn't hear from Justin at all, and it was midafternoon when Craig texted me. *I'll be home later. Got a busy week at work and need to be on point.*

On point? I thought. It was such a businesslike way to talk to me. *OK. Missed you. Glad you'll be home,* I typed back.

I did laundry and went for a run in the evening to keep myself from drinking. I rehearsed all the different ways I could apologize and tried to anticipate his reactions. I knew there would be tough times ahead for us but couldn't imagine us splitting up, no matter how many scenarios I ran in my head.

By the time he pulled up around nine o'clock, my stomach was in knots. There was something comforting in listening to him move through his usual routine as he parked, checked the mailbox, and came back through the garage and into the kitchen. I had left the mail in the box on purpose so he could go through it the way he liked.

His expression was impassive.

I walked into the kitchen and stood at the counter while he sorted the mail. "Hi, welcome back. How was the drive?"

"Fine. No problems," he said, without looking at me.

"Good, good." He wasn't giving me very much to work with. "Are you hungry? I made some chicken, and there's zucchini and rice."

"I ate," he said simply.

"OK, good. Um…"

"I have to work tomorrow," he said suddenly, cutting me off. "I drove a long way, and I'm tired, so I don't want to get into anything, OK?"

"OK." I was half disappointed and half relieved. I felt like we needed to have a knock-down, drag-out fight to get it out of the way, so we could move on to the rebuilding part of our relationship, but I was dreading it just the same.

"You can stay in the spare room, right?" he said, staring at the granite countertop that lay between us.

"Sure, of course," I said, my heart dropping a little.

He nodded, and I thought he looked like he might cry, but he took his duffel bag and went upstairs without saying anything else.

I sat back down on the couch and cried a little. I had waited and waited for him to come home, but now that he was here, nothing was any different, and I felt even worse. I curled up and stared at the TV until I fell asleep. I couldn't bear the thought of sleeping in the spare room alone.

I woke up around five and waited for the sound of his feet on the floor overhead. I listened to him move from room to room, shave, take a shower, and get dressed. I could picture him going through each action as he had done a thousand times before. Everything was the same. Nothing was the same.

He looked at me as he passed and went in to make his breakfast. I just lay on the couch and watched him without saying a word.

He stood at the counter with his back to me, drinking coffee and eating, and then he cleaned up and left, and the house went quiet again.

My day passed slowly; I worked on revisions to my articles that my editor had sent me and took another run and contemplated texting Justin while I waited for Craig to return home. It was racquetball night, which meant that he wasn't coming home until late. It also usually meant that we would be having sex, but I knew that probably wouldn't happen tonight. I wondered if I would ever have sex with him again. I just wanted to know where I stood and what he was thinking, and by the end of the day, I grew impatient and texted him. *Are you playing racquetball tonight?*

Why?

Just wondered.

I play racquetball on Mondays, he replied.

I know. I didn't know what else to say. He was not going to make this easy for me.

I called Paula and caught her up on all the drama and soaked up her sympathies and laughed while she told me stories of when she broke up with her first husband and how he filmed her having sex with her boyfriend, so he could prove she was cheating and how he filed a restraining order against her when she punched him after he showed her the tape.

When Craig came home, he immediately went upstairs and showered, and I wondered if he did want sex after all. Old habits were hard to break, and he was a creature of habit. I pictured us fucking on the couch, maybe him getting a little rough to get back at me, and then us ending up hugging and crying in each other's arms.

He came down the stairs and walked directly over to me and said, "I've got meetings all morning, but then I'm free after two. Are you going to be around?"

"Yeah, I'm free."

"OK. I'll come home, and we can talk." He turned and went back upstairs for the rest of the night.

I tossed and turned all night and finally got up at three and drank half a bottle of wine to relax myself. I slept two or three hours more and then woke up and again watched Craig go through his morning routine and leave without acknowledging me.

The day crawled by at a sickeningly slow pace, and I spent most of it sitting on the deck and staring at the trees. I didn't bother to come inside when I heard Craig pull up; I just waited outside and tried to calm my breathing.

He still had the same impassive, resolute expression on his face. His jaw was tight, and his eyes looked tired as he sat next to me and said, "I didn't want any of this. I hope you know that."

I almost started crying but held back. "I know. You don't deserve this."

"No, I don't," he said sharply. "I never cheated on you. Never even thought about it."

I tried to remember how I had rehearsed it and spoke slowly. "I don't have an explanation or an excuse for what I did. It just happened. I don't know if that makes it better or worse; I don't know how else to explain it. I know that I love you, and I never stopped loving you."

"That's a pretty piss-poor excuse coming from a writer. I would have thought you could have come up with some kind of fancy justification using lots of adjectives and ten-dollar words." He laughed cynically.

"Sorry, I guess I'm full of disappointments these days."

"Thing is, I liked that wild streak in you. It's one of the things that made me want you, but I thought you would have grown out of it by now."

"I have grown out of it," I protested.

"Not so much. You've spent eleven years partying with your friends and traveling around doing God knows what and avoiding having a family and apparently fucking other guys," he challenged.

"That's not true. I haven't been with other guys, just this one guy, and I only met him a month ago, so it's not like it's been going on. We've been building our life together—you know that, Craig! I've been here with you building our home and our careers."

"I don't know anything anymore," he said and exhaled hard.

"I'm sorry, I'm sorry, I'm sorry. I know that doesn't mean much, but I don't know what else to say to you," I pleaded, trying to get him to look me in the eyes.

"You'll have to move out," he said suddenly.

All the breath left my body, and I felt like I'd been kicked in the stomach. "What?" was all I could manage.

Craig looked at me now, looked at me hard, and said, "I'm the only one who can afford this house, so you'll have to move out. I'll have to buy you out, so you'll have something to start with if you want to get a condo or something. You can stay in the spare room until you figure it out, but I don't want this to drag on and on, you know?"

As I listened, I realized that I wasn't the only one who had rehearsed what she was going to say. Craig had obviously thought things through and maybe even consulted a lawyer. I sat there and blinked and tried to think of something to say.

"It's what I want," he said, nodding as if to reaffirm it to himself.

"I don't want to split up. We can get through this," I choked out.

"And then what? Have a baby? No, you don't want a family. You and I haven't been on the same page with that in a very long time." He stood up and began pacing around the deck.

"That's not true. We were always going to have a family. We can do it now," I offered.

"This is the worst reason in the world to get pregnant, to try to save our marriage. I've had friends who have been through this, and it's a mess. They all have visitation every other weekend now, and I don't want that, and I don't want to waste three more years figuring that out."

There was a calmness in his voice that bothered me more than anything. He was being very logical and reasonable, and I knew that he had made his choice. I also knew that this had been building for a long time. It wasn't just a reaction to my affair; it was an ending he had contemplated before.

"Maybe we should go to counseling for a while," I suggested. "You know, take six months to invest in our marriage. I think it's worth saving. I think we should at least try."

He sat in a lawn chair across from me and shook his head. "There's nothing wrong with you, you know? There's nothing wrong with me. We are just on different paths now. I don't think we need a counselor to help us see that. You know it. Be honest with yourself."

A bit of anger flared up in me. "Well, you sure seem like you've made up your mind. Sounds to me like you've been thinking about this for a lot longer than a weekend."

"Says the person whose been sleeping with someone else? Really? Seems like your mind has been elsewhere, too, eh?"

I moved into the spare bedroom that night. Craig and I walked carefully around each other for the next several weeks. We had gone from a married couple to two strangers almost overnight. Whatever connection we had once shared evaporated so quickly that it made me doubt whether it had ever really existed at all. I clung to the hope that he would soften and change his mind, but things between us only got more awkward as the weeks passed. When he brought the papers home, I looked at the lump-sum settlement that included my part of our savings and the buyout for my half of the house and signed them and left them on the dining-room table.

CHAPTER THIRTY-TWO

When the article was finally published, I hand carried a few copies to Mr. and Mrs. Strumble. A metal wheelchair ramp now led up to the front door and looked very out of place against the charming Craftsman house. Inside, some of the doorways had been widened to accommodate the wheelchair. There were still a few places where the patched drywall needed to be painted, and Mrs. Strumble explained that their son, Mike, had been working on it each weekend.

Mr. Strumble looked a little thinner and frailer than I remembered him, but he still greeted me with a smile and invited me to watch the rest of *Midway* with him. I complied and peppered him with questions about World War II and marveled at his ability to recall so many details. To me, the ability to remember so many details and statistics rarely came in handy and often opened me to the scorn of those around me. For him, knowing those details was his way of connecting to a world that he no longer felt connected with. It was ironic that memory both separated and connected him to the world at this stage of his life.

After leaving them, I made my way across town to the Normans' house. Much to my relief, all three Normans were exactly as I had left them. Linda was in the kitchen, cooking lasagna and rolling her eyes as her father paced the floor and complained about hedges that had been removed from the front yard. Linda told me to ignore him and informed me that the hedges had been removed many years ago. Mrs. Norman sat in her usual chair with a newspaper folded to the crossword puzzle in her lap. The TV was blasting to compete with Mr. Norman's tirade about the hedges. I spent a few minutes with them in the relative chaos of their house and left with a smile on my face.

I contemplated driving a copy over to the Dittmers' house but ended up stopping at the post office and sending one via snail mail instead. Justin and I were still texting periodically, but we hadn't seen each other since my last visit to his grandmother, and I just couldn't bring myself to face him.

I drove to my new home, which was a small apartment that I was renting over a garage near the lake. I had looked at condos in the area, but the beige carpet and off-white walls reminded me of the Phillipses' condo, and I knew I would never be able to shake that feeling, no matter how many coats of paint I used.

My new place was private and cozy and had a small balcony that sat under the shade of an enormous maple tree. Craig let me take whatever furniture I wanted and even helped me move it up the narrow staircase one hot July day.

After a few ups and downs, our relationship had settled into a comfortable place. A few weeks after I had moved out, he showed up unexpectedly on a Monday night, and we had sex. It felt great and familiar, but I took it for what it was—an echo from the past—and I refused to let myself read too much into it. He came back the next week and the week after that before announcing that it probably wasn't healthy for either one of us to get into a pattern, and he suggested we stop seeing each other again. I didn't argue.

Since I was now a woman living on a single income, I picked up some freelance technical-writing projects and was able to connect with another travel magazine that hired me to do a piece on Cuba. I was so excited to go to Cuba before it became too commercialized that I would have worked for free, but luckily, the pay was good. So I brushed up on my Spanish and prepared to take one of the educational tours that were currently sanctioned by the government as approved travel.

Newly single, in a new home with new job prospects and a trip to Cuba a mere few weeks away, I was finally settling into my new life. I was sitting outside on my balcony enjoying the cool fall evening and reading a *People* magazine when my phone rang. I looked down and was surprised to see Justin's name. I had not spoken to him in months and debated answering before I finally hit *accept* and said hi.

"Well, hello there." I could hear the smile in his voice, and an instant warmth spread throughout my body.

"Hello right back, Justin," I said in a bit of a whisper.

"How have you been?" he asked seriously.

"Terrible because I haven't seen you," I said, unable to stop myself from flirting.

"Well, whose fault is that?" he joked.

"I know. Complicated times, my friend, complicated times. How are you?"

"I'm good, but I called to tell you that Gram-Gram passed a few days ago," he said.

"Oh no, no, that is so sad. I'm sorry, Justin." Tears sprung to my eyes, and I immediately wished that I had gone by to see her again once the article was finished.

"Thanks. It's for the best. She was sleeping a lot at the end, and one day she just didn't wake up. Sam was here that day, and he told me that he thought she was close, so we all stayed by her bed, and then it was just...over."

"She went at home, like she wanted. You were a good grandson to her, Justin," I said, dabbing the tears out of my eyes.

"I tried my best. She was a hell of lady, and she deserved everything she got and more."

"That's for sure," I agreed. I wanted to go to him and hoped he would invite me over.

"Anyway, the service is Saturday morning at eleven at Holy Cross, and I wanted you to know in case you wanted to come by. I would have called you earlier, but I had to move some stuff out of the basement before my mom and dad and the rest of the family showed up, if you get my meaning," he said, and I remembered the enormous grow room he had set up in his grandmother's basement.

I laughed. "Oh my, that had to be quite the situation. You didn't trash the stuff, did you?"

"Are you kidding? No way! But my buddy Ryan has it now, and he'll smoke every bit of it if I don't get it out of there soon, so I'm looking now."

"Is your family there already?" I asked.

"Yep. Came in today. House is full of people. It's kind of weird. I'm hiding in my room with a beer and blunt right now," he admitted.

"Good luck with all of that. Thanks for letting me know. I'll come by on Saturday for sure," I said.

"I miss you, you know?" he said.

"Same. I'll see you Saturday, and we can catch up, OK?"

"Roger that," he said, and we both hung up.

CHAPTER THIRTY-THREE

All funerals reminded me of Chelsea's funeral, even this one that was the complete opposite. Chelsea had been young, and her funeral home was overflowing with distraught family and teenagers, flowers, and photo boards. Mrs. Dittmer was old and had outlived most of her friends, so her casket was laid out in one of the smaller rooms and had two large flower arrangements from the family on each side. There were a handful of people, including her three caregivers, her sister from Novi, and Justin and his mom and dad.

I almost didn't recognize Justin in his navy-blue suit and tie and brown dress shoes. His hair and beard were neatly trimmed, and I couldn't believe how hard my heart started beating as soon as I saw him.

He was watching the door when I came in, and he immediately came over and gave me a hug. I was just as attracted to him as I was the first day I met him standing in the doorway of his grandmother's house, and I was no closer to figuring out why.

His blue eyes sparkled as he looked me up and down. "A dress, eh? Wow, you clean up good, girl!"

"So do you. They don't make brown leather toe shoes, I take it?"

"Ha! I'm thinking of going into the Secret Service with this suit. What do you think?" He put a pair of sunglasses on and stood very straight and looked off into the distance.

"I think you're a goof!" I said, and we both laughed quietly.

"Come on, you wanna meet the fam?" He took me by the hand and then held it up and looked to see if I still had a wedding ring on my finger. When he saw that my finger was empty, he kissed it and smiled at me.

Justin walked me over to the couch where his mother and father were sitting with his aunt Patricia. His mother was tall and slender, and her brown hair had blond tips that could only be from the sun. She wore a sleeveless black dress and had a large medallion of the sun on a black ribbon around her neck. I got a hippie vibe off her almost immediately, and I could envision her jogging down the street in San Diego and drinking a wheatgrass smoothie. She noticed us holding hands and gave me a warm, if slightly cautious, greeting.

His father was the same height as his wife and built a little sturdier than Justin. It was obvious from the athletic build I could see under his black suit that he had a pretty serious fitness routine. He had the same blue eyes as Justin but without the hint of a smile that Justin's always had. He gave my hand a firm and quick shake.

His aunt Patricia showed no interest in getting up and shook my hand by grabbing the tips of my fingers and gently shaking them. She then turned to Justin's mother. "It's nice the help showed up, but do they get paid to be here?" she said, referring to Sam, Dee, and Amparo, who were talking near the casket. I immediately decided that I didn't like her.

"Come on; let's visit Gram-Gram," I said, and walked with Justin over to the casket.

The funeral director had done a nice job giving her face a little more volume and adding color with makeup. She looked peaceful lying there in a light-blue dress with a little stuffed dog in her hands. I couldn't help but tear up. "I think she looks nice."

"She does. She looks more like she used to look before she got real sick. Do you like the dog? I put that there this morning," he said.

"Yes, it's cute."

"She loved her dogs. That little dog was on her bedside table. I have no idea where it came from, but she might as well take it with her." He reached out and patted the top of her hands. I realized that he was crying, and I turned and gave him a big hug.

I used my Kleenex to wipe his eyes, and he leaned over and gave me a soft kiss on the cheek. "I guess I did miss you," he whispered in my ear.

"Same," I said.

He took my hand and led me away from the casket and over to a table that had several framed photographs of his grandmother and the family. A few were the ones that I had seen before, and a few were new to me, and I looked at each one carefully, trying to merge the woman I knew with the woman in the images.

"There's a luncheon after the service today. Will you be my date?" Justin asked.

"Of course. I would be happy to come with you. Just don't sit me next to your aunt."

"I know; she's a bitch, right?"

"I'll sit with 'the help,'" I said, using my fingers to make quotation marks in the air.

Justin moved close to me and pretended to look at the photo in my hand and said, "And after lunch, will you come back to the house with me and get in my bed and let me do all kinds of stuff to you?"

I flushed and pushed my back against him. "Really? Are you sure that's a good idea?"

"No, it's not a good idea; it's a great idea," he said with confidence.

"Well, what if one of the other girls you 'hang out with' shows up today?" It was the best way I could think to ask the question.

"Stop," he said, and turned me to look in my eyes. "I haven't seen anyone in a couple of months, if that's what you want to know."

"That's what I want to know," I said back.

He took my hand and walked me over to another table to look at some more photos. "And you—is everything OK between you and your ex?" he asked.

"I am officially divorced and haven't seen him in a while, if that's what you want to know," I answered.

"I was just wondering. Sometimes people get back together, you know."

"Well, this isn't one of those cases, unless you are referring to us getting back together," I said and squeezed his hand.

He squeezed mine back and held it up and kissed it. "We never broke up; we just hit *pause*."

"Am I supposed to say something clever about hitting *play* now?" I joked.

He smiled at me. "Let's go talk to 'the help,'" he suggested, using air quotes.

"Do you wanna go to Cuba with me in two weeks?" I asked suddenly.

"What? Cuba? For real?" he asked incredulously.

"Yes. You have a passport, right?"

"I do."

"It's for work. I'm taking a tour on assignment, and I can bring someone, so come to Cuba with me for the week."

"You don't have to ask me twice. I'm there, baby!" He grabbed me and hugged me again, and I felt my heart fill up.

"Excellent. We're going to have a blast," I said.

"Can I bring weed into Cuba?" he asked seriously.

"Oh my God, they just decided to let us ugly Americans in. Can we do it without causing an international incident, please?" I playfully pushed him away from me.

"Well, I'm going to have to do my research on this."

"Justin?" his mother called from across the room. "Justin, I think everyone is here now, and it's almost two."

Justin looked up and smoothed his jacket and tie down. "OK, Mom." And then he looked at me. "Come on, you can sit next to me." And he took my hand and led me over to a piano that I hadn't noticed earlier. He guided me into a high-back chair near the piano bench and then sat down at the piano.

His father busied himself closing the doors to the parlor, and his mother stood up and said, "Everyone, everyone, please take a seat over here." She motioned with her hands, and the few people standing made their way over to the couches and sat down.

"As you all may know or not know, my son, Justin, lived with my mother in the last years of her life, and he played music for her every day. In the end, when she was almost gone, it was one of the few things that she connected with and enjoyed. Today, Justin is going to play a little medley of her favorite songs for her for the last time. Please enjoy." And with that, she gestured to Justin, and he began playing.

I couldn't stop the tears from welling up, and I wished that he hadn't sat me up so close to him. I would have rather hidden in the back of the room. I watched his hands move across the keys and was overwhelmed by my feelings for him. It was as if not a day had passed since we last had seen each other, and despite the sadness of the occasion, I felt happy. His grandmother had brought us together twice in this lifetime. Maybe fate was at work after all.

Justin moved from song to song with ease, and his audience nodded and smiled with recognition at each selection. Mrs. Dittmer's mouth didn't smile, and her hands and feet remained still this time, but her presence filled the room just the same.

ABOUT THE AUTHOR

Tracy Nadeau was born just outside of Detroit. A graduate of Wayne State University, her career as a marketing event producer has allowed her to indulge her two great passions: travel and meeting new people. She splits her time between homes in Michigan and Florida, where she lives with her husband and two golden retrievers.

www.ingramcontent.com/pod-product-compliance
Lightning Source LLC
Chambersburg PA
CBHW061609170626
46811CB00001B/368

* 9 780692 850053 *